CLOSED CIRCLES

ALSO BY VIVECA STEN IN THE
SANDHAMN MURDERS SERIES

Still Waters

VIVECA STEN

CLOSED CIRCLES

TRANSLATED BY LAURA A. WIDEBURG

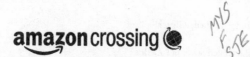

MYS
F
STE

Previously published as *I den innersta kretsen* in Sweden in 2009. Translated from Swedish by Laura A. Wideburg. First published in English by AmazonCrossing in 2016.

Published by AmazonCrossing, Seattle

www.apub.com

Amazon, the Amazon logo, and AmazonCrossing are trademarks of Amazon.com, Inc., or its affiliates.

ISBN-13: 9781503953888

ISBN-10: 1503953882

Cover design by Kimberly Glyder

Printed in the United States of America

To the kindest Alexander in the world

SUNDAY

CHAPTER 1

The woman's voice slowly counted down over Channel 16 on the marine radio: "Ten, nine, eight . . ."

The water churned with boats. Several large racing sailboats, meant for the open sea with their enormous sails and shining hulls, crowded the starting line a few nautical miles from Sandhamn. Beyond the starting area, observers maneuvered their boats to get the best view, prepared to follow the spectacle with binoculars.

The starting vessel, a minesweeper on loan from the navy, was positioned to the starboard of the starting line. Everywhere, large sails ballooned to capture the slight breeze.

The scene was perfectly set for an exciting race.

The voice continued: "Seven, six . . ."

It was a miracle that the competing boats didn't collide as they navigated into position. At times, they were only a few inches apart as they jockeyed for the closest position to the orange windward flag.

"Five, four . . ."

The start pistol would go off with three seconds to spare to account for the time it would take for the sound to reach the boats.

The first vice chairman of the Royal Swedish Yacht Club (RSYC), well-known business lawyer Oscar Juliander, stood confidently, his knees slightly bent, behind the wheel of his beautiful Swan, an elegant beauty called *Emerald Gin*. She measured sixty-one feet and had a crew of fifteen. She'd cost a small fortune—over ten million kronor—when he'd purchased her from the Nautor yard in Finland.

But she's worth it, Oscar Juliander thought. *She'll definitely be the first across the starting line today.* This was the summer when he'd finally be victorious in the Round Gotland Race, no matter what the cost.

Adrenaline pumped through his veins. *Dear Lord, how I love sailing!* he thought.

He glanced out over the water and noticed with satisfaction that there was a TV helicopter circling overhead. There'd be great pictures of the *Emerald Gin* as she headed across the starting line in the lead.

As usual, he didn't mind being in the media, and the media didn't mind turning their cameras on him. All he had to do was make sure he maintained his coveted position high on the windward side, the position everyone was jockeying for right now.

He clenched his fists. Soon, very soon, they'd be off on their way to Gotland.

The water churned as they closed in on the last few feet from the starting line. They were not allowed to cross the line ahead of time, or they'd be forced to turn around and start over—a shame that would not only cost them in terms of lost minutes but might also determine the outcome of the entire race.

He held his breath as the last seconds were counted down. They were so close now he could almost reach out and touch the start buoy.

Then smoke from the starting pistol could be seen in the sky. A moment later, the sound of the shot reached them across the water.

First vice chairman of the board Oscar Juliander slumped forward. His hands released the wheel, and blood streamed from a wound in his chest. His unseeing eyes never even had a chance to register that the race had begun. He was unconscious before his body landed heavily on the deck.

The shot that killed Oscar Juliander was timed perfectly to coincide with the one signaling the start of the race.

The *Emerald Gin* was the first boat in her class to cross the starting line.

CHAPTER 2

"What are they doing?" asked Detective Inspector Thomas Andreasson.

Thomas was on board one of the finest police boats in the flotilla, a fifty-two-foot Stridsbåt 90 that could reach speeds of forty knots.

Thomas had been her captain during the years he'd worked with the maritime police, but his best friend, Peter Lagerlöf, commanded her now that Thomas had joined the crime unit at the Nacka police station.

When Peter had asked him if he wanted to come watch the start of the Round Gotland Race, he hadn't hesitated. One never said no to a day on the water, especially when it included Sweden's largest offshore race.

Now his trained policeman's eyes noticed that something was going on at the starting line. A magnificent Swan 601, the first in its class, rounded up in the wind and headed away from the starting area. It was a strange and unexpected maneuver when she should be on a straight course toward Almagrundet on her way to Gotland.

"Hand me the binoculars," he said, his hand already outstretched to receive them. He lifted the black Zeiss binoculars to his eyes and rose to his full height for a better view.

The Swan was now headed into the wind just beyond the starting line. She'd lost the lead and was already last in the field, the others sailing swiftly ahead.

One of the crewmembers on deck was waving both arms high over his head.

A classic emergency signal on the water.

Thomas could see the crewmember's desperate face through his binoculars. His stomach churned. Something was seriously wrong on board.

"What do you see?" Peter asked, squinting into the sharp sunlight.

"Something's happened in the cockpit. There's a crowd standing by the wheel." Thomas focused the binoculars. "Someone seems to be lying on the deck and not moving, but it's hard to tell."

Peter turned to his subordinate at the wheel.

"Head over to the Swan."

His colleague swiftly changed their course and sheered toward the sailboat.

As they approached, the young man on the foredeck yelled to them, "Our skipper has been shot!" He gestured wildly. "Some damned idiot is shooting at us!"

He stopped yelling as he realized they could still be in danger. He crouched down and pressed himself as close to the mast as he could, his eyes filled with fear and confusion.

Thomas looked around without knowing what he might find. It was impossible to spot a threat in the throng of boats.

The spectators on nearby boats didn't seem to understand what had just happened. They were busy watching the sailboats head off into the distance. Sunshine danced on the surface of the water, and behind them the huge starting vessel loomed. The outline of Sandhamn and Korsö Tower could barely be seen.

Thomas realized how serious this was.

He had just witnessed a murder, along with hundreds of competitors and audience members, during one of the most important sailing races in the world.

This was going to become a media circus of giant proportions.

An enormous yacht approached. She was a Storebro 500, fifty feet long with many stories. The finely polished mahogany glistened. Through the bright sunlight, Thomas could make out a group of men and women looking down on them from the flybridge, an outdoor space with a set of controls from which the boat could be maneuvered.

A middle-aged man with a captain's cap and a sweater with the Royal Swedish Yacht Club emblem stood at the wheel. When they were just ten yards from the police vessel, he leaned down to speak to Peter.

"What's the matter?" he yelled.

"Keep your distance!" Peter answered.

It was not easy to maneuver so that neither the Swan nor the yacht came too close. A collision was the last thing they needed.

"We have Juliander's wife on board. How is her husband?"

In the cockpit of the *Emerald Gin*, a man in his fifties with silver hair and glasses stood up. His sweater was flecked with red, and he appeared dazed and shocked by what he'd just seen.

"Someone shot Oscar!" he yelled to the man in the captain's hat. "Oscar's dead."

Thomas noticed a woman with light-brown hair lift her hands to her face before she moved out of sight. Then the thunder of a helicopter overhead cut off all communication.

CHAPTER 3

Nora Linde grabbed the iron handle of the old-fashioned white gate and pushed it open to the beautiful but already overgrown garden.

She stood at the bottom of the stairs to the entrance to the Brand house, perhaps the most beautiful house in all of Sandhamn. Situated high up on Kvarnberg Hill, right before the inlet, the house had views in all directions. Near the sound, one of the Waxholmsbolaget ferries sailed toward the steamboat landing. It was tourist season, and the ferry was packed. Nora could see passengers leaning against the railing and staring at Sandhamn, their eyes filled with expectation.

A breeze blew through Nora's light hair, which had grown during the winter and now reached her shoulders. In one swift and habitual movement, she pulled it into a ponytail.

From a distance, Nora could be mistaken for a teenager, with her boyish figure and long brown legs. Only from close-up could someone tell she was a grown woman—a mother of two children, in fact. Still, her light-blue linen shirt hung loosely around her stomach.

She'd just turned thirty-eight. She had some new crow's-feet around her eyes and a few gray strands in her strawberry-blond hair. Freckles from the summer sun dappled her nose.

Her gray eyes were dark with anguish.

She'd dreaded this moment all day. Earlier, she'd screamed at her two boys and been short with Henrik. Her son Simon, just seven, had asked if she was so angry because someone had been mean to her. Her other son, Adam, had stood next to him nodding in agreement.

It'd hurt.

She'd taken a deep breath and promised not to let the situation influence her so much. At the very least, she would not take it out on her family.

Nora's surprise over her neighbor Signe Brand leaving the Brand house to her had already diminished. Yet her grief over what Aunt Signe had done was still fresh and raw.

Last summer, Signe had killed both her nephew and his cousin when they'd demanded their share of the great mansion. Nora had almost died of insulin shock when Signe, not understanding the danger, had locked her inside Grönskär's lighthouse. If Henrik and her best friend, Thomas, had not found her, she would have lost her life.

Nora shivered.

She took a deep breath and tried to calm down. The knot in her stomach wouldn't go away, but it was time to go inside. She would have to decide what she was going to do with the house. Today was as good a day as any.

She walked slowly up the few stairs and put the key in the lock. It stuck slightly, which was not unusual for such an old house. Then the door opened, and Nora saw the familiar sights she had enjoyed since she was a girl.

The roomy entryway led to a large dining room that overlooked the sea, which was so close one could almost smell it. Beautiful old lace curtains framed the high windows. A dark-green Swedish tile oven rested at one end of the dining room. Gold curlicues adorned the tiles.

Past the dining room was a large living space with an old-fashioned sofa set, as well as a veranda with transom windows. This was where

Aunt Signe had been found unconscious before she'd died from taking a mixture of morphine and painkillers.

The house was completely quiet. Too quiet.

Nora realized what was missing: the ticking of the old clock in the dining room. Signe had always been careful to wind this clock. Her grandfather Alarik Brand had had it sent to the house at the end of the nineteenth century.

Nora walked over to the gray cabinet in the corner and took out the key. She knew quite well where Signe kept it—the top left drawer. She carefully opened the glass door and wound the clock. Its familiar ticking brought a smile to her face and tears to her eyes.

She blinked them away quickly. She had to get through this.

The night before, she and Henrik had been close to quarreling. Henrik thought they should sell the Brand house as soon as possible. Then they could get on with their lives.

They were lying in bed talking after the boys had gone to sleep. She rested her chin on her elbow as she listened to him. Only one of the nightstand lamps was on, and it cast long shadows on the patterned blue wallpaper. The heat was oppressive despite the open windows.

A serious expression came over Henrik's handsome face, and his brown eyes filled with concern. As she watched him, she noticed how good-looking he still was. His thick dark-brown hair held a touch of gray, but it hadn't thinned out the way it had with most of the men they knew. His hair parted in the center, complementing his chiseled features.

It still often surprised Nora that such an attractive and extroverted man had fallen for a girl like her.

She was introverted—shy, even. She had little social confidence, and she admired Henrik's ease in all situations. He was the center of attention, while she just listened in on his lively discussions. Still, she loved standing next to him and watching their friends as they laughed at his jokes and comments.

While he spoke, she let her fingers glide along his arm. She breathed in his familiar scent—one she'd known for fifteen years.

"You almost died, Nora," he said. "If we hadn't broken into the lighthouse, it would have been the end of you. Perhaps you would have suffered permanent brain damage. How could you even think of living in her house after that?"

If it were only so simple, Nora thought, bringing herself back to the present.

She left the dining room and walked up the stairs. Four large bedrooms occupied most of the second floor. The original fifth bedroom had been turned into a bathroom with a big claw-foot tub.

Signe had lived alone in this house and only used the southernmost bedroom. The others had stood empty for as long as Nora could remember, though they were still decorated with furniture from the early twentieth century, when Signe had grown up. The furniture was old-fashioned and heavy but suited the house. Many pieces were handmade, real works of art.

One of the rooms contained a fantastic old Swedish sofa bed made of delicately carved wood and upholstered in black velvet. Signe had told her once how her brother had almost suffocated in that bed when he'd gone to sleep and it had closed on him. His mother, hearing his desperate shrieks, had found him just in time.

Nora stopped in front of a portrait of Signe's parents. They stared straight into the camera with serious expressions typical of the time. Signe's mother wore black and sat in an armchair. Her father stood behind her with an authoritative look. The green Swedish tile oven was visible in the dining room behind them.

Nora could not stop her tears any longer. The reason for Signe's death and the aftermath of her passing were unbearable. The loss was a weight on her chest.

And she must decide what to do with this house.

CHAPTER 4

"Business lawyer Oscar Juliander, who was also the vice chairman of the Royal Swedish Yacht Club, was murdered while participating in the Round Gotland Race."

The television reporter calmly described the incident as the camera swept over a glittering sea filled with sailboats heading for Gotland.

"Oscar Juliander was a well-known partner in the law firm Kalling, one of the most important firms in Sweden. Over the years, he made a name for himself as one of Sweden's most trusted bankruptcy lawyers."

The screen showed a man in his sixties with a serious expression staring back at the camera. He wore glasses and a dark-blue piqué sweater, and his forehead was red and shiny from time spent on the water in harsh sunshine.

"We are, of course, extremely shocked," a Hans Rosensjöö said. According to the box in the corner of the screen, he was the spokesman for the Royal Swedish Yacht Club. "Our thoughts go out to his wife, Sylvia, and their children in this difficult time."

"What can you tell us about the deceased?" the reporter asked. He stuck the microphone uncomfortably close to Rosensjöö's nose.

Hans Rosensjöö appeared to take offense, perhaps finding the question in bad taste.

"Oscar was a true competitive sailor and a valuable friend. Those of us in the Yacht Club mourn his passing."

"Do you have any idea who might have killed him?" the reporter asked.

"That is the job of the police," Rosensjöö said. He clearly wanted to end this conversation.

He took a step backward as if he needed to defend himself.

"Are you going to cancel the race now?" the reporter asked. He spoke with excitement. "Do you dare continue the race after what has happened? Is there a killer at large on the high seas?"

"The race will continue as planned. That is what Oscar would have wanted. I have nothing more to say on the matter." Hans Rosensjöö did not bother to hide his irritation anymore.

The reporter pointed to the harbor, where motorboats and sailboats were docked side by side.

"Right here in the paradise of Stockholm's archipelago, members of the sailing community are wondering if they are risking their lives when they set sail. The police have not yet announced a motive behind the murder, but today Sandhamn is an island in shock. Speculation is running wild."

The camera panned over the water and rested for a moment on Lökholmen, the large island with a great harbor across from Sandhamn. On the left, Telegrafholmen framed the harbor, creating a wind-protected location that made this sailing metropolis famous. The camera continued until it reached Oscar Juliander's Swan docked alone at one of the pontoons. Its green hull shone in the sun. The *Emerald Gin* looked lost and abandoned, like a thoroughbred left in the stables after the race has begun.

Blue-and-white crime scene tape blocked off the edge of the dock. The words "Entry Forbidden" were written on a yellow sheet of paper that also listed the law forbidding curious bystanders from coming any closer. A police vessel bobbed on the waves nearby.

With one final panoramic view of the Falu red clubhouse, where the flag hung at half-mast, the news spot concluded.

"Did you hear that, Ingmar?" Isabelle von Hahne asked her husband as they watched the television in their suite in the Yacht Hotel. "Good old Hans didn't manage the interview very well. That old man needs to learn how to deal with the media."

She took in the view beyond the balcony door before she turned off the TV.

As usual, her blond pageboy hairstyle looked flawless, with discreet highlights woven in. On her little finger, she wore a ring bearing the yellow-and-blue crest of her noble Baltic family. She noticed it needed to be cleaned, along with her diamond wedding ring. Then she shrugged and began to flip through a magazine.

Ingmar von Hahne shook his head.

"What can you expect on a day like this? After what happened?"

He took a miniature whisky bottle from the minibar.

"Do you really have to take a drink now?" Isabelle asked.

Ingmar looked at the woman who'd been his wife for the past thirty years. He decided not to comment.

"We'll need to hold an extra board meeting later this evening," he said. "Hans asked me to call around and find as many members as possible. We'll put out a press release and discuss how to handle this situation."

"Doesn't he have a secretary who can handle this?"

"I am the secretary of the club," Ingmar said. "It is part of my job to handle a crisis like this."

He poured the contents of the small whisky bottle into a glass.

"We'll meet at eight o'clock in the members' lounge. You'll have to dine without me. Maybe you can have dinner with Britta? I wouldn't be good company tonight anyway."

Isabelle sighed and turned on the TV again.

"Britta Rosensjöö only wants to talk about her grandchildren."

Ingmar sipped his whisky.

"By the way," Isabelle said, "has anyone talked to Sylvia since she came ashore?"

Her husband shook his head. "Not that I know of, but I'm sure Hans gave her something to calm her down. He was going to call the children. If they aren't here already, they're on their way."

"He can call the children we know about, at least," Isabelle mumbled.

Ingmar shot her a quick look. "I know that Oscar wasn't the best of men, but he doesn't deserve comments like that."

Ingmar pictured his friend the last time they'd talked, at the skippers' meeting the night before. All the skippers had gathered for a briefing on the competition.

Oscar had stood by the flagpole at the large dock, smiling and tan as ever. His thick, sun-bleached hair had not yet turned completely gray. The sun had also bleached his red sailing shorts a light pink. He'd been in a wonderful mood, strong and energetic as he laughed and joked with his crew.

Ingmar von Hahne went to the minibar again.

"Nora, have you heard what happened?"

Henrik entered the house with an agitated expression. Nora had fallen asleep on the sofa. Visiting Signe's house had taken all of her energy.

She woke instantly and looked up at Henrik.

"What happened?"

"Somebody shot Oscar Juliander."

"What?"

"The lawyer. The Royal Yacht Club vice chairman. He was killed the minute the starting gun went off."

"You're kidding!"

"No. Do you remember when we looked at his boat yesterday? The *Emerald Gin*. It was the Swan at the large dock in the harbor."

"The green one?"

"That's it."

Nora's thoughts circled back to the events of the previous summer. Another murder at Sandhamn. Her stomach hurt. She hoped Henrik was mistaken.

"Are you absolutely sure?"

"Yes, I'm sure. It's been on the news."

He took the remote and turned on Text-TV, the Swedish channel listing the news of the day. "See for yourself."

The green letters stood out against the black background. The words described the day's events as they slowly crossed the screen.

Nora felt tears start to form. Terrible memories swept over her.

"It's a damn shame, this story," Henrik said. He did not notice her reaction. He picked up the phone. "I'm going to call my parents. Juliander's summer place on Ingarö is close to theirs."

Nora heard him start speaking as he disappeared into the kitchen.

She sank back into the sofa. She did not want to believe this was happening.

CHAPTER 5

"What is wrong with the people on that island?"

Göran Persson, the head of the criminal unit of the Nacka police, couldn't keep his anger under control.

It was six thirty on Sunday evening. Thomas had gone back to the mainland, and now his younger colleagues Kalle Lidwall and Erik Blom joined him at the station. They'd been called in for a meeting. Carina Persson, the chief's daughter, sat beside them. For the past two years, she'd worked as their administrative assistant while trying to get into the police academy. She'd finally been admitted this fall.

"Last summer that crazy old lady killed people right and left because of some old house. This summer somebody shot a sailor on the high seas. The journalists are going nuts. Do you have any idea how many calls we're getting?"

Persson's face was red and his forehead sweaty. His body looked too large for his desk chair. A thunderstorm rumbled in the distance, and dark-gray clouds covered the sky.

"Another summer gone straight to hell because some trigger-happy idiot can't control himself."

It's not your summer going to hell, Detective Inspector Margit Grankvist thought. She sipped her coffee, which tasted like stale grounds, even though it was fresh from the machine.

Last summer's aborted vacation weighed on her mind. She'd had to leave her husband and daughters on the west coast while she took part in the investigation of the Sandhamn murders.

This year, she'd been wise enough to rent a cabin on Djurö, just three quarters of an hour away from the police station in Nacka. Keeping her daughters away from the moped gang they'd met down in the province of Halland certainly played a part in her decision.

She'd been on vacation for three weeks already. A healthy tan softened her narrow features. Years of police work and irregular working hours had left their mark. Her deep eyes were always on alert. Planning her vacation better this year was a small consolation.

"Thomas, you were at the scene of the crime. What can you tell us?" Persson asked.

Thomas lifted his gaze from his notebook and looked around.

He was also tan, his hair almost white blond around his temples. The lines at the corners of his eyes were lighter. He wore a light-blue shirt with rolled-up sleeves. The back pocket of his jeans showed the imprint of his wallet, a mark made by years of use. Although the murder had transformed a relaxing day on the water into intensive police work, he appeared fresh and rested.

He stretched and then tried to summarize what had happened earlier that day.

Half the day had passed by the time they'd gotten the *Emerald Gin* docked and called in doctors and criminal technicians. Oscar Juliander's body had been transported to the forensic laboratory in Solna for an autopsy and further tests. The vessel remained in the Sandhamn harbor, waiting to be moved to the police shipyard for a more thorough examination.

Thomas and Peter had secured a conference room at the hotel. There they interviewed a number of eyewitnesses who had been on board the *Emerald Gin*.

"Nobody seems to have seen or heard much. According to Fredrik Winbergh, the crewmember who was standing closest to Juliander, everything happened extremely quickly. One second everyone was focused on crossing the starting line first, and the next moment the victim collapsed right in front of their eyes."

"Can Winbergh be the killer?" asked Margit.

"We can't exclude anyone at this time," Thomas said. "At least fifteen people were on board, and many of them were close to the cockpit."

"It's hardly possible that one of them could draw a pistol and shoot him in front of the others," Margit said, answering her own question.

"It would have been smarter to wait until nightfall, or until they'd gone ashore," Erik added. "Why make it harder?"

"We've collected all the clothes from the crew of the *Emerald Gin*. We'll be looking for powder stains and other evidence of a pistol firing at close range," Thomas said.

"What are the alternatives?" Margit asked. "Was the killer on another boat? Perhaps one of the other racers?"

Thomas nodded.

"Well," she said. "That's like looking for a needle in a haystack."

Thomas had nothing to say to that. It was physically impossible to check each and every boat in the area. There were hundreds, and the perpetrator could have fired from any one of them.

He looked down at his notebook.

"Winbergh first thought Juliander might have had a stroke," he said. "Until he saw the blood. Even then, he didn't realize the man had been shot."

"What about the boats not in the race?" Margit asked. "Did anyone see what happened?"

Thomas shook his head.

"Not directly. We spoke to several witnesses. They are RSYC members who were on board a Storebro motor yacht. The vessel was close to the starting line at the time of the shooting. We'll question them thoroughly tomorrow. We didn't have time today." He glanced over his notes. "Juliander's wife, Sylvia, was on board with them. We weren't able to speak to her because of her shock. Hans Rosensjöö and his wife were also on board."

"Isn't he the chairman of the club?" Persson asked.

"That's right. He's a bank director. His wife is Britta. He was watching the sailboats as they approached the starting line, but he was looking at the sails, not the cockpit of Juliander's boat."

"Who else was on board?" asked Margit.

"Let's see," Thomas said. "Ingmar and Isabelle von Hahne, another married couple."

"Nobility, of course," Persson muttered.

"The guy who owns the Storebro is a doctor by the name of Axel Bjärring," Thomas continued as if he hadn't been interrupted. "His wife, Lena, is also a doctor. She was the one who boarded the *Emerald Gin* and determined that Juliander was dead. Their teenage daughter was on board, too. Judging by the wineglasses, not all of the passengers were entirely sober."

"What more do we know about the victim?" asked Margit. "I've seen him on TV a few times. He was quite well known."

"According to Winbergh, he'd participated in fifteen Round Gotland Races," Thomas said. "This year, he put all his money into winning and bought this new Swan from a shipyard in Finland. He was a bigwig in the RSYC, active in the sailing world, and a favorite in this race."

"Did he have enemies?" asked Erik.

"Any lawyer that well known must have a few enemies," Thomas said. "The question is whether or not one of his enemies did this."

"It's still rare that people murder lawyers," Margit said. "And this was a spectacular way to kill someone, I have to say. What a scene."

Kalle nodded in agreement.

"Are there any possible motives?" asked Persson.

Thomas shook his head.

"Well, the usual. Love. Hate. Money," Margit said.

"When will forensics finish the autopsy?" Persson asked.

"We're in luck." There was a trace of self-satisfaction in Margit's voice. "They can look at him on Tuesday."

She glanced at Thomas, who nodded in appreciation. Margit had pressured them to look at the victim quickly. Thomas and Margit had worked seamlessly together since the murders last summer. By now they knew each other well.

Thomas would listen patiently as Margit complained about her two teenage daughters and their constant arguments. In return, Margit kept an eye on Thomas and made sure he didn't work too many long days in a row.

"We must to talk to Juliander's wife as soon as she's ready," Thomas said. "We also need to question his colleagues at the firm and the leaders of the RSYC. They are all on Sandhamn at the moment because of the race, so we'll head out there early tomorrow morning."

He turned to Carina.

"Call Swedish Television and request their film footage from the start of the race. Perhaps we'll find something useful."

"Sure, I'll do it as soon as we're done here."

Persson looked thoughtful, as if he'd just made a decision.

"I'm going to ask the county commissioner for a media spokesperson this time around. We need somebody who can handle journalists. Otherwise we'll never get the space we need to work. This is a big deal. I'm sure you all realize this already."

Nobody said a word. An unpleasant feeling from last summer settled over them. The black headlines broadcasting every development must have influenced Persson's decision.

"Are we going to bring in the National Bureau?" asked Margit.

"Let's keep it all in the family for now," Persson said. "Here's what we'll do. Margit and Thomas, you're in charge of the investigation. Margit will stay in touch with the prosecutor. I don't know who's been awarded that role yet. Kalle and Erik, you're backup. It worked well last summer."

Persson's eyes roamed from Margit to Thomas and back again. He smiled and took a deep breath.

"I'm sure neither of you has a problem delaying your vacation by a few weeks? Just like last year? Another summer investigation at exclusive Sandhamn?"

Margit had booked a dream trip to the Canary Islands at the end of August in addition to the three weeks she'd already taken off. She smiled back at Persson, unconcerned.

CHAPTER 6

It was already past eight in the evening, and the heat in the room was still oppressive. Thunder rumbled in the distance.

Hans Rosensjöö discreetly wiped his forehead with a cotton handkerchief. The back of his polo shirt was damp, even though he'd just showered.

To his left, the chair of the first vice chairman of the board sat glaringly empty.

Someone had pushed together several smaller tables to form a larger one. Eleven of the fifteen board members were present. *Not bad,* Rosensjöö thought. *Though most of them were already on Sandhamn because of the race.* The Round Gotland Race, their largest, was the most important source of income for the Yacht Club.

As a small boy, Hans Rosensjöö had accompanied his father to Sandhamn to watch the formal awards ceremony. Back in those days, majestic mahogany vessels competed in the Round Gotland Race. They carried dignified names, like *Refanut*, *Barracuda*, and *Beatrice Aurora*. Today, the vessels were named after sponsors: *Eriksson* and *Volvo* and whatnot. Hans sniffed. *What kind of names were those for offshore racing boats?*

In the good old days, red velvet covered the sofas in the cabin and the faint aroma of cigars wafted around the skipper. Three-course meals accompanied by glasses of schnapps and good wine were standard fare.

Nowadays, Hans thought, *racing sailboats are empty shells. There aren't even bunks for everyone, because the crew work in shifts anyway.*

In the modern era, the Round Gotland Race had become an enormous event that brought in millions of Swedish kronor. The first Sunday after Midsummer, the entire sailing world focused on the start of the race in Sandhamn. The spectator area on the southeast of the island was filled with guests of the sponsors, tourists, and other enthusiasts. Exclusive yachts competed for space with small outboards. Whether celebrating with champagne or with a cheese sandwich brought from home, everyone wanted to participate in this racing festival.

Today, Hans thought the word *festival* was nothing but a mockery.

Despite heavy emotions, he had handled the chaos following the unhappy event with character and resolve. The telephone rang constantly. When it wasn't a journalist asking questions, it was a shocked spectator or some club official checking in.

Rosensjöö was an upright and traditional man who adopted the motto of the old king, "Duty Above All." He'd attained the rank of lieutenant commander as a reserve officer in the navy and was considered a dependable and honorable person with a high moral code.

He never expected that the cold-blooded murder of his successor would cloud his last months of service as the head of the RSYC.

Never before had he felt so powerless and uneasy at the start of a board meeting. He banged the venerable old gavel on the table, calling the proceedings to order.

To his right sat Ingmar von Hahne, the secretary and second vice chairman. An untouched pad of paper and two sharpened pencils rested in front of him. Ingmar fastened his gaze on the gleaming white paper. A signet ring with his family crest glittered on his left pinkie finger.

Here we have a man whose greatest talent lies in his family background and his social graces, Rosensjöö thought. At official dinners, no one charmed women or danced as elegantly as Ingmar. He was the queen's favorite at all the Yacht Club parties. But he was not a man of action, one who could take Oscar's place.

Hans Rosensjöö's eyes wandered until they rested on the head of the Facilities Committee, Martin Nyrén, who was drawing tiny figures on his own pad of paper. Next to him sat Arvid Welin, the head of the club committee, a corpulent man well known in the world of finance. Both board members appeared resolute.

Hans Rosensjöö cleared his throat.

"Let us begin with a moment of silence for our departed friend, Oscar Juliander," he said.

He lowered his head and managed some forty-five seconds. That felt like enough.

"Thank you all for coming on such short notice," he began. "Unfortunately, we are completely unprepared for a situation like this."

He fell silent as he searched for the right words.

"The first thing we must consider is how to proceed with the race and preserve the good name of the Royal Swedish Yacht Club. There are a few decisions we must make."

He cleared his throat again.

"Does anyone object to allowing the race to continue? We can honor Oscar by making sure the race goes on."

Everyone in the room nodded in approval. So far, not a single man in the room had spoken. The silence unnerved Hans, though he did not know why.

"I believe that is what Oscar would have wanted," he added.

Then he took a deep breath and regarded the board members.

"I hardly need to mention that we must cooperate with the police in every way possible."

"Mr. Chairman," Arvid Welin said. His face was sweaty. "Who will we elect as the next chairman of the board at our annual meeting in September? Oscar had been nominated for the position, and you won't be eligible any longer."

Hans Rosensjöö felt a wave of irritation rise. *Arvid is such a stickler for formalities! Who cares about the election on a day like this?*

"Let's take things one step at a time," he said. "We'll deal with that problem later, one way or another."

He was seven years old the first and only time he came home crying during lunch. He'd just started first grade at the Broms School in the Östermalm District of Stockholm. His family lived only a few hundred yards away, in an exclusive apartment complex by Karlaplan.

Full of despair, he threw himself into his mother's arms as she opened the door. His tiny body shook with sobs.

He stiffened as he caught sight of his father in the hallway. Why was he home at this hour?

The large figure in a dark suit gave him a disapproving look.

"Why are you crying, boy?" His father's voice sounded cold and distant.

Through his sobs, he tried to explain that one of the bigger boys had taken his best marble, the one made from blue glass, while they were playing in the schoolyard.

He stammered as he explained why he'd run away. Willie Bonnevier was two grades ahead. It did no good to argue with him. He couldn't think of anything to do but leave the schoolyard.

The slap almost knocked him off his feet. He was so shocked that he stopped crying.

A large red mark spread over his left cheek. Nobody spoke.

He looked at his mother, but she turned away. In the doorway to the kitchen, his beloved nanny, Elsa, stood perfectly still and silent.

When the head of the household was in that kind of mood, it was best that everyone kept quiet.

Elsa wrung her hands. Her heart ached as she watched the little boy shaking in front of his father.

"You will return to school and get your marble back. In our family, we do not accept such treatment. Remember who we are. And stop crying. Immediately."

"Yes, Father," he whispered.

He bent his head and put his jacket back on, trying in vain to catch his mother's eye.

He walked slowly down the green marble steps and out through the heavy front door.

He feared his father more than he feared any older schoolmates.

Almost sick from anxiety, he demanded his marble back. Willie pressed it into his hand, either surprised that Hans had stood up for himself or simply bored with the new treasure. Hans would never know.

When he returned home that evening, his father did not ask about the marble.

He wet his bed again that night.

MONDAY,
THE FIRST WEEK

CHAPTER 7

The red boat taxi pulled away from the dock in Stavsnäs just as Thomas and Margit came running from the overcrowded parking lot.

The skipper saw them coming and brought the ferry in so they could jump on board.

"Thanks," Thomas called, nodding to the skipper.

They walked down the stairs to the passenger area and found a table in the half-full dining space. Thomas paid the cashier for their tickets. The aroma from the grill made Thomas hungry.

"What smells so good?" he asked the pleasant woman behind the cash register.

"Grilled sandwiches," she said. "Would you like one? They're pretty good, if I do say so myself."

She showed him a sample plate.

Easily persuaded, Thomas ordered one for Margit and one for himself. He added two bottles of light beer and carried them to Margit along with two glasses.

He heard a familiar voice behind him.

"Well, if it isn't Thomas! How are you doing?"

Thomas looked up to find one of his neighbors from Harö. Hasse Pettersson was seventy years old, a weather-beaten man who spent most of his postretirement time on Harö, where he'd been born and raised. His worn jeans were oil stained on one thigh. Pettersson knew everything worth knowing about engines. He was the man to turn to in any emergency and a neighborhood guru any time something needed fixing. All work done under the table, of course.

"Hey, there, Pettersson. How are you doing?" Thomas stood up to shake hands.

"Just fine. Won't you be going on vacation soon? I ran into your father a few days ago, and he said you were planning to come out."

"Not yet." Thomas shook his head. "I'm on my way to Sandhamn right now. On the job. You probably heard about the shooting yesterday? We're heading out to talk to some of the people there."

"The great lawyer, Oscar Juliander." Pettersson practically spat out the name. "As far as I'm concerned, it's no great loss. He was an ugly bastard, that Juliander."

Pettersson nodded emphatically as he packed some snuff under his lip and sat down at their table, holding his cup of coffee.

"You've met him?" Margit asked.

"Many times. He tried to cheat me out of a lot of money once."

As he put his snuff tin into his back pocket, Pettersson snorted to show his displeasure. His right forefinger was stained from nicotine, and a black half-moon of snuff lined his fingernail.

"How'd he try to do that?" said Margit.

"He wanted to buy a piece of property of mine on Runmarö. There were building restrictions on it because of beach protection, so it wasn't that valuable. He got in touch and offered next to nothing."

"Did he say why?"

"He said he wanted it for timber."

"What's that? A tree farm?" Margit asked.

"No, it's a piece of property where you can haul away fallen trees and stuff," Thomas explained. "But you can't build any kind of structure on it, not even a shed."

"So what happened?" Margit asked.

"Let me tell you! It turned out that the district was thinking of redesignating some property as buildable after all because somebody complained to the European Union. If I understand correctly, some stubborn devil wasn't content to own beachfront property if he couldn't build on it."

"The district office probably wasn't expecting that," Thomas said.

Pettersson dried his mouth with the back of his hand as he shook his head.

"With permission to build, that property would be worth a few million, not the measly one hundred and fifty thousand Juliander offered."

He turned in his seat and spit the wad of snuff into a nearby garbage can. Without blinking, he pulled out his tin and stuffed another wad behind his lip, then slurped down the last of his coffee.

"So, did you sell it to him?" asked Thomas.

A smile of contentment spread over Pettersson's face.

"I had intended to, but my boy thought there was something fishy about the whole deal."

"I can see why," said Margit.

"Yep." Pettersson chuckled. "Why in the world would a city lawyer want to pick up fallen wood? My boy was suspicious, so he checked with a friend down at the district office, who clued him in. After that I lost interest in selling to Mr. Big Shot Lawyer."

"Did he give up?"

Pettersson shook his head.

"Oh, no, he tried all kinds of tricks. He said we shook hands on it and claimed we had an oral agreement just as binding as a written contract. Finally he upped his offer to half a million. But I told him to stick his offer where the sun don't shine. I didn't hear from him again."

"And then he was shot," Margit said.

The old man flinched.

"Perhaps he tried to cheat somebody else, somebody who wasn't as forgiving as me."

"Well, here we are again," Margit said. They'd arrived at Sandhamn and were walking down the gangway at the Steam Boat Dock. "Perhaps we should call it a summer rerun?"

She looked around the harbor. Sailboats and motorboats crowded into the slips. As usual, a sandwich board displaying the day's headlines stood next to the newsstand.

The Round Gotland murder dominated the headlines. Speculations abounded in thick black fonts.

Commerce was in full swing despite the threat of rain hanging in the air. Crowds of tourists picked through racks of clothing at a store called the Summer Shop. A few retired folks sat on the two park benches, watching people go by.

As far back as Thomas could remember, elderly Sandhamn inhabitants had sat on those benches and commented on passersby. They were as much a part of the surroundings as the white ferryboats. For a moment, time stood still, and Thomas remembered how impatient he'd been as a boy, waiting for his father to finish chatting with some old guys sitting there.

"Come on," he said. He headed toward the Yacht Hotel.

"They've arranged for a conference room for us. We might as well get started. It'll take at least the rest of the day to talk to all the people we've lined up."

Chapter 8

The narrow conference room didn't look much different to Thomas than others, except for the view stretching east for miles, magnificent as a painting.

Thomas and Margit sat on one side of a conference table, leaving an empty chair for the visitors across from them.

Hans Rosensjöö had just left the room after confirming his short statement from the day before. Everyone aboard Bjärring's Storebro when Oscar Juliander had been murdered told the same story. Just like them, Hans Rosensjöö could not remember exactly which boats were near the *Emerald Gin* at the moment the race started. Shock and a few glasses of wine had dulled his observations.

Because the race had begun so far out on the open sea, the perpetrator must have been aboard a boat, either Juliander's or someone else's. At least that much was clear.

Something occurred to Thomas as he reached for a bottle of mineral water. If he could find witnesses who could help him determine the angle of the shot that had killed Juliander, he might be able to limit the number of boats that could have had the shooter on board. They could then narrow down the search.

The thought gave Thomas some relief. He smiled at Britta Rosensjöö as she entered the room.

She looked like a frightened teacher called into the principal's office for some mysterious infraction. Her thin blond hair, streaked with gray, had been cut into a pageboy that didn't suit her at all. Her deeply tanned face, dry and wrinkled, showed she'd spent a great deal of time at sea. Thomas put her age at about sixty, but she could be sixty-five or even older.

Britta Rosensjöö hesitated before sitting in the chair still warm from her husband.

"What do you remember from yesterday's incident? Can you tell us?" Margit began.

Britta Rosensjöö's eyes filled with tears.

Thomas recalled yesterday's unsuccessful attempt to speak with her. She'd been hysterical, just like Sylvia Juliander. He hoped today she could collect herself and provide some answers.

She dried the tears running down her brown cheeks with an embroidered handkerchief.

"Would you like some water?" Margit asked. She held out a full glass.

"I'm sorry," Britta said. "I just don't understand how Oscar was shot down right before our eyes and we couldn't do a single thing about it. The whole ordeal is so terrible." Her eyes watered again, but she swallowed hard and continued. "I'd been taking photos of his beautiful *Emerald Gin* just as it neared the starting line. And then that horrible thing happened. I can't comprehend it."

She dried more tears with her handkerchief.

Thomas, now interested, leaned forward.

"You said you were taking photographs?"

"Yes, I often bring my camera along when I go to these events with Hans. I've got several dozen photo albums at home from the regattas we've attended over the years."

"Could we see your photos?"

Britta looked unhappy.

"I would have brought them with me today, but I must have misplaced my camera." She smiled apologetically. "I'm forgetful sometimes. But it has to be here at the hotel. We're on the third floor, in one of the suites facing the harbor. It's probably there with all of our other things."

"Britta," Thomas said softly. "We definitely need to borrow your camera for a while. Or, I should probably say, the memory card, as soon as you find it."

Britta Rosensjöö smiled at them as if begging forgiveness. "I'm sorry, but it's not one of those modern digital ones. It's an old-fashioned camera that uses film. You see, I've never bothered to learn about many of these newfangled technologies."

"That's all right. But we do need that film. It could definitely help us. Can you search again as thoroughly as possible?"

Britta nodded but didn't say anything.

"Was there anything else you took pictures of that day?" asked Margit.

"Quite a few of the magnificent racing boats, actually. It's always such a wonderful sight. It was this year, too . . . until we realized Oscar was dead."

She fell silent and sighed deeply.

"I can't stop thinking of poor Sylvia. What is she going to do now?"

Tears returned as she looked down at her lap, her handkerchief now completely damp.

"I know Oscar had his faults, but I've known him and Sylvia for thirty years."

"How was their marriage?" Margit asked.

"They've been married a long time. They have three children."

Britta's voice died away as she looked out the window.

"I believe Oscar neglected Sylvia sometimes."

"Neglected her how?" Margit asked.

"He was gone a lot. And he wasn't the kind to stay within the bonds of marriage, if you know what I mean."

Britta smiled at Margit, embarrassed.

"I don't want to speak ill of the dead, but Oscar had a roving eye. It was no secret. He'd probably visited greener pastures many times."

"Did Sylvia know?"

Britta looked away.

"I don't know," she said. "I assume she did."

So jealousy could be a motive, Thomas thought. *How angry does a woman need to be to kill the man she loves? And how common would it be to shoot him? Especially with a gun across the open sea.*

Thomas knew that on average about one hundred fifty murders occurred in Sweden each year, and women usually committed no more than ten of those. The most common weapons were handguns or knives. These crimes were often impulsive or acts of self-defense.

Most of the murders women committed were rooted in abusive situations that continued for years before they became unbearable. Such cases were seldom premeditated. They were desperate last resorts.

The known details about this murder did not point to a spurned lover or a betrayed spouse.

This looks like a well-thought-out operation, Thomas thought. *The killer would need a great deal of experience in marksmanship, familiarity with the sea, and access to a boat and a gun.*

Only a damned good motive would drive someone to go to so much trouble.

CHAPTER 9

Thomas vanished for ten minutes after they'd finished with Britta Rosensjöö, and returned with a long roll of paper.

"Where did you go?" Margit asked. She looked at the roll of paper. "And what's that?"

"It's a nautical chart."

Thomas unrolled the blue-and-yellow chart on the conference table. He took four bottles of mineral water and placed one on each corner to keep it from rolling back up.

Margit leaned forward for a better look. She wasn't much of a boat person and certainly wasn't familiar with navigational charts.

"What are we looking at?"

"This is the area where the Round Gotland Race began. I got it from the woman down at the harbor. Look here." Thomas pointed to a spot on the upper half of the chart. "Here is Sandhamn. Southeast of Sandhamn we have the lighthouse that marks the shallows on Revengegrundet. Outside of that, we have the starting line."

"In the middle of the open sea?"

"That's right."

Thomas picked up a pen and drew two small crosses. "Between these positions we have the starting line the day Juliander was killed. This left cross is the windward flag, and the right one is the leeward flag. The sailboats try to keep as close as possible to the windward flag at the moment the starting gun goes off."

"Why is that?"

"Because there they will have the best wind."

Margit nodded, although she still seemed a little confused.

There was a knock at the door, and a gray-haired man looked in.

"Oh, sorry," he said. "I didn't mean to interrupt you."

He remained in the doorway waiting for a reply.

Thomas shook his head and waved him in.

"Come in," he said. "We were just going over the chart for the starting area, and you're exactly the man we need right now."

Fredrik Winbergh stepped inside. He wore jeans and a light-blue polo shirt with a blue sweater draped over his shoulders. Behind his horn-rimmed glasses, his eyes were sharp and intelligent.

He greeted them both and then looked down at the chart.

"So, how can I help you?" he asked. Though he didn't look as shocked as he had the day before, he still seemed shaken from his loss. His eyes were slightly swollen.

Thomas gave him a reassuring smile.

"I'd like you to mark where you were at the starting line. Can you estimate the distance?"

Fredrik Winbergh nodded. Without a word, he took the pen from Thomas and drew a small dot just a few millimeters from the cross marking the windward flag. His hand was sure and deliberate. Then he smiled sadly at Thomas and Margit.

"I've been reading nautical charts my entire life. I was the navigator on board the *Emerald Gin*. That's how we usually worked it—Oscar was the skipper and I was the navigator. I can pin down angles and courses in my sleep if I have to."

"Excellent," Thomas said. "Now I need your help with a more difficult task. Where did you stand in relation to Juliander at the moment he was shot?"

Fredrik Winbergh nodded again. His eyes darkened as if replaying the scene of his close friend getting shot to death in front of him.

"I stood a few feet to his right, slightly behind."

"How sure are you of where you stood?"

"I clearly remember resting my right knee on the starboard bench. I have an old meniscus injury that hurts my knee sometimes, like when I have to maintain my balance at sea. So I try to rest it whenever I can."

"All right," said Margit.

"Oscar was turned toward the leeward buoy," Winbergh continued. "He was concentrating on the start, and both of us were watching the other boats to make sure we didn't collide with anyone."

"Do you have any idea where the shot came from?" Thomas asked. "Take your time and think. Can you remember the angle between the starting flag and your own position?"

"That's not so simple," Fredrik Winbergh muttered as he studied the chart. "I'll do my best, but keep in mind it's just a guess."

"Anything you can remember will help us," Thomas reassured him. "We'll compare your information with the forensic analysis of the direction of the bullet. What you say might help us catch the person who did this."

Thomas looked directly into Fredrik Winbergh's eyes and then pointed to the chart.

"We're trying to determine if the shot was fired from another boat. We haven't found anything yet to indicate another possibility. We need to figure out where such a boat might have been in relation to the *Emerald Gin*."

Fredrik Winbergh closed his eyes to recreate in his mind those fateful moments between life and death. When he opened his eyes, he studied the chart carefully. Finally he picked up the pen.

With a steady hand he drew an upside-down pyramid with the point meeting at the dot indicating the position of the *Emerald Gin*. The base of the pyramid spread to the right, into the area reserved for the spectators.

He put down the pen and looked back up at Thomas and Margit.

"I'm afraid I can't do any better than that," he said. "Still, the shot must have come from somewhere to the right."

"What makes you say that?" Thomas asked.

"I believe I felt the draft of it passing. To port—that is, to the left of us—there were only the other participants. I find it hard to believe that the shot came from one of them."

"Because . . . ," Margit encouraged him.

"How could he have managed it during the start?" Winbergh countered. "In front of his crew?"

Thomas nodded at Winbergh in appreciation. "Thanks. If this agrees with what we get from forensics, we can definitely rule out any other participant, along with your own crew. That would reduce the number of suspects considerably."

"Do you have any other leads?" Fredrik Winbergh asked. He seemed to relax a bit.

"We're working as hard as we can," Margit said.

"By the way," Thomas asked. "Why did he name his sailboat the *Emerald Gin*?"

Fredrik gave a half smile.

"That was Oscar in a nutshell," he said. "He loved dry martinis. No matter what the season, that's what he drank. Do you know the best gin for a martini?"

Thomas shook his head. He preferred beer.

"Tanqueray. British. In a green bottle."

"And . . . ," Thomas said.

"Tanqueray sponsored us. They paid for our sails—green, of course—and gave us unlimited bottles of gin. We christened the boat

44

the *Emerald Gin* and painted the hull green. As a matter of fact, green is Oscar's favorite color."

"I see," Thomas remarked.

"Everyone was happy," Winbergh said.

"We must ask you one more question," Margit said. "Do you know if Oscar had any enemies?"

Winbergh shook his head.

"Not that I know of. Still, in his field, you could make a number of enemies. And, of course, he had extramarital affairs. That's bound to come out. You'll have to look into it all, I suppose."

"Was his wife aware of his infidelity?" asked Thomas.

"Hard to know. Oscar tried to be discreet, but it was common knowledge among his group of friends."

"Is there anything else you think we should know?" Thomas asked. "Again, think carefully. Every bit of information is important at this stage in our investigation."

Fredrik Winbergh had been leaning over the table, but now he sank slowly into a chair. His shoulders drooped slightly and he frowned.

Thomas and Margit exchanged a glance.

"Please tell us everything you can," Margit encouraged him. "We need to know as much as possible about Oscar in order to find the killer."

Winbergh hesitated, then seemed to reach a decision.

"I believe Oscar was involved in something shady."

"What makes you think that?" asked Margit.

"He seemed nervous lately. Wound up. Oscar always had a thousand irons in the fire, but there was something . . . something haunted . . . about him that I didn't recognize. I was starting to wonder whether he took . . ."

"Took . . . ?" asked Thomas. He didn't want to say the words for Winbergh.

"I'm not sure. Maybe drugs." Fredrik Winbergh seemed troubled.

"What kind of drugs?"

Winbergh shrugged. "Oscar didn't hit the bottle every day, exactly, but I've seen him drunk often enough to know how booze affected him. And alcohol wasn't the problem in the situations I'm thinking of now."

"How can you be sure?" asked Margit.

"Something in his personality changed. It was different from when he drank." Fredrik Winbergh nervously ran his hand through his hair. "He became even more Oscar-like. It's hard to explain. Extremely talkative. More dominant than usual. Almost manic. And in addition . . ."

"In addition?" Margit leaned forward to catch his gaze.

"I don't know . . . perhaps I'm only imagining this. Something he said one night when we were sitting in the cockpit on *Emerald Gin* bothered me." He fell silent for a minute. "Something about how it cost a fortune to keep a vessel like that going. All his expenses . . . He said he'd have to find more ways to afford his lifestyle—more than those permitted by the government."

"And that stuck in your mind?" Margit asked.

Fredrik Winbergh nodded reluctantly, as though he hated every word he'd just uttered.

"It was so out of character for Oscar."

"In what way?" Margit asked.

"He was a lawyer. He'd witnessed people trying to bend the law to suit their own purposes. He told all kinds of stories about people avoiding the taxman or creditors. So it felt strange to learn he was thinking along those lines himself. He didn't sound like the Oscar I knew."

"And then what happened?" asked Thomas.

"Nothing," Fredrik Winbergh said. "It was late. We'd been drinking. The next day he didn't mention it. But now . . ." He made a frustrated gesture.

"Now you can't stop thinking about it," Margit said.

"Yes. It kept tumbling around in my head last night. Maybe he'd been serious. Maybe he'd gotten involved in something criminal that made someone want to kill him."

He looked at Margit and Thomas, torn between loyalty to his friend and a desire to help the police find the killer.

"I've sailed with Oscar for almost thirty-five years. Ever since we went to college together. He actually died in my arms."

He choked up for a moment and tightly laced his fingers together to regain his composure.

"He was standing at the wheel, full of life, with a huge smile. Invincible. And then he fell down right in front of me. Do you have any idea how that feels?"

He looked fiercely at Thomas. Then he slammed his fist against the table.

"I've never felt so helpless in my life. Can you understand that?"

Thomas met his eyes.

He'd once held the lifeless body of his three-month-old daughter in his arms, unable to do a damned thing.

He knew exactly how it felt.

Chapter 10

Thomas and Margit took a break before interviewing the von Hahne couple. In the meantime, someone came into the room to clear the bottles and water glasses. The window had been opened to air out the room, but it remained hot and humid. Thomas felt his shirt starting to stick to his back.

Ingmar von Hahne, however, appeared comfortable when he entered the room for the interview. He wore a short-sleeved shirt and a pair of khaki shorts with seams down the front. He began the conversation by describing his work as a dealer specializing in early twentieth-century art. He chose his words carefully. He pushed aside a lock of blond hair that kept falling over his forehead.

"How well did you know Oscar Juliander?" Thomas asked.

"Fairly well. We moved in the same circles. We celebrated Midsummer together. We were both on the board of the Royal Swedish Yacht Club for many years." He had a slight accent typical of the Swedish upper class.

"Do you know if he'd had a quarrel with anyone?"

"Not that I'm aware. Oscar was well liked. He was outgoing and involved in many things. But you never know about lawyers. He could have stepped on someone's toes."

"Tell us about your work on the RSYC Board," Margit said.

"Oh, that's a long story," Ingmar said. He flashed a winning smile. "My father was vice chairman back in the day and extremely involved in the club. That's back when they wore sailing uniforms and called each other 'dear old chap.'"

He winked at Margit.

"My family always owned sailboats, and I've competed in races since I was a child. It didn't matter how much I threw up in rough waters. I had to keep on going. My father was not the kind of man to let anyone give up."

He paused over this memory and shook his head.

"I was asked to join a committee—the club committee, I believe—and I moved up from there. We all have our cross to bear."

The last words he said with a disrespectful tone, as if trying to get a rise out of them.

"And now you're the secretary and second vice chairman," Margit said.

"Oscar was the first vice chairman."

"So perhaps now you'll be Hans Rosensjöö's successor?" Thomas asked.

Ingmar von Hahne shrugged.

"Our annual meeting happens soon. Hans cannot be reelected as chairman since he's been on the board for as long as they allow. I'm not jockeying for the position, but I won't say no if I'm asked. In this situation, everyone has to pull his weight, right?"

He brushed an invisible piece of fluff from his shirt and leaned back in the chair.

* * *

Isabelle von Hahne smiled as she entered the conference room. A pair of black sunglasses held her blond hair back from her face, and a few gold bracelets dangled from her right arm.

She likes expensive things, Thomas thought.

"How can I help you?" Isabelle asked. She sat in the chair across from them.

"Would you like something to drink?" Margit asked.

Isabelle von Hahne nodded, and Margit poured her a glass of water.

"Can you tell us about yesterday? You were a spectator on one of the boats closest to Juliander's when the shot was fired," Margit said.

"Yes, what a terrible day. Because Oscar was killed, of course. My husband and I—he's the RSYC secretary—accompanied the Bjärring family on their boat. We've done this for so many years that it's tradition. We eat well, drink some wine, and watch the start of the race."

She shut her eyes as she realized her description was disrespectful under the circumstances. She'd made a tragic day sound like a charming outing.

"And then that horrible thing happened," she added.

"What do you remember about the actual start?" Margit asked.

Isabelle von Hahne took a sip from her glass and paused to think.

"What I remember from the start? Everyone was focused on the sailboats as they jockeyed for position. I know we hadn't eaten yet, since we planned to begin once the large-class vessels had started. Some of our company used binoculars to see better, and Lena brought out a good Italian wine that we barely had a chance to taste."

She fell silent and twisted her wedding ring.

"We were excited to see if Oscar would be the first across the starting line. That new Swan is a fine boat," she continued. "He's—he was—an extremely competitive person. This year he believed he'd bring home the trophy. It was all he talked about these past few months."

She smiled at the thought of Oscar winning.

"Where were you when the starting gun went off?"

"With all the others on the flybridge. There's a lot of room, enough for a table in the middle. Even though there were quite a few of us, we all fit comfortably and enjoyed the wonderful view. We were having so much fun. Everyone was in a good mood, telling jokes and laughing."

"You were there the whole time?" Thomas asked.

"Yes, of course. Except when I went to the bathroom."

"Could you see Juliander's boat from where you sat?"

"Absolutely. We could see the whole starting lineup."

"How far were you from Juliander's boat?"

She studied her manicured nails.

"Maybe seventy, eighty yards. Maybe one hundred. It's hard for me to say for sure."

"Do you remember anything else?" Margit asked.

"Oscar was placed well. I remember that. I was admiring the entire starting line, however. That's what we were there to see, after all. Those big racing yachts are so beautiful."

"When did you realize what had happened?" asked Margit.

Isabelle von Hahne took another sip of water. Her brow tightened with concern.

"It was probably when the *Emerald Gin* rounded off and stopped sailing."

"What did you do then?" asked Margit.

"Axel turned the boat around so we could get closer and see what was happening. Then made his way to the police boat nearby. You were on board, weren't you?"

She looked at Thomas, who nodded.

"What were you thinking then?" asked Margit.

"What was I thinking?" Isabelle said. She put her elbow on the table and rested her head on her hand.

Thomas watched her closely.

"I really don't know," she said. "I probably thought that something had broken on board the *Emerald Gin*. A rudder or a sail. Something that made it impossible for the boat to compete."

She straightened up and looked right at Thomas.

"Not in my wildest dreams would I have imagined someone shot Oscar."

CHAPTER 11

Cognac spilled slowly from the heavy Martell bottle into the crystal glass. Martin Nyrén placed the bottle back in the bar cabinet. After a day filled with telephone calls to RSYC colleagues and acquaintances, he deserved a strong drink.

As the head of the Facilities Committee, it was his job to call each member of the committee to inform them of Oscar Juliander's death. Thanks to the media, the news did not come as a surprise. Still, a personal call was good form.

Martin Nyrén shivered. *What kind of sick mind would dream up something like this? Who would shoot someone to death in his happiest moment?*

Now he regretted not taking his vacation on July 1, like most of his colleagues. He'd thought it would be pleasant to remain a few more weeks after the tumult had quieted down. Plus, it was always best to have someone from the board on hand until the middle of July. Not much happened at the National Board of Trade during the summer, but you never knew . . .

At any rate, it was now too late.

His sailboat, a stylish Omega 36 with a white hull, waited for him at Bullandö Marina. The boat was the apple of his eye, and he would be able to get it soon. He would sail it alone if no friends or relatives wanted to keep him company.

He took a hefty swig of cognac. The warm amber liquid spread through his body, and he started to relax.

Holding the cognac, he walked into his home office—more of an alcove by the bedroom—and turned on his computer. He'd purchased this three-room apartment in the Birkastaden District in the early nineties, and he liked it. Real-estate prices had been low then, so even a government bureaucrat could afford to buy an apartment in the center of the capital.

He swiveled the glass between his hands as he thought about Juliander. He didn't have much to do with Oscar, except for the board meetings, of course. The Facilities Committee was not as glamorous as Juliander's Offshore Racing Committee.

Nyrén's duties involved managing the club's various properties and making sure they were properly kept up. His committee oversaw the maintenance of the docks and the buildings. It wasn't very exciting work, but it suited him.

The computer screen blinked on, and Martin Nyrén made a few quick keystrokes to check his mail. As a government employee, he was careful to not receive private e-mail at work, since all incoming mail was considered an official document. Because of his relationship with Indi, he'd installed an extra security screen on his private computer.

He took a quick glance at his in-box. He found nothing but ads, except for a message from his brother wondering when they'd get together for a week of sailing. He also read an official memo from the government office telling employees about Oscar's death.

He shivered as he thought about the gunshot.

Dreadful.

He scrolled down the list of messages. Nothing from Indi today either. Most likely the family was in the country. Not so easy to send a message to a secret lover, Nyrén realized. Still, he was disappointed. Even a short message would please him. He considered sending a text message, but it was late and a text might draw too much attention. Someone else might see it. Someone who had to be kept in the dark. No matter what.

That had been the one condition of the affair. Nonnegotiable.

If their love were revealed, the consequences would be unimaginable. Indi was vigilant. The family must not be affected. The children came first.

Martin turned off his computer and sighed. He hated these weeks of vacation when everyone else spent time with relatives and friends. Vacation meant a long string of barbecues no one truly wanted to attend. Half of the couples at these events politely lifted their glasses to one another while thinking about someone they were seeing on the side.

After observing all these seemingly happy couples, he was glad he'd never married. He'd rather be single for the rest of his life than live a lie. It was better to wait for an honest e-mail than to participate in a hypocritical marriage.

He downed his cognac and went to pour himself another glass.

Tuesday,
THE FIRST WEEK

CHAPTER 12

As soon as his eyes opened, Thomas was wide awake. He lay on the edge of the double bed that dominated the corner of Carina's small studio apartment in Jarlaberg, not far from the Nacka police station.

Carina was rolled up in a tight ball on the left side of the bed. Her dark hair covered half of her face. Her dimples were invisible when she slept. She looked more like a teenager than a twenty-five-year-old woman.

They were fourteen years apart in age, a gap that seemed much greater at times. The youth and enthusiasm that had first drawn him to her now made him feel old. He was closer to forty than to thirty. Before long, he'd be middle aged.

Looking back, he was no longer sure how this relationship with Carina Persson, the boss's daughter, had begun. He hadn't chased her. In fact she wasn't really his type, if he had any type at all.

His ex-wife, Pernilla, had been tall and thin like him. They'd met at a pub one evening while he was out with some friends from the police academy. They'd started hanging out after that. She'd studied at Berghs School of Communication and then taken a job as a project leader at an advertising firm. They'd finished their studies at the same time. They'd moved in together shortly after that and gotten married. The only thing missing had been a child.

They'd tried for years to conceive, deciding finally to join the wait for artificial insemination. Before they'd reached their turn in line, the miracle had happened.

He remembered the magical moment when Pernilla had held a stick with two blue lines in her shaking hand. It had seemed so incomprehensible. Finally, finally—a small life was taking shape in her womb.

Then the catastrophe. They couldn't deal with it. Everything they'd waited for, everything they'd hoped for—all gone. If Emily hadn't died from SIDS, perhaps they'd still be married, but grief and guilt had destroyed their marriage. They'd divorced almost two years ago.

For a long time, he couldn't look at another woman. His long-time friend Nora kept trying to match him up with various single friends, but he had no interest. He felt only indifference.

Carina was always at the police station. She'd had to put in a massive amount of overtime during their murder investigation last summer. She never complained, even when the days were long. She'd worked through endless lists and compilations in their hunt for information.

One day she'd invited him to lunch. After a few lunches, she'd suggested dinner. After that, they'd gone to the movies. One thing led to another, and now he slept at her place several days a week.

Thomas looked over at her.

She didn't resemble her fat father in the least. She didn't have his bad moods either. She was cute as a button, petite with dark hair and a nice figure.

Thomas insisted they keep their relationship quiet at the station. He didn't want his colleagues to know, and certainly not her parents. Carina had gone along with this so far, but she was beginning to question the secrecy. She planned to leave her job at the station soon. Then they would no longer be colleagues.

He felt like an alien in her apartment. It was a feminine place with fluffy, embroidered pillows scattered about and a light-blue sofa, a color he'd never have chosen. It looked more like a girl's bedroom than an adult's apartment.

What was he doing here with a woman who was so much younger—not just in body but also in soul?

He didn't know whether to feel embarrassed or flattered that a woman her age wanted him. Perhaps he was unwilling to face the situation—the thrill of infatuation was fading, leaving no deeper feelings behind.

Nora might have understood, but she'd had so much to think about the last year. She'd always known what he felt before he did, like a little sister.

This special friendship with Nora had existed for a long time. Pernilla had never questioned it, unlike Nora's husband, Henrik. But Thomas and Henrik had never been close.

From the start, Thomas had seen Henrik as a spoiled, upper-class medical student. But Nora had fallen in love with him, and Henrik had reined in his worst behavior. Later, Thomas had figured out how to handle Henrik, but they'd never been comfortable around each other. These days, he often met Nora alone, or together with Simon, Nora's youngest boy. Simon was also his godson, and Thomas was very fond of him.

Thomas glanced at his alarm clock. It would be twenty minutes before it went off, but it seemed already bright as midday outside. Carina's white curtains let in more light than they kept out.

As Thomas rolled onto his back, his thoughts turned to the investigation. Obviously Oscar Juliander was a strong, virile man who liked the company of women. This meant that both his wife and his lovers had reason to kill him. Or why not some cuckolded husband? Jealousy was a powerful motive.

On the other hand, why would a wife get rid of the husband who provided everything for her? Apparently she'd put up with his extramarital affairs for years, so why would she take such drastic revenge on this particular day?

Regardless, they needed to talk to his wife as soon as possible. Thomas hoped she'd recovered enough to speak with them. Last Sunday, in Sandhamn, she'd not been capable of dealing with anything, and her doctor had not allowed them to interview her.

Thomas thought about the client list the law firm had provided. They'd handled hundreds of bankruptcies in the past few years. Juliander must have made a fortune. How he'd found the time to juggle work, women, and sailing was another question.

Thomas decided he'd assign Carina to check Juliander's bank accounts. Money often revealed motive. He wondered if lawyers were generally honest, or if they simply hid illegal funds better since they knew how to work the system.

Thomas glanced at his alarm clock again. Time to get out of bed and take a shower. First on today's list: a visit to the Kalling law firm.

CHAPTER 13

Nora stared at her cell phone. The message in her voice mail was painfully clear, yet she didn't want to admit what it meant. The man from the Outer Islands Real Estate Agency said he would be in Sandhamn the next day to appraise the property. Would someone be there to meet him on the steamboat landing?

The property had to be the Brand house! Henrik must have gone behind her back and contacted an agent without speaking to her first. She didn't want to believe that, but who else could have arranged such a meeting?

Nora sank into her wicker chair on the glass-enclosed veranda. The Mårbacka geraniums crowded the windowsill, though the pots were dry. The sun had shined on them all morning, and they needed watering.

How could Henrik do such a thing?

She let her gaze drift out the windows toward the Brand house. The building towered over theirs, standing on the hill just a stone's throw away. She could almost smell the roses growing along the outer wall. Aunt Signe had loved those roses like children.

Last fall, Nora had declined a dream job in Malmö as the bank's regional lawyer. Henrik did not want to leave Stockholm.

After what she'd been through last summer, it hadn't been difficult to refuse the offer. She'd felt fragile and depressed. Henrik had even urged her to keep her old job at the bank's central law office. "You're not up to a big change right now," he'd said. "You need rest first."

As she slowly began to regain her balance during the winter, she wondered why Henrik assumed his job was more important and that the family should remain in Stockholm. Couldn't he follow her for once? Why was there so little room for her own ambitions?

If Henrik had been offered an exciting position in another city, moving vans would be pulling up to the door.

Declining the job had left a thorn inside her that wouldn't go away. It pricked at her. No matter how much she tried to reason with herself, neither facts nor logic eased her discontent. It was difficult to accept remaining at the same job with the same overbearing, incompetent boss—a constant reminder why the job offer in Malmö had made her so happy.

She stood up and plucked a few yellowing leaves from the geraniums. She couldn't avoid confronting Henrik about this message. She already dreaded asking the question.

She went into the kitchen to prepare lunch for the boys. Swedish cultured sour milk, cornflakes, and cheese sandwiches. She didn't have the energy to make anything else. Sometimes, it seemed that summer vacation was nothing more than a food preparation marathon. Between making breakfast, lunch, dinner, and snacks, there was not much time left for her to enjoy vacation.

As usual, Henrik was down at the docks working on his boat, a six-meter class that he raced at every opportunity during the summer. It would be hours before he'd be home.

Nora decided to bring up the question in a quiet moment. They'd already fought a lot this past winter, and she had no desire to start their vacation with another quarrel. She would be neutral, not aggressive.

There must be a reasonable explanation. Henrik deserved the chance to explain before she accused him of deception.

She put the thought out of her mind for the moment and walked outside to call the boys in for lunch.

CHAPTER 14

The entrance door to the fin-de-siècle building at the center of Norrmalm Square opened more easily than Thomas had expected.

The door squeaked a bit as it opened. On the wall inside, a brass plaque informed Thomas and Margit that the Kalling law firm had offices on all floors, but the reception was on the third floor. A red carpet led to the elevator.

From behind an expensive dark-wood reception desk, a cute girl in a modest white blouse and blue skirt greeted them. She asked how she could help them. They explained their business, and a few minutes later a well-dressed woman in her fifties approached them.

"Mr. Hallén, our managing partner, can see you now," she said. "Please follow me."

She led them through the hallway to a conference room with a large mahogany table. In the middle sat a row of sparkling waters in several flavors and a tray with coffee cups in blue-and-white Danish porcelain next to a plate of cookies and a bowl of expensive dark chocolate.

"Are they inviting us for coffee?" Margit whispered to Thomas.

The middle-aged man who entered the room matched every one of their prejudices about lawyers.

He wore a dark custom-made suit with thin chalk-white stripes. His breast pocket held a light-blue silk handkerchief that matched his tie, and his white shirt had been perfectly pressed.

"What a terrible incident," Ivar Hallén said. He shook hands with Thomas and Margit. "Absolutely dreadful. Oscar was an esteemed colleague here in our firm. He took our big cases. He was much in demand and generated substantial business." He gestured to them to take a seat.

"Did Juliander have any conflicts with any clients?" asked Thomas.

Hallén turned the question over in his mind.

"Not that I'm aware of," he said. "He's a bankruptcy lawyer, so there is little chance of conflict with clients. The company is already insolvent, if you get my drift. The bankruptcy administrator is a neutral party called in once bankruptcy has become a reality."

"Was Oscar Juliander popular here at the firm?" asked Margit.

Hallén took his time before answering. He pressed his palms together and looked down at the table before he began to speak.

"Popular is probably not the right word. He was respected and valued as a lawyer. Still, he was a bit of a prima donna. He was always happy in the spotlight, no matter what the occasion."

The lawyer fell silent for a moment before continuing.

"Some people thought he took credit for himself at the expense of the firm. He put in many hours and ruled the associates with an iron fist. His team was always the first in the office and the last to leave."

"So he earned a great deal of money," Margit said.

"Yes, he brought in the largest fees."

"How do you share the profits here?" Thomas asked.

"We have a true partnership."

"What does that mean?"

"We share everything equally. Once all bills are settled, the profits are split among the partners."

"Do the partners bring in the same income?" asked Margit.

"Not at all," Hallén said. "There's a great deal of difference in the amounts each partner makes."

"If that's the case, why do you have an even split?"

Hallén shrugged.

"That's a good question. The point of a true partnership is that lawyers don't compete for clients so that they can maximize their personal profit. Instead, the client gets the partner best suited for his case."

"This wasn't to Juliander's advantage?"

"That's correct." Hallén took a sip of coffee from one of the blue-and-white cups before he continued. "Oscar was not pleased with our system. To be honest, he strongly objected—he was the one who brought in the most money, so he wanted the greatest share of the profits."

"What did the other partners think?" asked Margit.

Hallén gazed at a point on the wall above Margit's head. A few seconds passed before he continued.

"Conflict was in the air. Oscar threatened to leave our firm if he didn't get his way."

"How much money are we talking about?" asked Thomas.

"Oscar's income would have increased by several million kronor."

Margit knew it was common for people to want more money. But that was not the most important issue here.

"Was this a major problem?" she asked. "Important enough for someone to want to kill Oscar Juliander?"

Hallén twisted in his chair. Experienced lawyer that he was, he appeared to regret sharing this information. All at once, he no longer wanted to talk.

"I would hardly call it a problem, more like a disagreement among the partners. By no means would it have led to violence. Absolutely not." He shook his head emphatically.

Thomas glanced at Margit as if to indicate it was time to finish this conversation.

"We would like to speak to Oscar Juliander's secretary, if you wouldn't mind," she said.

"Absolutely. Not a problem. Please stay here, and I'll bring her to you."

Hallén walked to an intercom and spoke a few short sentences, and then he turned to Thomas and Margit.

"Eva will be right here. Oscar's secretary's full name is Eva Timell," he added. "She's worked for him for as long as I can remember."

He'd barely finished when someone knocked on the door.

A dark-haired woman in a dark-blue dress and trim pumps entered. She wore a discreet pearl necklace but no wedding ring. Her eyes were red rimmed, and she held a crumpled handkerchief in her hand, as if she'd been crying.

"I'll leave you now," Hallén said. He shook their hands. "Don't hesitate to contact me if you need anything else. The Kalling firm will do its utmost to help your investigation. The person who killed Oscar Juliander must not escape justice."

Eva Timell sat silently at the other end of the table and looked at Thomas and Margit.

"How long did you work for Oscar Juliander?" Margit asked.

"For more than twenty years," Eva said. "I started with the firm just as he made partner, near the end of the eighties."

She tried to hide a sob but was not successful.

"Please excuse me," she said. "I'm all worn out. The phones have been ringing off the hook. Everyone wants to know what happened and how his cases will be handled. And all his colleagues are in shock."

"How much did you know about Juliander's caseload?" asked Thomas.

Eva Timell straightened up.

"I was aware of everything Oscar did," she said.

"Can you describe this a bit more?" asked Margit.

"Oscar often said he'd never make it through the day without me. I had access to his e-mail and correspondence. Not to mention his cell phone, which he was always forgetting."

"You were his right-hand man, so to speak," Thomas said.

"I was the one who kept his life in order, both at work and in private."

"In private?" Margit asked.

"Oscar had too much to do to keep up with his private affairs. He was extremely busy."

"So you helped him out?"

"Yes, of course, whenever necessary. I bought birthday presents, sent flowers, accepted invitations. You know," she said, with a look at Margit.

Margit had no idea. *I certainly don't have anyone helping me buy birthday presents or sending flowers,* she thought.

"Did your boss have conflicts with anyone?" asked Thomas.

Eva Timell considered the question. Then she shook her head.

"Not that I know of. Oscar was a highly respected lawyer. You probably know he was on the board of the Swedish Bar Association."

"If he had any enemies, you would have known," Thomas stated.

Eva Timell nodded. "Oscar would have told me."

Margit walked over to the window. Norrmalm Square spread out before her, alive with tourists and office workers walking among the flower shops and cafés. In one corner of the square, she saw an ice cream shop with a long line.

She turned back to the room and looked at Eva Timell.

"How was his marriage? Did you know his wife?"

Eva's eyes wavered.

"His marriage . . ." She stopped speaking, as if carefully choosing what she wanted to say.

"Were they happily married?" Margit asked.

Eva Timell sighed and began to speak again.

"Not exactly. It had been quite some time since their marriage was a happy one. But it is possible"—she drew out her words—"that they weren't altogether unhappy either."

"What do you mean by that?" asked Thomas.

Eva Timell grimaced and then looked at him.

"He was a successful lawyer, and she was a housewife who took care of the children. They had a huge house in Saltsjöbaden and a summerhouse on Ingarö. As long as he could come and go as he pleased, she enjoyed the social status and a standard of living that many would envy. Sylvia wanted for nothing. They had an agreement, you could say. A personal contract."

"Did he see anyone outside of his marriage?" asked Margit.

The corners of Eva's mouth lifted slightly, as if the question was funny.

"Did he see anyone? Of course he did. Quite a few, in fact."

"Are you sure?" asked Margit.

"I sent flowers to various women on his behalf. You surely can't believe that a man like him would be satisfied with one woman for thirty years?"

"But how did he get away with it?" asked Margit. An image of her own spouse went through her mind. Bertil spent most of his evenings in front of the television. They'd been married for twenty years.

Eva Timell looked at Margit as if she found the question completely naïve.

"Oscar Juliander was rarely home during the week and sometimes not even on the weekends. How could his wife have known if he were in an important meeting at work, having a board meeting with the RSYC, or meeting up with his mistress? What do you think he was doing whenever he was out of town on business trips—watching CNN?"

Eva smiled and shook her head.

"He also raced extensively. Morals go out the window when you make it back to port. Successful men are very attractive, especially if they have gravitas and a fat wallet."

She looked at her intertwined fingers.

"But he was loyal to Sylvia, as far as I know. He never wanted to embarrass her. He was always very discreet."

"With your help."

Margit regretted the words the moment they left her mouth, but she couldn't help herself.

Eva Timell sank back into her chair. The silence in the room became oppressive. Finally she said, "Oscar was my employer. I made a point of being as effective and loyal as possible."

"Would you please make a list of the women you know your employer had been involved with?" Thomas asked.

He handed her his card.

"We will likely be back with more questions. If you think of anything before then, we'd be grateful if you contacted us."

Eva Timell nodded and looked at Thomas with sorrow in her eyes.

"I still can't believe he's dead," she whispered. Then she got up and walked out the door.

CHAPTER 15

Henrik came home right after lunch, catching Nora off guard. Before she could mention the phone message, he smiled and told her he'd made an appointment with a real-estate agent for the next day.

The realization made her cold inside. Did he not know how she felt, or did he not want to understand?

While she tried to form a response, she realized he was looking for praise besides.

"It wasn't that easy, believe me, right in the middle of the summer and all," he said. He looked pleased. "Especially if you're looking for a really good guy."

"But shouldn't you have asked me first at least?" Nora said.

They were standing in the kitchen. The boys had already run into the yard. Nora began wiping down the counters forcefully so she wouldn't have to look at him.

Henrik seemed surprised. Then anger flooded his face.

"I thought you'd be happy," he said. "It's hard to know what you want these days. I'm trying, I really am."

He opened his mouth as if he wanted to say more, but then he shut it again.

Nora smiled in an attempt to pacify him.

"I was just a little surprised," she said. She put down the gray dish-rag. It was on its last legs, and she made a mental note to pick up more at Westerberg's Grocery Store the next time she had to go shopping. "Perhaps it's not a bad idea to get a professional opinion. As long as he won't feel we're wasting his time."

Henrik looked at her.

"What do you mean by that?"

"We haven't decided whether we're going to sell—we've only made a few offhand remarks about it."

"You can't be serious about us moving in there," he said. "Do you really want to live in a house that belonged to a murderer?" He crossed his arms over his chest and leaned against the countertop.

Nora felt her body go rigid. Through the window she saw a guide leading a group of tourists through the village. He was likely telling them Sandhamn's history and how the population used to live long ago.

She wondered if life was easier then. Probably not. Just different.

Her instinct was to become defensive.

"Don't call her a murderer! Aunt Signe was a fine person." She spoke more sharply than she'd intended. "She didn't will the property to me to sell it. She wanted me to take care of it. She loved the Brand house more than anything else."

"Get a grip," Henrik said. "She killed two people, or have you forgotten that? Don't be so goddamn loyal. Two people are dead because she didn't want to share her property."

Henrik could not hide his frustration. Nora shot him an unhappy look. She felt torn between her loyalty to Aunt Signe and keeping the peace at home. She didn't want to quarrel with Henrik again.

"Sweetheart," she said. "Let's not argue about this. Let's meet the agent and see what he has to say."

She snuggled close to him and tried to relax. He smelled like coffee and cologne, a familiar scent that made her feel better immediately. She buried her face in the crook of his neck and felt him soften as well.

"That's just what I've already said. You'll see this is the right thing, Nora." He stroked her hair as he spoke. "All I want is what's best for us and for the children. Can't you understand that?"

CHAPTER 16

Thomas drummed his fingers impatiently on the green fence surrounding the entrance to the Department of Medical Forensics in Solna. They'd driven there right after visiting the Kalling law firm.

The department was just north of Stockholm, on the campus of Karolinska University Hospital. The redbrick building looked like any other in the area. Students sauntered across the lawns. Presumably taking summer courses.

"How long can it take to open the door?" asked Thomas. He didn't expect an answer.

"About as long as it takes to walk the length of the place," Margit said. The autopsy rooms were on the other side of the building. "He'll be here any minute. Just be glad that he took our case first so we don't have to wait until the end of the week for results."

Thomas didn't reply, but he stopped drumming his fingers.

Behind the glass door's white ruffled curtain, a shadow appeared shortly before Dr. Oscar-Henrik Sachsen emerged.

"Sorry it took me so long," he said. "There's no one around to open the door in July."

Margit and Thomas followed him through the long hallway, down a spiral staircase, and into another long hallway. Finally they arrived at a collection of silent, neutral spaces, where the pale linoleum matched the gray walls: the autopsy rooms. Various instruments and stainless-steel bowls were arranged on a counter.

They greeted Dr. Sachsen's assistant with a nod. The assistant wore a long white coat and was busy entering something into a computer.

A body rested under a white sheet on an examination table nearby.

"Would you like to take a look?" Dr. Sachsen asked.

Without waiting for an answer, he pulled the sheet off of Oscar Juliander.

The bullet hole looked remarkably neat, like a small incision below his left nipple.

"He's a good-looking guy," Margit said. "He must have gone to the gym quite a bit to stay in shape like that."

They recognized his face from television and newspaper photos. Juliander had frequently appeared in the media during the real-estate crash in the nineties, when many businesses went bankrupt. Since then, whenever a similar case had come up, he had been called in to give his opinion.

"I assume there's no doubt about the cause of death," Thomas said.

"No, no need to put much time into figuring that out," Dr. Sachsen said. "His death must have been instantaneous."

He leaned forward and pointed.

"The bullet went straight through the heart's right ventricle, although the shot was not direct. The bullet's trajectory indicates it entered the victim's body from the front right."

Thomas remembered Fredrik Winbergh's statement.

With a pair of tweezers Dr. Sachsen picked up an object less than a centimeter long and five millimeters in diameter.

"Here's the bullet. It appears to be from a rifle, half-jacketed, and it matches the wound."

"So, not a handgun," Margit said.

Dr. Sachsen shook his head. "I don't believe so. A handgun would have left more residue by the entrance wound. Still, we'll have to wait for the ballistic analysis to say for sure. Did you find any cartridges at the scene?"

"No, nothing," Thomas said. "Is there any other evidence it was a rifle?"

"The shot was fired from a distance," Dr. Sachsen said. "Otherwise, the area around the wound would have been more torn."

Margit studied the object after Dr. Sachsen set it down in a bowl.

"It's a small-caliber bullet," Dr. Sachsen said. "Most likely a .22."

"What does that tell us?" Margit asked.

"Well, I'm not a ballistics expert, but I've brought down a deer or two. These bullets are often used in hunting."

"Why is that?"

"These bullets expand when they enter the body. That's why it has this mushroom appearance at the top."

"To cause more damage," Margit muttered to herself.

"It's also unusual to use lead-tipped ammunition in a handgun," Dr. Sachsen continued. "Which would further indicate a rifle."

Dr. Sachsen picked up the bullet again so they could study it more carefully.

"Look here. Here's the lead tip. Only the casing is copper. Typical hunting ammunition. The bullet stays in the body and causes the maximum injury possible, just as you said, Margit."

He slowly set the bullet down.

"If I were you, I would look for a rifle designed to hunt small animals."

"If a rifle was used, the shooter could not have been aboard the *Emerald Gin*."

Thomas found himself coming to the conclusion as he uttered the words.

Since the bullet had entered Juliander's chest from the right, the killer must have been on a boat to his windward side. In other words, from the spectator boats.

It fit their theory.

He closed his eyes to better visualize the start of the race. The police boat was behind the starting line, with the big starting vessel right in front of them. There were hundreds of spectators.

"At least two people must have been involved," Thomas started to think out loud. "One steering the boat and the other taking the shot. It would be too difficult to do both at once, especially since the shot was so precise."

"Is it even possible to shoot accurately from a moving boat?" asked Margit.

"You'd have to be very good to hit such a target," Dr. Sachsen said. "But in the right position, with the right weapon, it could be done. What was the weather like that day?"

"Very calm," Thomas said. "A light breeze. An ideal summer day."

"Perfect circumstances for aiming a rifle accurately," Dr. Sachsen said. "You could do it from any deck."

"Someone should have heard the shot." Margit looked skeptical.

"Not if the sound of the starting gun masked it," Thomas said. "That's a loud bang, believe me."

"But how could someone time it so well? It's less than a second."

"A real ace could manage it," Dr. Sachsen said.

"Perhaps he used a silencer," Margit said. "That sound wouldn't have carried far."

Thomas nodded. "Especially if he synchronized it with the starting gun. Even if someone else heard, they might have thought it was just an echo."

"A silencer works well with small-caliber ammunition," Dr. Sachsen said. "But it's harder with larger calibers. You can't dampen the sound so well. With a .22, there's nothing but a dull thud."

"Hardly noticeable at sea," Thomas said.

Again, he remembered Juliander on the deck after the race began, and the confusion that broke out when the crew realized their skipper was dead.

Thomas took one final look at the bluish-white body on the examination table.

"We're dealing with a cold-blooded killer," he said.

CHAPTER 17

The drive from Solna to Saltsjöbaden usually took about thirty minutes if it wasn't rush hour. Thomas drove while Margit sank into thought. They passed Fisksätra, a crowded group of shabby apartment buildings built in the seventies. They stood in stark contrast to the fashionable houses in Saltsjö-Duvnäs and Saltsjöbaden.

A few minutes later, they reached Saltsjö Square and turned west toward Neglinge. The Juliander house sat on the other side of Hotel Bay and the historic Grand Hotel. The winding road led them past huge mansions with exquisite gardens sitting next to some white brick town houses from the sixties.

Out on the spit, they could see the RSYC yellow clubhouse.

Only fifteen minutes from the center of Stockholm and they found themselves in the middle of the countryside. The water sparkled in this lush landscape. Some houses were completely covered in ivy. Hundred-year-old oaks stood in many of the yards, a clear indication that Saltsjöbaden was one of the first suburbs of Stockholm. The industrial Wallenberg family had founded it, and their influence was still felt throughout the area.

Thomas turned onto Amiralsvägen, and they soon caught sight of the large gray mansion. It had a fantastic view of Saltsjö Lake. In the driveway, a Land Rover was parked next to a silver Lexus, while another car, a black Porsche, rested in the shade.

"Not a bad place," Margit said. "I wonder how long it takes to clean it."

"You mean for the maids? I doubt they pick up a vacuum cleaner themselves," Thomas said.

They walked to the white front door, and Thomas rang the bell. A young man in jeans and a red shirt with a well-known logo opened the door immediately. He introduced himself as David Juliander, Oscar's youngest son.

Margit remembered that the lawyer had three children: two sons and a daughter. The daughter was studying abroad. Paris, if Margit had her facts right. The youngest was following in his father's footsteps and studying law. The oldest son worked in IT. So David was the one studying law.

Thomas expressed his sympathies and asked for David's mother. The young man invited them to sit down in the living room. He said that his mother was still resting, but he'd let her know they were there.

They sat on the large corner sofa upholstered in an unusual material resembling suede. It faced the water so one could enjoy the view.

While they waited, Margit wondered about the woman they were going to meet. How did she feel as she wandered through this house while her husband was off having his adventures? The children must have been busy with their own lives.

She could imagine Sylvia moving from room to room waiting for her husband. She must have known what was going on. Perhaps she'd even confronted Oscar and then learned to swallow the bitter truth to preserve the marriage.

She must have been lonely, especially after the children left, Margit thought.

* * *

A few minutes later, Sylvia Juliander entered the room. She looked pale but composed. Her brown hair framed her narrow face. It was obvious that the past few days had taken a toll on her.

Her son sat next to her and watched his mother with concern. It was obvious he wanted to take care of her, as if he were the parent instead of the child.

"You have some questions for me," Sylvia said. She spoke in a quiet voice. She fidgeted with a loose thread on her blue cardigan. Her well-trimmed fingernails were painted a neutral color. She wore a large sapphire ring as well as a simple golden wedding band on her left ring finger.

Thomas broke the silence.

"As you know, our highest priority is to find the person who murdered your husband. Therefore, we must ask some questions that may seem unpleasant or unusual. We apologize for any distress."

Sylvia nodded.

"Do you know if your husband had any enemies?"

The pale woman looked frightened.

"Why would he have any enemies? Oscar was a business lawyer. People liked him. He was in great demand."

"It's important that you consider the possibility, no matter how strange it seems," Thomas said. "We need to create a picture of your husband's public and private lives."

Thomas gave her an encouraging smile.

"I understand. Still, I've never heard him mention any enemies," Sylvia said. "Actually, I know very little about my husband's business. He said he didn't want to bore me with his work. I wouldn't understand much of it, anyway."

David Juliander's face twisted, and he leaned forward.

"My dad received threatening letters," he said.

Thomas studied the sad young man. Despite the tan, he looked worn and tired.

"Who sent them?" Thomas asked.

"I think it was called Property something. I don't really remember. Something to do with real estate."

"How do you know?" asked Thomas.

"I happened to open a letter by mistake. My dad told me it was a company who'd employed him during some bankruptcy proceedings. He told me the previous owners had owed the Russian mafia money. The mafia wanted to pillage the company, but they went into bankruptcy before that happened."

"Are you sure about this?" Margit asked.

David seemed to hesitate.

He's just a boy who's recently lost his father, Thomas thought.

"Pretty sure. When they found out about the court proceedings, they told my dad to stop the bankruptcy case. But the court had already ruled on the matter."

The young man was familiar with legal terms. He clearly went to law school.

"What happened to the letters?" Margit asked.

"He said he'd given them to the police." David seemed unsure. "I don't remember that well. It was last year, or maybe even the year before. My dad told me not to worry about them."

He cleared his throat and went on.

"My dad laughed it off," he said. "I asked if he was scared. He told me that such threats happened occasionally to lawyers, but it was nothing to worry about. I'd forgotten all about it until now."

Thomas made a note to check if Juliander had filed a report about the threatening letters. He also noted that the letters had been sent to the home address, even though the family had an unlisted telephone number.

Margit turned to Sylvia and asked, "How was your relationship with your husband? Were you happily married?"

Sylvia appeared insulted by such a private question.

"We've been married for almost thirty years. We have three children."

"Please answer my question," Margit said. "How would you describe your marriage?"

Sylvia stared at Margit for a moment. Then with a sigh and a quick look at her son, she decided to speak.

"I was alone most of the time," she said. "Oscar traveled a great deal. He had work and many other duties as well. The Swedish Bar Association, the RSYC."

"Tell us about his sailing," Thomas said.

Sylvia's entire face transformed. As she smiled, the worn contours disappeared. She was still a beautiful woman.

"Oscar loved sailing," she said. "He's loved it since he was a teenager. He's always raced. The bigger the boat, the better. I think his best memories were made at sea. He found peace there, even though he always focused on winning."

"Do you like to sail?" Margit asked.

Sylvia laughed. Her smile disappeared.

"No. I don't like sailing. I get seasick the moment I see a mast." She pulled her cardigan tighter around her body. "But it was Oscar's life. Our eldest son loves it, too. But not David. Right, darling?"

She looked at her son, who nodded in agreement and squeezed her hand.

"What did you do while your husband was at sea?" Thomas asked.

Sylvia shrugged hopelessly.

"I'd wait for him in port. Or I'd stay at our summerhouse on Ingarö. I often found myself waiting for Oscar. It became part of our marriage."

"Were you also active in RSYC?" Margit asked.

"Not really." She shook her head. "Oscar wanted me to become more involved. I did my best, but I wasn't really interested."

"Did your husband expect to be elected chairman this fall?" Thomas asked.

"Yes. But I wasn't really paying attention. It wasn't that important to me." She spread her hands. "Becoming chairman was just one more duty that would take him away from us."

"Why do they need a house on Ingarö when they already have one with such a wonderful view of the water here in Saltsjöbaden?" asked Margit as they left. "Going from one water view to the other. What's the point?"

Thomas turned the Volvo around and started back. He simply smiled.

"What do you make of those threatening letters? The Russian mafia has their methods, but that's not usually one of them," Margit said.

"I hope the letters are still around. That is, if Juliander actually filed a police report. It's not certain that he did. We'll have Erik check for it."

Margit nodded.

"If the letters exist, we'll have to find out where they came from," she said.

Thomas's telephone rang. He picked up the call.

"Hello, this is Britta Rosensjöö. We met on Monday."

Thomas pictured the distraught woman who'd constantly twisted her damp handkerchief between her fingers.

"Hello," he said.

"Well, yes," she said. "I want to tell you something . . . if you're not busy, that is."

"Not to worry," he said. "What's up? Did you find your camera?"

"No, I haven't, but I'm sure it'll turn up. It's not the first time I've misplaced something."

She fell silent for a few moments.

"The thing is, I think someone broke into our hotel room. Hans says I'm imagining it, but I still wanted to call and tell you."

"A break-in?" Thomas asked.

"Yes, that's right. It looks like someone was in the room."

"Is anything missing?"

"Not a thing. But it's not the way I left it."

"Do you think the cleaning lady might have moved things around?" Thomas asked.

"That could be it." She hesitated for a moment. "But still, it feels like someone has been in our room. I can't shake that feeling."

"But nothing is missing, you say?"

"That's right."

"Perhaps it's nothing to worry about. If you find something more, that something has gone missing, give me a call."

Thomas hung up and told Margit about Britta's concerns.

"What do you think?"

"I think it probably has nothing to do with the investigation. She seemed a bit confused last Monday, and she's still pretty shaken by what happened."

Margit looked out the window. They passed the square and were heading back to the highway.

"I'm sure you're right. Just a cleaning lady moving things."

CHAPTER 18

A strange feeling came over Martin Nyrén when he opened the front door. He stood in the hallway and looked around.

The long, blue-patterned Persian runner was still in place. On the hall table, beneath the Balinese mirror he'd bought on a trip to Asia, everything was in its proper place. Below the mail slot, a few white envelopes and ads lay on the floor.

Still, something made him hesitate.

He walked into his living room without taking off his shoes. His beautiful Italian leather sofa was there, and the windows were properly shut. He noticed he'd forgotten to close the curtains when he'd left that morning, and the orchids were wilting in the bright sun.

Then he realized what he'd been sensing: an unfamiliar scent. A smell that didn't belong.

He furrowed his brow as he tried to identify it. A mixture of exotic spices? Nutmeg, perhaps, or cloves.

He walked back into the hallway and hung up his jacket.

Where had this scent come from? Had somebody been in his home?

He walked around his apartment again. Everything appeared normal, nothing missing or out of place.

He sniffed the air again. Was he imagining things? It was hard to tell.

He shook his head and let go of the thought. It was probably the smell of flowers in the hot air. The apartment was certainly stuffy.

He opened the window as wide as possible to let in the cool evening air.

Then he poured himself a glass of whisky and water.

Their loud voices woke him in the middle of the night. He'd turned thirteen that summer, but wetting the bed still woke him up. He'd try to scrub the sheets clean in the sink so nobody would notice.

This time, something else startled him from his dreams. His father's muffled voice came through the thin walls between the bedrooms of the summerhouse. He heard his mother's desperate pleading.

"I'm begging you. Please stop seeing that woman!"

His mother cried. She was drunk. Of course.

She thought nobody noticed when she poured herself glass after glass of sherry. Everyone in the household knew what she was doing. But nobody said anything, especially not his father.

"Don't stick your nose into things that don't concern you!" his father yelled. "If you weren't sloshed all the time, I wouldn't have to go to her."

He pulled up his blankets and put his pillow over his head so he wouldn't have to listen. The lump in his throat hurt.

When he got up in the morning to eat breakfast, Elsa told him that his father had already gone back to Stockholm for important business and his mother had such a migraine she needed to be alone.

WEDNESDAY,
THE FIRST WEEK

CHAPTER 19

Persson cleared his throat to indicate that it was time to get the meeting started, and people took their seats, coffee mugs in hand.

It was eight in the morning—exactly two days and twenty minutes since Oscar Juliander had been shot to death a few nautical miles southeast of Stockholm. Rain beat against the windows. The temperature had dropped to sixty degrees as dark clouds rolled in. *Typical Swedish summer,* Thomas thought.

Thomas and Margit sat on one side of the conference table while Kalle and Erik took chairs at the short end, with Carina next to them.

Persson cleared his throat again. "Well, it's time to draw some conclusions. Who wants to start?"

He looked directly at Margit and Thomas.

"So, you two went out to Sandhamn. What did you find out so far?"

Margit walked over to the whiteboard. The first marker she picked up was dried out, but the second one worked.

As she wrote, she discussed the main conclusions that she and Thomas had arrived at.

When she was done, Margit pointed to the list on the whiteboard:

Jealousy
Mistresses
Wife?
Cuckolded husband
Financial crimes
Russian mafia
Drugs

"Why did you put a question mark after *wife*?" asked Persson.

Margit took a few moments to think before she replied.

"She certainly has a motive, but she also has an alibi. Seven people described her drinking Italian wine on the Storebro when the shot was fired. Every single person on board that boat can back each other up. She also appears to have no experience with guns, let alone a permit to own one."

Margit reached for her coffee cup.

"I don't see what she'd have to gain," she said. "I believe we can eliminate her as a suspect at this time."

"Nobody will be eliminated until I say so," Persson muttered. "I understand there are several mistresses involved."

A number of meaningful looks were exchanged around the table.

"You could say that," Erik said quietly.

"Are you jealous?" Margit smiled.

"No, I'm doing quite all right with the ladies," Erik responded. Everyone around the table believed him. He was a young man, almost thirty, with a boyish smile and a muscular body.

Kalle held up the list of mistresses from Eva Timell. Over a dozen women were listed by name and address.

"So he enjoyed the good things in life." Persson chuckled.

"That's one way to look at it," Margit said. "If you find a man cheating on his wife funny."

"Let's focus," Persson said. "Divide the list among yourselves and contact these women. We can leave the wife out of it for now. Next, what can you tell me about the financial situation?"

Thomas turned to Carina.

"How did it go? Did you locate his financial records?"

The prosecutor had granted them permission to examine Juliander's bank accounts.

"I've just begun," Carina said. "It'll take some time since it's hard to reach people in July. I'll know more by the end of the week."

"We're also going through his legal caseload to see if anything comes up," Thomas said.

"I see. What about the Russian mafia hypothesis?"

Persson turned to Margit and Thomas, who, in turn, looked at Erik Blom. Erik flipped through his notebook.

"We found no police report, so it appears he did not bring the letters his son mentioned to our attention. According to Eva Timell, the letters may be connected to the bankruptcy of a company called Eastern Property. It's been a few years since Juliander handled the case."

"That may be why he didn't take the letters seriously," Thomas said.

"Or he didn't dare report it," Margit said.

"I spoke to a former colleague in Financial Crimes yesterday," Erik said. "I asked if he recognized the name Eastern Property or anyone who may have been involved."

He flipped through a few more pages and looked up.

"My colleague checked the names against their records."

"What did he find?" asked Margit.

"He didn't find anything in the crime records, nor in the list of banned economic activities."

"If the Russian mafia was involved, they might have used a fall guy."

"A fall guy?" Carina asked. She looked embarrassed as she realized everyone else knew what the term meant.

"It's the person who takes the fall if a company goes bankrupt, especially if there were any financial crimes. They find a man on the board to take the blame."

"Are there really people who'd do that?" Carina asked.

Thomas couldn't decide if her question was serious or if she was really that naïve. Then he felt a little disloyal for questioning his girlfriend—or whatever she was to him.

"You'd be surprised," Margit replied. "If you only knew what a guy down on his luck would do for a few thousand kronor. Somebody on unemployment would be glad to sign his name on a business contract for next to nothing."

"Whatever," Erik said. "If the mafia used a fall guy, it won't be easy to find them."

"How does the Russian mafia usually operate?" asked Persson. "Does this match their methods?"

There were a few moments of silence until Thomas spoke up.

"I'm not an expert, but it doesn't seem like it. Waiting a whole year just to get rid of a troublesome bankruptcy lawyer? It's a stretch."

He was doodling a few pictures in his notebook.

"If they were really unhappy with Juliander, they would have sent some thug to beat the shit out of him."

"They would have had many ways to get rid of him," Margit agreed. "A car crash, a shot in the night, a knife in the back in a dark place. Take your pick."

She leaned over the table.

"This was a sophisticated murder that required care and planning. Our Russian friends are not known for their finesse. Why go all the way to the seafront when it's easy enough to take him out after work some dark night?"

She sank back into her chair and crossed her arms. She looked like an angry wasp with her short dyed-red hair. It wasn't pretty, but it inspired a certain respect.

"Maybe they wanted to send a message," Persson speculated.

"So long after the letters?" Margit raised an eyebrow. "Who would they be targeting? All the bankruptcy lawyers in Sweden? Those gangs tend to keep to their own kind. They avoid lawyers and the courts. It's a bad idea to draw attention by attacking the judicial system."

"I can buy that," Persson said. "So let's put the Russian connection to the side for now."

He rocked in his chair, which creaked under his weight.

"In my opinion," Thomas said, "*how* Juliander was killed is as important as the fact that he *was* killed."

Persson turned toward Thomas.

"Go on."

"As Margit mentioned, this murder was very carefully planned. So I believe the way he was killed is important. It had a purpose. Juliander was taken down in a moment of triumph."

"Yes," Margit said. "It was almost an execution if you think about it."

"That's right," said Thomas.

"Would a scorned woman go to so much trouble to kill her lover?" asked Persson.

"Doubtful. But what about a jealous husband?" Thomas asked. "A competitive sailor, perhaps active in RSYC, who would be at the start of the race anyway. Someone who had access to both a boat and a rifle."

"That's worth looking into," said Persson. "Keep following that lead." He changed the subject. "Drugs. What can we say about that?"

Thomas summarized his conversation with Winbergh and his suspicions of drug use.

"So Juliander was a drug user?" Persson asked. "Any other evidence for this?"

"We haven't found any so far."

"So the charming lawyer did have a few secrets. By the way, what have we found out about the murder weapon?"

Erik pointed to a tall stack of printouts in front of him.

"We're comparing all gun permits with the names of the people around Juliander. We're especially looking for persons who had licenses for small-caliber weapons and ammunition."

"Be sure to include the entire RSYC gang," Persson said.

"How many people are we talking about?" asked Margit.

"There are about six hundred and fifty thousand gun owners in Sweden and over a million gun permits." Erik grimaced. "At least we have Sachsen to thank for ruling out shotguns."

He winked at Carina, who winked back. She went to the window and opened it wide. The fresh air was a relief in the oxygen-starved room.

Persson collected his papers. Nobody said a word.

"I think that's enough for now. Everyone knows what to do for the rest of the week?"

Persson started to get up from his chair, then sat down again.

"By the way," he said. "Keep the prosecutor in the loop. Otherwise things will get hairy."

"We'll be meeting with her tomorrow morning," Margit said. "We'll take care of it. Don't worry, Charlotte Öhman's on the case, and we know her."

CHAPTER 20

Nora disliked the real-estate agent from the moment he set foot on Sandhamn. She couldn't decide which was worse: his dapper jacket, his polished shoes shining from across the dock, or the fact that he wore a tie in the outer archipelago.

His youth surprised her. He smiled like this was the opportunity of his life. *An ambitious young man,* Nora thought to herself. *Ready to impress his superiors.*

Svante Severin wasn't dissuaded by Nora's cool reception. He flashed a well-practiced smile and shook her hand far too long. With Henrik, he acted as if they'd known each other for years. A constant stream of words flowed from his mouth in the ten minutes it took them to walk to Aunt Signe's house.

When they reached the house, he used every superlative imaginable to describe the property.

The kitchen had an irresistible, old-fashioned charm. The Swedish tile oven in the dining room entranced him. The old-fashioned veranda took his breath away. Even the old bathroom, with its claw-foot tub, received its share of breathless admiration, though it was obvious the room needed a complete renovation.

Nora bit her tongue and delivered a stiff smile.

"Were you listening?" Henrik asked.

"What was that?"

Lost in thought, Nora had not heard a word they'd said as she followed them down the stairs and back into the dining room.

"You have to pay more attention, darling. Svante said they'd adjust the fee since this is such a unique property."

Nora crossed her arms and looked at Svante Severin and Henrik.

"Fee?"

"They have to be paid for their work, of course. But Svante here is ready to waive his normal fee of four percent for a fixed sum. Doesn't that sound great?"

Henrik wrapped a protective arm around Nora's shoulders while nodding to the real-estate agent.

"Absolutely," the man said. "It would be an honor to market a cultural treasure like your house. I'm sure we can come to an agreement that benefits everyone."

He smiled as if to reassure them. "I wouldn't haggle about percentages in a case like this."

The situation was bizarre. Nora searched for a sign that Henrik understood she was far from ready to sell.

She pulled away from Henrik and walked to the window. The view amazed her, as always. Through the inner window, she could see the old wicker chair on the veranda where Signe used to sit in the evenings. For a moment, she almost thought she heard the thud of a tail on the floor, the sound of Signe's dog, Kajsa, who'd always slept at her feet.

"I think it's too soon to discuss all this," Nora said. "Henrik, we need to talk this over first."

Henrik continued as if she hadn't spoken.

"Listen, Nora. Svante says there's already been an offer."

"An offer?"

"A good offer. This house is in demand."

Nora touched the old Mora grandfather clock in the dining room. It had stopped ticking.

"How can there be an offer? We haven't even put the house on the market."

Severin looked at them with surprise.

"You see, after Henrik and I talked, I searched our customer register. Sandhamn is very attractive, especially for Swedes living abroad. We have a list of customers who have already expressed an interest in buying older homes here."

"I still don't understand," Nora said.

"After our conversation, I found an interested family. They're Swedes living in Switzerland. When they heard about the Brand house, they jumped at the chance to buy it."

Nora was furious. She couldn't decide who made her angrier: her husband or his real-estate agent. But she had reached her limit.

"How much money are we talking about here?" Henrik said.

"I believe"—Severin paused for effect—"we're talking about several million here. It's an extraordinary house in an extraordinary location. It's all about location, you know," he said.

"Wow, that's a fortune," Henrik said. "And all for something that just dropped in our laps." He turned to Nora. "Unbelievable, right? Just think what we could do with that kind of money! We'd have all kinds of possibilities!"

He beamed at the real-estate agent.

"Henrik, we have to think about this," Nora said. "We haven't even decided to sell yet."

Nora gave her husband a thunderous look, and then she turned to the agent.

"Thank you for taking the time to come to the island. We really have to think about this. Both of us." She glared again at her husband, but he seemed lost in thought about the money.

She led the agent to the door.

"We'll be in touch," she said.

Chapter 21

They divided the list between former and present mistresses. Thomas took one half and Margit the other.

Some of the women were businesswomen and others were people Thomas had never heard of. Two of them were flight attendants. *How typical,* Thomas thought. Others were married to prominent men and would hardly welcome a visit from the police asking about a murdered lover.

Though it was summertime and people were vacationing, it had been surprisingly easy to find out where each woman had been at the time of the murder. Thomas decided to interview Oscar Juliander's latest *conquest*—as Erik had called her—the woman on his speed dial.

Diana Söder was thirty-nine years old. She hadn't yet left for vacation, and Thomas hoped he could catch her at her workplace on Strandvägen.

Thomas parked his car in an expensive garage. He walked down Birger Jarlsgatan past the Royal Dramatic Theater, where tourists sat on the stairs watching the crowds go by. Then he turned in the direction of Djurgården.

"Strandvägen Art Gallery" was elegantly scripted on the glass of the front door. Two large landscapes in heavy golden frames hung in the window.

He walked into a long, narrow space with white walls covered in works of art. Ceiling spots lit up the artwork. To the right of the entrance were two comfortable club chairs in forest-green leather with a glass table holding art magazines between them.

What Thomas knew about art could be written on a note card. He realized he had no idea if the art on the walls was worth ten kronor or ten thousand.

An attractive woman sat at an antique desk near the back of the gallery. She was speaking on the phone but quickly ended her conversation when she saw him.

"What can I do for you?" she asked.

She wore a rose summer dress and a pearl necklace. Her hair was gathered behind her neck in a clasp. When she smiled, the trace of a dimple appeared on one cheek.

Thomas introduced himself and showed her his police badge.

"I have a few questions about Oscar Juliander."

The woman's face turned a bit pale, but she nodded and offered him a seat in one of the club chairs.

"What would you like to ask me?" she said quietly, sitting down.

Thomas pulled out his notebook and flipped to a new page. Diana Söder watched him nervously.

"Could you describe your relationship to Oscar Juliander?" he began.

"We were friends."

"Very good friends, from what we understand," Thomas said.

He could tell by her expression that Diana Söder didn't want to answer. But Thomas waited, he could afford to be patient.

"We had a relationship," Diana Söder finally said. She looked at the floor and fiddled nervously with the ring on her right hand. It was made of intertwining gold and silver strands.

Thomas had a thought.

"That's a beautiful ring," he said. "Is it new?"

Diana Söder nodded.

"Did *he* give it to you?"

Her hands stopped moving as a tear slid down her cheek.

"For my birthday. This past June. He had it specially made for me."

"How did you two meet?"

"At work. The gallery has a December party for customers and important people who like to be seen and heard. My boss's wife organizes it."

"So you met at this party?"

"Yes, a year and a half ago, the day before the Saint Lucia's Day celebration. Isabelle always invites many guests, including the entire board of the Royal Swedish Yacht Club and their wives. But Oscar came alone."

RSYC. Isabelle. This got Thomas's attention.

"What's the name of your boss?"

"Ingmar von Hahne."

Thomas tried to hide his surprise. How could he have missed the fact that Ingmar von Hahne was her boss? Now he remembered that von Hahne had mentioned that he worked in the art world.

"Ingmar owns the gallery. He started it just about twenty-five years ago. He's a real art lover but not a salesman." She smiled slightly. "He loves the art too much to sell it."

What a remarkable coincidence that Juliander's latest mistress worked for Ingmar von Hahne, Thomas thought. Did it mean something?

"What happened at the party?"

"We started talking. Then he called me a few days later and asked me to lunch."

She sighed slightly and let her eyes wander to the window.

"Things just went on from there. Oscar could be very stubborn when he knew what he wanted."

"Did you know he was married?"

Diana Söder avoided looking at Thomas.

"Yes," she said. "I knew. Oscar said he and his wife had an agreement. As soon as the children finished their studies, he was going to divorce Sylvia."

A note of defiance crept into her voice, as if she was daring him to contradict what she'd just said.

What a familiar line—the children needed to grow up before the unfaithful husband could leave his wife. Convincing his mistress that his children had to finish their university studies took it one step further.

Thomas tried to understand why an attractive woman like Diana Söder would be in a secret relationship with a married man, especially a womanizer like Oscar Juliander.

"Were you planning a future together?"

"I was hoping to. I loved him very much."

Her voice was so low that Thomas had to strain to hear the words.

"I need to know where you were last Sunday when Oscar Juliander was killed."

She clasped her hands in her lap before she answered, almost like she was praying.

"I was with my brother and his family at their summer place on Skarpö. I heard what happened on the news . . . that he was killed."

"Can your brother confirm that?"

"Of course. It was horrible, finding out about it on TV." Her eyes filled with tears, and she tried to hide them by running her forefinger beneath each lid. "Why would anybody want to kill Oscar? It's incomprehensible," she said.

"That's what we're trying to find out," Thomas said. He leaned toward Diana Söder. "Was Oscar acting any differently lately?"

She thought about it for a moment.

"He seemed harried. Stressed. I thought he just had a great deal to do at work. But all through this past spring, he was more moody."

"Do you know if he had any financial trouble?"

She shook her head.

"Not anything he discussed with me. In fact, he was always generous whenever we met. We took trips together and always stayed at elegant hotels." She fell silent for a moment and then asked Thomas, "Do you think this is all about money?"

"I don't know. And I can't discuss the investigation."

Diana Söder sank back into her chair. Her eyes were shiny with tears.

"Do you know if Oscar Juliander used drugs?" Thomas asked. He kept his voice as calm as possible. He didn't want to frighten Diana.

It was so quiet in the room that they could hear a woman with a baby carriage walking by on the street outside. They could even hear the pinging of the rattle hanging from the carriage.

"Yes, sometimes," Diana said. "He did cocaine every now and then."

"What did you think about that? Did you do it with him?" asked Thomas.

Diana Söder shook her head.

"Not on your life. Oscar wanted me to try, but I refused. I have my son to think about."

"But Oscar still did it?"

"He said it helped him concentrate, made him think more clearly. We argued about it. He thought I was being ridiculous."

"How long had he been doing drugs?"

"I have no idea. He first used in front of me about a year ago."

"Where were you then?"

"In my home. I'd gone to the bathroom, and when I came back he showed me some white powder on a pocket mirror. He asked me to try."

"And you did?"

"No, I already told you." Diana Söder's voice was sharp.

"What happened then?"

"He told me not to worry about it. He said lots of people use cocaine. It wasn't any worse than alcohol."

"You never thought about leaving him?"

"I loved him. I trusted him when he said he had it under control."

"How did it affect him?"

"Not badly, really. He got louder and his eyes were shinier. He'd get wound up. Never aggressive, just more intense." She smiled a sad smile. "That was Oscar, always full of life."

Then she glanced at her watch, a discreet gold band on her wrist.

"I have a customer coming in ten minutes. Do you think we'll be finished soon? I'll have to pull myself together. I can't look like this when he arrives."

"Just one last question. Do you know if Oscar had any enemies?"

She shook her head.

"None that I know of. But he could be really condescending at times to people he didn't like, especially to other lawyers."

"What do you mean?"

"He'd rant on and on about their incompetence. Called them idiots. Sometimes he'd say that someone never should have been admitted to the Swedish Bar Association. Or that he should be kicked out."

"Did he say things like that in public?"

"He could be sharp when he showed that side of himself."

Sharp enough to attract a mortal enemy? Thomas thought. *Had Oscar Juliander been so rude that someone decided to kill him?*

"Do you know of any contact with the Russian mafia?"

Diana Söder looked at him in surprise.

"Why would you ask a question like that?"

"He may have received some threatening letters from them."

"I've never heard about anything like that. But he probably wouldn't have told me."

Thomas stood up.

"I think we're finished now. Thank you for taking the time to talk to me. I'm sorry for your loss."

Diana Söder tried to smile as she said good-bye, but her expression looked more like a grimace. As Thomas closed the door behind him, she disappeared into a room at the back of the gallery. He thought he heard a muffled sob as he stepped outside.

CHAPTER 22

This must be the first time we awarded the Round Gotland prize with flags flying at half-mast, Hans Rosensjöö thought.

The stage had been erected between the harbor office and the large dock. Hans stood next to Ingmar von Hahne, waiting for the ceremony to begin.

A large table with a blue velvet tablecloth bearing the club's emblem held the prizes. Rows of silver trophies stood beside magnums of champagne and plaques for the second- and third-place winners. An enormous flower arrangement topped off the display.

Hans Rosensjöö, as chairman, would award the prizes. The race coordinator and Ingmar's sweet daughter Emma would help him. It was always pleasant to have a female participate, especially since men dominated the competition by 90 percent.

But the atmosphere was not festive, given the circumstances. The Yacht Club's restaurant was usually fully booked, but they'd received a stream of cancellations. This displeased the maître d'. They'd had to rearrange the tables to make the restaurant look less empty.

Hans Rosensjöö wished he could have stayed away, too. But since they'd decided that the race would continue, they had to go through the formalities: the awards ceremony, the exclusive dinner, the whole bit. They owed that much to the other participants who'd completed the race.

Hans glanced at his watch. Ten more minutes until the official gunshot went off, indicating the beginning of the awards ceremony.

Britta Rosensjöö was chatting with Isabelle von Hahne and a few others, and, as usual, Isabelle dominated the conversation. Britta sipped her champagne. *Where does Isabelle get all her energy? How does she keep up with all these committees and volunteer organizations? The woman needs a real job.*

But that wouldn't have been acceptable in her upper-class family, Britta realized. Though she and Hans moved in high circles, Isabelle's were even higher. In the fifties, her father had been one of the most important industrial giants in Sweden. Her family would never have allowed a beautiful daughter an education or a career. Instead Isabelle had married a nobleman to acquire even higher social status and a title.

Britta almost felt sorry for Isabelle. She'd met her father several times before his death and remembered him as stiff and tradition bound. He'd ruled his family with an iron fist.

Britta glanced at her husband over by the awards table. He looked tired and worn out. These past days had been difficult, and she was concerned. He would be sixty soon. No longer a young man. It was time to put his health before his duties. She'd never told him how glad she was that he was leaving the board. She was counting the days.

To tell the truth, she never liked Oscar that much. He was too full of himself. He'd already started to act like the RSYC chairman that summer, though Hans had not yet stepped down.

Britta found Oscar's behavior presumptuous, although she didn't discuss this with her husband.

She had always preferred Sylvia, a pleasant person who came from a better family than Oscar. But Sylvia often stayed behind in their summerhouse on Ingarö. She never seemed comfortable at these kinds of events, where Oscar's ringing laughter and endless sailing stories dominated every conversation. And Oscar probably didn't mind Sylvia staying home and letting him take center stage.

"Right, Britta?"

Britta shrugged vaguely at Isabelle's question. She'd been lost in her own thoughts.

"I'm sorry, what were you saying?" she said. "I didn't hear you. I'm so scatterbrained this week. The other day I lost my camera, and this morning I lost my sunglasses."

Isabelle smiled at Britta.

"I was just saying I hope the awards ceremony doesn't go on too long. It would be nice to get this evening over with as quickly as possible."

Britta nodded in agreement. She took another sip of champagne and discovered her drink had grown warm. But the thought that Hans would soon be done with all of this cheered her up. She smiled as she imagined never having to attend another function like this again.

THURSDAY,
THE FIRST WEEK

CHAPTER 23

"Take a look at this," Kalle said. He pulled some sheets of paper from the fax machine.

It was almost four in the afternoon, and they were the last people left on the floor. So many had left on vacation or were off working on the Juliander case.

As Erik looked over the pages, he recognized the logo of the National Forensic Laboratory in the top corner.

"So, Linköping sent their autopsy analysis."

"Yep," Kalle said.

Erik sat in a chair near Kalle's desk and quickly read the three-page report.

"I see," he said. He scratched his head. His dark hair was combed back with a touch of gel, and his white short-sleeved shirt rode up in the back, revealing a patch of suntanned skin above the waist of his jeans.

"Not much doubt about it." He held out page two.

"Not much."

"Traces of cocaine in Juliander's blood."

"So Winbergh's suspicions were correct."

"But does it mean anything?"

"That's the question, isn't it?"

* * *

"That's such wonderful news, Nora! Just think how great it will be!"

Monica Linde sounded so excited that Nora had to hold the phone away from her ear for a moment.

"Henrik told me! Now you can buy that big house in Saltsjöbaden. All I can say is congratulations. Something good came out of that woman's despicable behavior. Every cloud has a silver lining!"

Nora's snobby and tactless mother-in-law knew exactly how to irritate her daughter-in-law.

Nora had never been fond of Henrik's mother; Monica tended to boast about all the important friends she'd made during her long stint as a diplomat's wife, and name-dropping was not one of Nora's favorite pastimes.

Nora took a deep breath and managed to control herself.

"I don't understand," she said. "What did Henrik tell you?"

"That you're selling the Brand house, of course! And you've gotten a fantastic offer!"

"That's what he told you?"

Monica ignored Nora's chilly tone.

"That town house you have—it always felt so dull. So boxed in. And your neighbors have neither class nor style."

Monica paused to catch her breath.

"Henrik has always enjoyed spacious living quarters, ever since he was a child. I could never understand how he deals with that little house of yours. It's absolutely wonderful that you can buy something bigger now."

"We like where we live just fine," Nora said.

She wanted to end the call, but she'd hear about it for years if she hung up on her mother-in-law. She considered pretending her battery was dying.

"I'm so upset about Oscar's death," Monica continued. "So upset! What's this world coming to? Have you seen the evening papers?"

"Yes, I have."

"How can such a handsome man be killed like that? It's incomprehensible. And the police aren't doing a thing about it, of course. No matter how much tax money they spend. They're so incompetent."

Her son Simon came running through the doorway, and Nora seized her chance to escape.

"Simon wants to say hi to you," she said. She pushed the phone into her son's hand without saying good-bye.

After he'd hung up, Nora gave her son a quick peck on the forehead to thank him for being patient with his grandmother. She knew she needed to talk to someone besides Henrik about selling the Brand house, and she needed someone who would understand. Thomas. He knew the whole story of the house and Aunt Signe.

Nora wrote a text message:

```
Call me when you have a chance to talk.
```

He responded right away:

```
On Sandhamn already. Something happen?
```

Nora smiled. Quick and efficient. Typical Thomas.

```
How about a beer at the Divers Bar at six?
```

She clicked "Send."
The reply was immediate.

```
OK -T.
```

CHAPTER 24

"So, how are things going?" Nora asked.

Thomas set down his beer. He'd drunk half of it in one fell swoop, and now he let out a discreet burp.

"What do you want to know?"

"You know I'm curious! All of Sandhamn is wondering who killed Oscar Juliander! It's been in all the papers the last few days!"

"You think I'm going to spill the beans about an investigation just because you're curious?" Thomas smiled halfheartedly. He was tired after interviewing witnesses all day with Margit.

Nora looked better rested than she had for a while. Thomas noticed she wasn't as thin as she'd been the past winter. A few freckles were sprinkled across her perky nose, and the dark rings under her eyes had mostly vanished. Her slightly longer hairstyle gave her a softer look.

"Come on," Nora said. "You don't have to say anything. But Juliander was so well known; why wouldn't I want to ask about it?"

"Did you know him?" Thomas snacked on some peanuts the waitress set before them. He'd ordered a club sandwich that had not yet arrived. Nora sipped her beer. She'd invited Thomas to eat dinner with her family, but he'd declined. He had to catch the last ferry to Stavsnäs at seven thirty.

"I've met him a few times. He was a real bigwig in RSYC. Henrik's parents knew him."

"Did you ever work with him?"

"No. But he was well established in the elite Stockholm judicial circles," she said. "Kalling is a well-known old firm, and Oscar Juliander was one of Sweden's leading bankruptcy lawyers."

"Explain to me what a bankruptcy lawyer really does," Thomas said.

The waitress brought his order. He grabbed the ketchup and poured a healthy portion onto his plate.

"A bankruptcy lawyer," Nora said as she swiveled her glass between her palms. "He's the person who takes over the operation when a company declares bankruptcy."

"I understand that. But what does he *do*?"

"After a bankruptcy, the board or the management has no more access to the operation. They have lost the right to dispose of the assets."

Thomas looked at Nora, and she saw the fatigue in his eyes. Sometimes lawyers used jargon without realizing it was gibberish to outsiders.

"Can you speak in normal Swedish, please? What did you just say?"

Nora smiled. "The courts kick out the president, and the board puts a lawyer in his place. This lawyer's job is to close down the company and settle assets and liabilities."

"How does he manage that?"

"It varies. Sometimes the assets are sold one by one. Sometimes the whole company is sold. Sometimes the former owners buy back the company from the bankruptcy court and start over."

"Is that allowed?"

"Why not? The goal is to pay back the creditors as much as possible. If you can get a better price by selling to the former owners, so be it. It's not forbidden, though it may be considered immoral."

Thomas looked at her. This sounded like something that should be declared illegal. But then, he wasn't a trained lawyer.

"So Oscar Juliander became a kind of temporary company executive for a number of businesses."

"Yes, that's what he did, more or less."

"Have you ever heard anything unfavorable about him? Something out of line with his public image?"

Nora leaned back in her chair. She thought about all the gossip in Stockholm. He'd definitely been a womanizer. At the Swedish Bar Association parties, he'd always flirt with the young female lawyers. But what else had she heard about Oscar Juliander?

She shook her head.

"Actually, he had a pretty good reputation. And lots of money, I think."

"You should have seen their house in Saltsjöbaden. Three cars in the driveway."

"That Swan boat, the *Emerald Gin*, must have cost a small fortune," Nora continued. "And their place on Ingarö is very nice and not so far from my dear parents-in-law's place."

She winked at Thomas. He was well acquainted with Harald and Monica Linde and knew exactly what she meant.

"But I assume lawyers at a firm like Kalling already earn good salaries?" Thomas asked. He stabbed his fork into his French fries. "We met their managing partner, or whatever he's called. He spoke of making millions. That should go pretty far."

"Maybe so," Nora said. "But Juliander must have logged some serious hours to earn so much. Do you know the saying about competitive racing?"

Thomas shook his head. "No. What?"

"Competing in sailing is like standing in the shower and ripping up thousand-krona bills."

Thomas grinned.

"I heard an air force general came up with that line in the seventies," Nora explained. "Competitive sailing is incredibly expensive. I know how much money Henrik and his crew put into their six-foot sailing boat, and they only race in Sweden."

"What kind of money are we talking about?"

"I imagine a Swan like that would cost ten to twelve million kronor. Not to mention the sails, fees, and transportation if you're competing abroad. Just the Round Gotland Race probably cost a hundred thousand kronor."

"You're kidding."

"And he probably had to hire a few professionals for his crew. Then you have food, matching uniforms embroidered with the name of the boat, the cost of the awards dinner—the skipper pays for everything. That's the tradition."

She took a sip of beer and looked out over the harbor.

The orange pilot boat came into the toll dock. Her son Simon had just learned to read and thought it was odd that the word "PILOT" was painted in big letters on the hull. He insisted that a pilot flew an airplane and was not someone who captained a boat. It didn't help when Nora tried to explain that the word *pilot* was English. He still thought it was ridiculous.

"So, how's it going with the investigation?" she asked.

Thomas shrugged.

"We haven't brought the case into home port, so to speak." He couldn't help grinning. "We still have too many loose threads and not a single suspect."

"Did you find anything unusual about his legal work?" Nora asked. "Anything sticking out? Do you know the case he was working on recently?"

"Take a look for yourself. You're a lawyer."

Thomas reached for his briefcase and took out a sheaf of papers clipped together. He handed them to Nora. She began to flip through them.

"What about this one?" she asked. She offered him the paper.

"Keep it. If you find anything interesting, give us a call." He held up his palm defensively. "The answer to your unasked question is yes, we have begun looking into it all, but we don't have enough personnel. We need more help from the Financial Crimes unit, but it's the middle of July. You know how things are when it's vacation time in Sweden."

He fell silent and hesitated a moment.

"Anything special we should be on the lookout for?" he asked.

Nora picked up the document and studied it more thoroughly.

"Run all the board members against the Swedish Company Registration Office to see if any have been banned from carrying out business under the trading prohibition act, if you haven't already done so. Do the same with all the CEOs and executives."

"Good idea," Thomas said. "Erik will talk to them. He has a contact there."

Nora looked at her watch.

"Is that it on Juliander?" she asked. "I have to head home soon, and I wanted to talk to you about something else."

She played with the tiny saltshaker on the table. The old feeling of being disloyal to Henrik came back. She decided to ignore it. She really needed to talk this thing through with someone.

"Henrik wants to sell Aunt Signe's house. He's already found a buyer."

CHAPTER 25

Silence overwhelmed the office. It had become an empty space that could be filled only by one familiar voice.

Eva Timell put her face in her hands and wondered what she would do with herself. Her head ached. It felt like glowing steel had been bent into a crescent moon and pressed along the brow of her eye socket. If she closed her eyes, she could almost see it.

She didn't want to take her migraine medicine, though it usually reduced the pain enough to get her back on her feet. The throbbing over her eye was still better than the pain she felt over Oscar's death.

She looked at Oscar's office door again and again. After so many years, she couldn't help it. Her head would simply turn in that direction out of habit. Beyond that door was *his* desk, an elegant antique piece from the nineteenth century that he'd found at a Bukowskis auction house. He'd held on to it even when the firm had brought in an expensive interior design company that suggested modern, streamlined furniture. Now it looked as lonely as an abandoned dog.

In the first days after his death, she'd cried more than she'd thought humanly possible. A furious flood of tears ran past her red, swollen eyelids. At night, she pressed her pillow to her face so her neighbors wouldn't hear her sobs. Her Persian cat, beautiful white Blofeld, had hidden under her bed, frightened by her weeping.

She wondered how Sylvia felt now. Sylvia had all the right in the world to cry in public. The grieving widow, comforted by relatives and friends. At least she still had her children to live for.

Eva Timell's mouth formed a bitter grimace. Sylvia had everything and Eva nothing. But Eva was the one who'd known Oscar better than anyone else. Eva had planned every moment of his waking life. She'd kept track of his meetings and engagements.

Eva had chosen every single Christmas present Oscar had given Sylvia for the past fifteen years, every bottle of perfume in its luxury packaging. Eva had even kept a list so that there would never be any duplicates.

And what thanks did she get? A life as a single woman, middle aged, without children.

When Eva started as Oscar's assistant, they'd had a passionate affair. She'd never felt as loved as she had back then. She'd wake up early, wanting only to see Oscar at the office.

She'd often lie in bed and remember their intimate moments together. Sometimes she'd think of small surprises for him. Sometimes she'd buy a card, write a sweet message, and tuck it into his morning mail. Then she'd wait for him to discover it. He'd come out to see her with that special smile.

She waited years for Oscar to get a divorce. Little by little, as the children grew and Oscar's attention turned elsewhere, she'd realized he would never divorce. His life was far too comfortable.

Sylvia filled the role of wife and mother perfectly. She took care of their home and family and was a major asset to a successful, ambitious man like Oscar. She came from a good family and was part of the social circle in Saltsjöbaden. She didn't protest when his personal needs came before family life. Instead, she took care of parent-teacher conferences,

arranged dinners and spring parties, and turned a blind eye to Oscar's
romantic conquests.

She never questioned him, rarely complained, and was always there.

As time went on, Eva and Sylvia reached an understanding. They
divided Oscar between themselves. Sylvia took charge of his family
time, and Eva managed everything else. They orbited Oscar like two
moons around a single sun.

It pained Eva deeply when their romantic relationship died out,
but something new replaced that passion. Eva held his attention in
other ways.

She made herself irreplaceable.

While he became one of Sweden's most famous lawyers, she became
an indispensable part of his success. She took care of the stream of
incoming clients. At receptions, she made sure he always had a glass
in hand. If his shirt became wrinkled, she had a fresh one at hand. If
he double-booked himself, she tactfully resolved the issue so that both
parties were placated.

At times, she'd played with the idea of starting over, finding another
position. She realized working for Oscar would lead only to loneliness.
She turned forty and saw her chances of starting her own family shrink-
ing. Still, she never found the will to leave him.

Now, with a sigh, she stood up. She needed to find some water for
the little pink pill she would take after all. Her migraine was pounding,
and the pain was becoming unbearable.

Eva Timell walked to the kitchen ten yards down the hall to get a
mineral water from the refrigerator. She then turned on her computer
to address the flow of messages that had come in as the news of Oscar's
murder had spread. She hadn't had the energy to go to work those first
few days, but it was time to pull herself together and sort through the
mail.

Going through her personal in-box took some time. Many people who had known Oscar also knew her, and they'd sent their condolences directly to her, perhaps to avoid disturbing Sylvia.

Next she started on Oscar's in-box. After thirty messages, she came across one different from the rest. The address was a collection of letters and numbers that did not reveal the sender's identity: ACV91@hotmail.com. No subject. She clicked on it. The text came up on the screen and she scanned the few lines.

Oscar,

You promised the money would be deposited today at the latest. I can't wait any longer.

Benny

Eva Timell stared at the message. The tone was unusual for communication between lawyers. If it had come from another firm, it would have had the firm's logo and address.

Of course, it could be from someone involved in Oscar's latest bankruptcy case. But something was still odd about the message. The last sentence felt like a threat.

She checked when it had been sent. Last Friday, the same day Oscar left for Sandhamn. Two days before he was shot.

She reached for the water bottle. It was empty, so she walked back to the kitchen for another. She considered contacting the police about this message. Could it be harmful to Oscar's reputation in any way?

She weighed the alternatives and decided to show it to the police. What if the message had come from Oscar's killer?

His white graduation cap, now a symbol of hope and freedom, flew through the air as he sang wholeheartedly with all the other graduates of Östra Real School.

"We've graduated! We've graduated! God damn, how great we are!"

The relief of not flunking out made him euphoric, and his body felt bubbly as a bottle of champagne. The future is mine! he thought.

He would never have overcome a failure. Being one of those miserable, sad students who had to slink out the back door behind the janitor, while his family and friends waited in vain in the schoolyard by the entrance.

I'd rather die, he had thought while the examiner deliberated.

It had taken forever. He had stood ramrod straight, fists clenched at his sides, on fire with impatience and agony.

The examiner had shuffled through his papers and made a note. Then he'd taken off his glasses, polished them with a small cloth, and replaced them before opening his mouth.

"I believe the candidate has passed," he said.

Now here he was, diploma in his hand, freshly graduated as he saw his parents approach.

His father wore a hat and an elegant dark-blue topcoat, even though it was almost seventy degrees out. His mother looked elegant in a light linen dress and matching hat decorated with a pink cloth rose. His mother's personal seamstress had created the ensemble.

"Darling!" she exclaimed. She threw her arms around him. "How handsome you look! You've done so well!"

Her eyes shone. When she kissed him on the cheek, he caught a whiff of sherry. She couldn't leave it alone, *he thought.* Not even today.

"Congratulations, my son," his father said. "You've succeeded after all. I'm pleased."

"Thank you, Father." He gave a slight, automatic bow.

"Here you are, then," said his father, handing him an envelope. "Have some fun. You're only young once."

He winked.

He took the envelope, but his father's attempt at manly camaraderie only made him uncomfortable.

Farther away, his younger brother shot a peashooter at an older lady in a lilac silk dress. She gave out a short shriek and looked around, but she couldn't determine where the pea had come from.

His brother was grinning.

He looked for Elsa, their housekeeper. She should have been here. She was the one who had helped him get through school.

He could not have survived without her unconditional love.

"Where's Elsa?" he asked.

"At home, of course," his mother said. "She's getting the buffet ready. Who do you think would set the places and prepare the food if she was here?"

She laughed a bit too loud and shrill.

Well, who else would it be? Not you, Mother, drinking your sherry all day long, *he thought.*

One of his schoolmates took him by the arm.

"Come on, you have to meet my parents. And my little sister. She's eager to meet you."

Friday,
THE FIRST WEEK

CHAPTER 26

On his way to the station, Thomas decided to see if the bullet analysis was finished. The forensic medical examiner had sent it to Stockholm's technical department, and they'd forwarded it to the National Forensic Laboratory in Linköping.

It should have arrived on Wednesday, or at least yesterday. So it was reasonable to expect results by today from Linköping. It wouldn't take long to run the data through the computer once they'd received the bullet.

Thomas punched the number into his phone with one hand. Someone answered on the first ring. Thomas didn't know the woman's name, so he explained who he was and what he wanted.

"Well, you're in luck," the woman said. Gunilla Bäcklund was her name. "If you'd called ten minutes later, you'd have had to wait until Monday. I'm on my way out the door for an all-day meeting. Thank God it's Friday, right?" She laughed at her own joke.

Her casual demeanor irritated him, but he decided to ignore it. The analysis was part of a murder investigation, and every bit of information should be reported as soon as possible. He turned off the car fan so he could hear her better—it was just blowing hot air anyway. When he'd bought the car, he couldn't afford adding air-conditioning. Now he wished he had. The morning sun turned his car into a sauna. He asked what she'd discovered.

"We've done a thorough analysis," Gunilla said. She spoke brightly, not at all put out by his short tone. "You're in luck here, too. We know it's a rifle, and not just any kind either."

"Oh? How's that?" Thomas switched the phone to his other hand and rested his elbow on the edge of the rolled-down window. It was as hot outside as inside the car, and he felt sweat starting to slide down his back. He squinted against the bright light and wished he hadn't left his sunglasses at the station.

"As you probably know, the grooves and lands in the barrel of a weapon imprint every bullet," she said. "You can scan the number and direction of the lands depending on whether the gun barrel has left- or right-twisting grooves."

She reminded Thomas of one of the lecturers at the police academy who was enthusiastic even though her listeners were bored out of their minds. He realized this conversation would take a great deal of patience.

"I understand," he said.

Gunilla Bäcklund would not let herself be rushed.

"Most weapons, even handguns, have five to eight grooves of varying widths. They can be used to identify a weapon, since they are specific to the weapon and its maker."

"Yes, I see," said Thomas.

"In addition, the FBI has created a huge database of land and groove data from almost all the rifles in the world. They call it the General Rifling Characteristics file, though everyone just says the GRC. That's much easier."

She paused to take a breath and continued before Thomas could respond.

"It's a wonderful tool. All the police forces in the EU use it. Between that and the German database, we have all types of guns covered."

"All right," Thomas said. "So what have you found out about this exact bullet?"

He tried to stay calm, but he couldn't help honking at the car in front of him that was lingering despite the green light. The driver flipped him the bird.

"If a bullet comes from a weapon with a common groove system, it's almost impossible to identify the exact type of rifle," she said. She paused to increase the effect of what she was about to say. "But *this* bullet, you see, comes from a special rifle."

"You wouldn't mind telling me what kind, would you?"

"Not at all!" Gunilla Bäcklund said happily. "This bullet wasn't shot from a rifle with five to six right-twisted grooves. It comes from one with twenty!"

It was clear to Thomas that Gunilla Bäcklund expected him to respond with surprise. She waited in silence.

Thomas worked up as much enthusiasm as he could. "That's very exciting," he said. "But what does it mean?"

Bäcklund giggled.

"It means we know both the exact kind of rifle and its manufacturer."

Thomas couldn't help smiling. This was good news, really good news.

"And what is it, if I may ask?"

"It's a Marlin."

"A Marlin," Thomas repeated. The name sounded familiar, but he couldn't place it.

"Oh, it's a very popular American rifle," Gunilla Bäcklund continued. "It's cheap and dependable. It uses Micro-Groove landing for its .22. Excellent for us as an identification mark. You ought to thank your lucky stars that your suspect didn't use a common Winchester."

Thomas gave it some thought.

"Could you put a telescopic sight on a Marlin?" he asked.

"Sure. Easily. Theirs is specially made for quick shots, kind of like the express sight on a British gun."

"What about a silencer? Can you use one?"

"Definitely."

That's why nobody had heard a second shot. Dr. Sachsen's theory was most likely correct.

"Thanks, Gunilla. That was very helpful," Thomas said before hanging up on the long-winded Ms. Bäcklund.

He tried to imagine how many registered Marlin owners there were in Sweden.

Five hundred? One thousand? They could probably find out through the central gun registry.

This had to be checked out as soon as possible.

CHAPTER 27

Henrik whistled as he cleaned the nets from the morning's fishing trip. He'd gotten four perch, one fine turbot, and five flounder.

He stood at the edge of the water, where he'd hung the nets on four tall spikes down by the dock. He folded them carefully to avoid tangles. Tangled nets were the worst, especially if you discovered your mistake when you were already out to sea.

He opened the door to the Falu-red boathouse at the base of the dock. It was barely two yards long by one and a half yards wide, but it was tall with enough room for the nets and the tools. Everything hung neatly from black iron hooks.

Henrik walked back to the dock and opened the fish keep. You could store caught fish there for a few days so they were fresh when you wanted to eat them.

He picked up the perch and tossed three of them into a bucket of water. He set the fourth fish on the makeshift cleaning table he'd put together himself. The sun was already hot, and he felt sweat on his back. He'd enjoy a dip once this was through.

Adam and Simon were busy jumping off the end of the dock. They'd helped him bring in the nets that morning.

"Cannonball!" yelled Adam as he leaped off the dock. Water splashed in all directions, and his brother choked with laughter.

Henrik cut deeply into the perch's neck so that the head was almost detached. Then he stuck his knife into the anal opening and split the belly all the way to the orange fins. With a sure hand, he cut along the spine on both sides until the fillets loosened. He removed the sharp rib bones and pulled the meat from the skin and then took the small, upright bones from the middle of the fillet. This last bit was called "taking the pants off" by the inhabitants of the archipelago.

"Well, then," he said. He contemplated the results of his work. "Not even the royal palace serves such fine food."

He whistled an ABBA tune as he picked up the next perch. He'd scraped the fish guts to the side. The seagulls would have a feast later. It was a spectacle the boys loved to watch.

As he continued to clean the fish, he began to dream about spending the millions they would make by selling the Brand house. It was incredible, better than winning the lottery.

Not that he didn't have a good salary. As a radiologist at one of Stockholm's major hospitals he earned more than the average Swede. He actually earned more than an average household with two incomes. But he didn't want to be an average person.

He compared himself to his classmates, the ones who'd gone on to study at Sweden's Harvard, the Stockholm School of Economics. Most of them had become bankers or ran venture capitalist companies. They earned millions in bonuses, which was as clear as day when they'd meet for a beer or go sailing together. Many of them were enthusiastic sailors just like he was, but there'd be plenty of chatter about fine cars and fast boats. They would gossip about who'd bought what exclusive mansion or who'd earned what tidy sum on an IPO.

His own employer, a state-run hospital, could not even spell the word *bonus*, that much was clear. If he wanted to earn as much as his friends, he'd have to change professions. But Henrik had not become a doctor just for the income. He'd dreamed of being a doctor since he was in secondary school. He didn't really know why. No one in the family worked in the medical field. He was an only child, so no sibling inspired him. His father had always been in the diplomatic corps and finished his career as an ambassador. His mother had put aside her own ambitions to help her husband achieve his goals.

When Henrik began med school, he'd planned on becoming an outstanding orthopedic surgeon who repaired broken bones and shattered spines. After his studies were complete, he spent some time in the radiology department while waiting for a residency. Something about the role of a radiologist appealed to him.

Perhaps it was the ability to understand and decipher something other doctors saw only as shadows and light, the thrill of finding the missing piece to a puzzle in a hazy picture. When he stood at the podium and explained the X-rays to the surgeons, his interpretation was the difference between life and death.

Secretly, he was also proud of his reputation as a nice and well-liked specialist doctor. He was especially popular among the nurses, who always seemed to gather around him when he was on a coffee break. And he did nothing to dissuade them.

Still, his profession would never lead to lots of money. Henrik understood the value of economic freedom. It was important to him to live the kind of life he'd enjoyed growing up.

When Nora became pregnant with Adam, they moved from their two-room apartment on the outskirts of the city. Nora fell in love with a yellow wooden house in Enskede, not far from where her parents lived in Älvsjö, but Henrik was determined to live in Saltsjöbaden, where he kept his sailboat. He'd lived there as a child when his father was not stationed abroad, and many of his school friends still lived there. He felt at home in the midst of the greenery surrounding the beautiful old mansions.

It was a more expensive location, however, and they could barely afford the small town house they'd chosen. It was far from the kind of mansion Henrik dreamed of.

Now he could change everything.

With the profits from Signe's house, they could settle in one of the fin-de-siècle mansions with money to spare. Visions of a new car glimmered in his imagination, but he pushed them away with a smile. One thing at a time.

If only Nora wasn't so obstinate about that house. Sometimes he had no clue what she was thinking. Like the time she'd gotten this crazy idea about moving to Malmö. That would uproot the family—how insane! Their parents lived in Stockholm. All their friends were there. Henrik had no desire to look for another job. They'd had a few bitter arguments about it.

Nora had mourned Signe as if she were her own grandmother. She'd been nearly inconsolable as they'd put Signe to rest in the small island cemetery, where most of the Sandhamn families buried their dead.

Henrik could not understand why Nora couldn't put the past behind her and move on. Instead, she let that terrible summer torment her all winter. She fell silent and kept to herself, spending most of her free time with the children. For a long time they hadn't even had guests over. Whenever Henrik brought up the idea of hosting a dinner, Nora objected. Months went by without them seeing anyone.

Now Henrik could see the light at the end of the tunnel. That insane woman's will was a silver lining to the cloud that had hung over them. In a new house, each boy would have a room of his own. They could have a real yard, not the lawn the size of a postage stamp that they had now. They'd have a real dining room, so guests wouldn't have to eat in the kitchen with the dirty dishes.

Again he struggled to follow Nora's thoughts. At first, she'd seemed happy that he'd taken the initiative and contacted Svante Severin. Then she'd done a one-eighty, becoming almost hostile when the man arrived.

Henrik later called the real-estate agent to make sure she hadn't insulted him, but Svante Severin remained enthusiastic. He reassured Henrik that he would put all his energy into the deal. He said the family from Switzerland had contacted him several times. They happened to be in the archipelago for the summer in a rented place on Ljusterö, another island not far from Sandhamn.

Henrik had called his mother to tell her about their plans. She'd understood immediately how important it was for him to leave the town house. Henrik knew Nora found Monica trying at times, but his mother was a great support. She'd welcomed Nora into the family and gone out of her way to make her feel at home. Besides, maybe a little tension between a mother-in-law and daughter-in-law was normal.

Henrik shrugged off these thoughts as he transformed another perch into delicious fillets. This evening he planned to fry them in butter and serve them with potatoes and a cold mustard sauce.

He whistled while he daydreamed about the part of Saltsjöbaden where he'd most like to live. Solsidan, perhaps, or why not by the Hotel Bay, on the waterfront?

CHAPTER 28

Thomas opened the meeting with a short summary of his conversation with Gunilla Bäcklund.

"Over one thousand licenses have been issued in Sweden for Marlin rifles," Kalle added. He'd checked before the meeting. "As soon as there are any suspects we can check them against the national gun registry."

"Excellent," said Persson. "How fast can you get us the list? Maybe we will recognize some names."

"When this meeting is over," Kalle said.

"How is it going with the mistresses? And the RSYC?" asked Thomas. "Also we discussed the possibility of a jealous husband."

Kalle nodded.

"We've reviewed the names on Eva Timell's list. We've also checked everyone on the RSYC Board, along with committee members. We discovered at least a third of them hunt. We've found licenses for all kinds of rifles—Class 1 rifles and Class 2 rifles, Blaser .30-06, .22 WMR . . . it's a real mix."

"Remind me of the difference," Margit said.

"Blaser is used for moose and deer. People use the Winchester for smaller animals, like foxes and badgers."

"Where does that leave us?" asked Margit.

"About thirty people in the RSYC leadership have access to guns with small-caliber bullets."

"Anyone own a Marlin?"

"We'll check on that as soon as we're done here." Kalle nodded.

"And the mistresses?" Thomas said.

"Nothing."

Margit held up an e-mail printout.

"This is a message sent to Juliander. His secretary contacted us." Margit passed the piece of paper around the table. "Perhaps an extortion attempt. No identifiable sender, of course."

"You can take this on, Carina," Persson said. He looked at his daughter, who sat the farthest from him. "See how far you get. We can always bring in the computer squad from Kronoberg to help."

The computer squad from Kronoberg belonged to a special unit of the National Bureau who knew how to access someone's computer or reconstruct a hard drive in the blink of an eye. They were often ridiculously young men with long, stringy hair and pale skin who spent their free time playing computer games. But if they secluded themselves with a trashed or locked computer for a day or two, they could work miracles. But Carina was also pretty skilled at uncovering such information.

"OK," she said. She tried in vain to catch Thomas's eye.

Yesterday evening, she'd texted him about plans for the upcoming weekend, but he hadn't replied.

He's probably too busy with this case, Carina thought. The start of an investigation was always the most critical. Every day that passed lessened their chances of catching the culprit. Thomas was so focused on the search, most likely he'd forgotten about his private life.

She sighed to herself.

"What are we doing about Juliander's drug habit?" asked Persson.

"I have more on that," Thomas said. He filled them in on what he'd gotten from Diana Söder. "He's used cocaine regularly for the past year."

"Do you think a dealer is involved?" asked Kalle. "Someone he owed money to?"

Thomas looked skeptical.

"Cocaine is not that expensive these days. For a wealthy lawyer like him, the cost would be negligible."

"How likely is it that a dealer would get a rifle and a boat to carry out a murder?" asked Margit.

"Not very."

"Erik will ask around and see what turns up," Persson said.

"By the way," Thomas said, "do we have that clip from the TV station yet? It should be here by now."

Kalle shook his head.

"I've called them twice. I'll call again after the meeting."

"Any tips from the general public?" asked Persson. "Anything useful at all?"

Erik shrugged.

"Same old story. People call in with all kinds of crazy stuff. Conspiracy theories. Suicide theories. Quite a few tips about Juliander's romantic affairs, but we know that already. We'll follow up on anything reasonable."

Persson nodded and stood up.

"That's it, then. Keep up the good work."

CHAPTER 29

As usual, the Friday-afternoon traffic on Värmdö highway was heavy as people were en route to their summerhouses. The July lull hadn't hit this crowded highway. The stop-and-go traffic began at the expressway exit and snaked along to Mölnvik shopping center. Hopefully, past there, things would start moving again.

Martin Nyrén glanced at his watch. It was just past four, but he was in no hurry. He had no schedule to worry about. His Omega 36 would wait for him at the Bullandö Marina until he cast off for his weekend excursion.

He didn't mind sailing alone. In fact, he preferred the silence. No voices breaking the quiet, nobody jockeying for his attention. His boat was set up for single-handed sailing. Indi was the only person he'd miss, but that was out of the question.

July was devoted to family life, and that was that.

He turned up the car's air-conditioning, trying to keep cool amid the glaring sun and exhaust fumes. This week felt more like April—sun shining one minute, rain the next. What was wrong with a stable high-pressure system for a change?

He settled back in his seat.

He'd had an unpleasant feeling the past few days—as if he were being followed.

Yesterday, while heading back to the office after lunch, he'd had the sensation that someone in the crowd was watching him. But when he'd looked around, he hadn't recognized anyone.

The same thing had happened on his way to work that morning. The feeling that someone was trailing him settled in. Then he sensed a movement behind his back. But when he stopped to look, no one was there—at least not anyone he knew.

He'd even paused in front of a display window to see if he could spot someone behind him in the reflection. Nobody was there, and he'd felt like an idiot.

Why would anybody be following him?

Oscar's murder was making him imagine ghosts in broad daylight.

He turned on the radio and forced the dark thoughts from his mind. It was Friday, and he would soon be on his way, setting course for the outer skerries. He had no reason to worry.

Still, his uneasiness did not lift, not even when traffic started moving again.

CHAPTER 30

"What's wrong, Mom? Are you sad? You look like you're crying." Fabian stared at Diana with concern and tried to pat her cheek with his soft hand.

He held his teddy bear under one arm.

Diana Söder hadn't heard her son come into the bedroom. She'd been so busy on the computer that she'd forgotten about his bedtime. Feeling guilty, she looked up from the screen and turned to him.

"Don't worry, sweetie," she said. She brushed away her tears as best she could. "I must have something in my eye."

She forced a smile and pulled him onto her lap. He smelled of soap from his bath, and she took comfort in the warmth from his little body. He was already outgrowing his light-blue pajamas with elephants—the legs ended above his ankles. She'd have to buy him some new ones.

Sometimes she wished he would never grow up.

Her son studied her and then looked at the screen in front of him.

"Did you get a mean e-mail? My teacher says we should tell a grown-up right away if somebody sends us mean e-mails."

His little-boy voice was so innocent. Diana Söder smiled through her tears. He had no idea how true his comment was.

She turned off the computer to keep him from seeing anything. At eight years old, he was already a good reader.

She did not want him to see the nasty words calling her a murderer or "a damned whore."

SATURDAY,
THE FIRST WEEK

CHAPTER 31

"Did you all see the headlines?" Persson threw the evening paper onto the table.

Silence settled over the room.

"How the hell did the press find out that Diana Söder had been involved with Oscar Juliander?"

Diana Söder's passport photo was on the front page under the headline "Jealousy the Motive for Murder?" Pages six and seven offered a comprehensive summary of Juliander's relationships with women.

Beneath the black letters "Juliander's lover's hideaway!" was a blurry picture of Diana Söder. She stood in front of some building with her hand held over her face as if trying to shield herself.

"I don't even need to tell you that this is totally unacceptable."

But you can't do a thing about it, Thomas thought. Anyone can report anything to a newspaper. You can't even find out who it was without breaking the law.

Thomas pictured again the unhappy woman twisting her ring around and around—the ring she'd received on her birthday.

"If I find out the leak came from this office . . ." Persson didn't have to finish.

"Don't bother," Margit was equally sharp. "There have been hundreds of people coming through this building. Some of them probably knew we were going to interview Diana Söder."

Persson stared hard at her.

"We've had extra personnel here to answer the phones and go through the gun registry," Margit continued. "Anyone could have overheard something by the coffee machine."

"We're going to get shit about this from both the police chief and the press secretary."

"It doesn't matter. We can't do anything about it right now."

The red color in Persson's face went down a bit. He reached for a cardamom twist and bit into it fiercely. He was still angry, but dropped the subject.

"Let's get on with it so we don't have to stay here all weekend." Margit took command. "Where are we now? Thomas?"

Thomas made his report short and sweet.

"We met all the women Juliander had affairs with. Most of them speak well of him, even though he dumped them."

"He must have been charming," Margit said with a wry smile.

"What about their alibis?" asked Persson.

"Every single one has a rock-solid alibi for the time of the murder. Many of them were actually abroad or at least not in Stockholm that day," Thomas explained.

"So we can eliminate jealousy as a motive?"

"We have alibis for everyone we spoke to," Thomas said. He turned to Kalle. "How's it going with the rifle search?"

"Here's a list of everyone with a license for a Marlin."

"Any names we recognize?"

Kalle nodded. "One."

"A lover?"

"One of the husbands."

"Then we'll pay him a visit today and search his house."

Thomas glanced over at Margit, who looked a little glum. This was part of the job, but it was clearly not how Margit wanted to spend the rest of her Saturday.

"Here's the address." Kalle slid it over.

Thomas read *Saltsjö-Duvnäs*. It was a suburb not far from Saltsjöbaden, where the Julianders lived.

"What are the chances that they're home on a Saturday afternoon in the middle of summer?" Margit said.

"It's one thirty now." Thomas glanced at his watch.

"So, doubtful. Perhaps we should call first?"

"Don't worry," Thomas said. "I can head there right after the meeting, and I don't mind going alone."

Thomas realized he'd just found a reason not to meet Carina later.

Persson turned his stare toward Erik, who shuffled through a stack of papers. Sugar from his pastry had fallen on the documents, and he tried to brush it off.

"What do you have for us?" Persson asked.

"We've gone through Juliander's bankruptcy caseload. There was one case where Juliander had reported tax evasion to the authorities. The company president was banned from engaging in business."

"Have you interviewed this guy?"

Erik fumbled with the papers and more sugar fell on the table.

Thomas wondered if Erik was qualified enough to look into such complicated proceedings, but there wasn't much of an alternative. The Financial Crimes unit was seriously understaffed at this time of the year.

Persson scanned the room.

"Nothing else? OK, we're done for the weekend. See you on Monday."

* * *

The woman who opened the door to the suburban house in Saltsjö-Duvnäs paled when Thomas held up his police ID. The house sat on a hill. Thomas could see the glittering water below.

"I just need to ask a few questions concerning the murder of Oscar Juliander," he said.

She looked like she might start weeping any minute.

"I already talked to the police last Wednesday," she said in a low voice. "My husband is home now . . . do you have to . . ." Her voice died out.

"Actually, he's the one I need to speak with," Thomas said.

"Who is it?"

A voice came from inside the house, and a well-built man of about fifty walked up to the door. He wore only swimming trunks. Thomas could see a turquoise swimming pool through the living room's sliding glass doors.

"May I come in?" Thomas asked. "I have a few questions about your gun license."

Sunday,

The first week

CHAPTER 32

Who would benefit from Oscar Juliander's death?

The question had tumbled around in Thomas's dreams during the night, and he woke up soaked in sweat. The sleeping loft in his Harö summerhouse felt suffocating, although it was barely eight o'clock in the morning.

He threw off the damp sheet and climbed down the ladder into the open kitchen, living room, and dining area below.

The house had once been an old barn, but Thomas and Pernilla had transformed it into a modern, winterized second home. For years the project swallowed up all their money and free time. They'd painted and hammered their way through most of it themselves. They'd used contractors only for the changes requiring skilled expertise, like plumbing and wiring. Thomas had even laid the tiles in the kitchen—not an easy task.

These days, Thomas spent as much free time as he could on the island, especially after Pernilla took the apartment in the city after the separation. His two-room apartment in Gustavsberg was nothing to boast about, and he could never summon the energy to improve it. He wasn't there often anyway. For the past year, Carina had demanded his attention, and they usually met at her place. But Thomas had never brought her to the house on Harö, where he and Pernilla had been so happy before they'd lost Emily.

Thomas took a towel from the bathroom and opened the front door. The house sat about ten yards from the water with a narrow path to the dock. Thomas walked to the edge of the dock and dived in. The cold water shocked and refreshed him. Moments like this reminded him why the Finns were always leaping from their saunas into snow banks. The blood circulated faster and the brain cleared. Exactly what he needed.

He climbed back onto the dock, rubbed himself all over with sea salt soap, and then jumped back in.

Nothing like a summer morning dip out in the archipelago.

A bit of seaweed had gotten between his toes, and he rubbed it off against the dock. Then he dried himself with the towel and walked back inside.

After getting dressed, he decided to swing past Sandhamn for some fresh bread at the well-known bakery. Sailors' sweet rolls were famous all over the archipelago. He might also see Nora and his godson if they were home.

His phone beeped. A text from Margit wondering about yesterday's interview.

The man in Saltsjö-Duvnäs had been surprised but had not hesitated to explain about his weapons: two rifles, one of which was a Marlin. The Marlin was broken, however, and he'd sent it in for repairs. He showed Thomas the receipt and then brought Thomas to his locked gun cabinet in the basement where the guns usually were kept. He seemed like a responsible person.

The weekend Juliander was shot, the man and his wife were in the south of Sweden visiting his sister and brother-in-law. He gave Thomas their number so he could check the alibi.

Only when the man began to question why Thomas was checking up on him did things get awkward.

"You should talk to your wife about that," he said. "She and Juliander were well acquainted a few years back."

Before the man could ask anything else, Thomas left. He did not want to participate in the discussion that was bound to follow.

By then, it was so late he had a good excuse to not see Carina that night.

Carina.

He'd have to do something about this whole situation, but not right now.

He texted a reply to Margit and then texted Carina. In a lame attempt to make her happy, he suggested they catch a movie Sunday evening. Then he pushed all thoughts of her to the back of his mind.

As he sat in the sunshine by the window with a cup of coffee in hand, his thoughts returned to the question that had troubled his dreams.

Who would benefit from Oscar Juliander's death?

Perhaps the answer lay in Juliander's profession. Perhaps he'd stumbled across something shady in a bankruptcy case. Thomas decided to speak with Nora when he got to Sandhamn. After all, she was a lawyer with one of the major banks. She knew about these things.

"Ask his secretary," Nora said. She took a big bite of the roll Thomas had brought from the Sandhamn bakery.

They sat on the dock enjoying the fine day. A line of light-gray clouds hung over the treetops of Eknö Sound, closer to the mainland, indicating bad weather on its way. But for now, the sun was shining.

The boys had eaten their breakfast rolls quickly and were busy jumping off the dock, their favorite activity on a day like this. Henrik was on his way into the city. He'd been on call, and there was an emergency at the hospital.

Thomas pictured the pale, unhappy face of Eva Timell. She'd been a great help to the investigation. He crumpled up the sticky paper from his roll and set it on the tray.

"Wouldn't you like a job as a police investigator?" he asked. "You always have good ideas. And you'd get away from that boss you're always complaining about."

Nora gave him a resentful look.

"I don't *always* complain! But he really is an idiot. Why they let him get away with the stunts he pulls is beyond me."

Simon ran toward them, dripping water everywhere. In one hand, he carried a full bucket. His intentions were clear.

Just before he reached Thomas, Simon took the bucket in both hands. But before he could lift it, Thomas picked him up and turned him upside down.

"You weren't really planning to dump a bucket of water over a cop, were you?" he said. He used a stern voice and frowned.

Simon wasn't the least bit afraid.

"Put me down!" he yelled. Then he begged Nora for help.

"Oh, no!" Nora said. "Get out of this one on your own! You tried to soak your godfather. You have only yourself to blame!"

Thomas lugged Simon to the edge of the dock, swung him back and forth, and threw him into the water.

Adam laughed so hard he almost fell in himself. Thomas walked toward him with open arms. Adam, still laughing, leaped into the water before Thomas could grab hold of him.

"You can't get us! You can't get us!" the boys called out.

Thomas pretended to reach for them again before walking back to Nora.

Nora looked at him and shook her head.

"How did you become so good with children, Thomas Andreasson?" she asked. "How did that happen?"

Thomas shrugged, an embarrassed smile on his face. "Please don't tell anybody."

He reached for his coffee cup and took the last sip.

"Do you have time to look over Signe's house with me before you go back?" asked Nora.

The afternoon sun lit up Nora's white kitchen as she loaded the dishwasher. Thomas was heading back to Harö and then taking the ferry to the city.

"Sure," Thomas said. "I'm not in a rush."

"Boys," Nora said. "You'll be on your own for a few minutes. I just want to show Thomas something."

They walked to the Brand house together, and Nora unlocked the front door to let them in. The house smelled stuffy. Abandoned.

Nora led them to the veranda. In an attempt to recreate the former atmosphere, she'd set out a few Mårbacka geraniums, but they'd wilted in the heat, making the space look even more forlorn.

"The real-estate agent called again and wants to bring that family from Switzerland here. They are positive they want to buy the house, he says."

Nora sank into one of the wicker chairs and looked out to sea. The clouds had come closer, and they would soon swallow up the sun. She stroked the knitted throw lying over the arm. It still held some dark strands of dog hair from Signe's Labrador.

"I don't know what to do. Henrik is completely obsessed with the idea of selling. The only thing he cares about is how much money we're going to get. I hardly even recognize him."

"Is it really that bad?"

"He wants us to buy some huge place in Saltsjöbaden. Something that fits his parents' ideals."

She sighed and leaned back in the chair.

Thomas didn't know what to say. He could understand why Henrik would be eager to unload Signe's house for a better home for his family. The Brand house was certainly a fine old merchant house, but it needed a great deal of work.

At the same time, he understood Nora's dilemma. He'd also known Signe and understood why she'd made Nora her heir.

"Wouldn't you be happier with something larger in Saltsjöbaden rather than two houses out here?" He chose his words carefully.

Nora's eyes flared with anger.

"Whose side are you on?" she asked.

Thomas tried again.

"Nora, look at the whole situation. Who is going to take care of this huge place? You already have a nice summerhouse here in Sandhamn. You work full-time, and Henrik's a doctor. Wouldn't it be better to invest in a permanent home instead?"

Nora bit her lip but slowly nodded. She got up from the chair and stood by the window. Now the whole sky had clouded over, and small white caps were scudding along the gray waves.

"If it was yours, what would you do?" she asked.

"I can't tell you that," Thomas replied. "It's your decision." He hesitated for a minute. "But I know this. Don't let anyone force you into something you'll regret one day."

Nora nodded again.

Then he said, "Why don't you rent it out for a while? You don't have to make a decision right this minute. Take your time."

Rent it out? Why hadn't she thought of that?

Every time Henrik had badgered her to sell, she'd gotten a knot in her stomach. She wasn't ready, that much was clear. Now she felt much better.

"Let's go," she said. "You should head back before the weather gets worse. The wind is really picking up."

Monday,
THE SECOND WEEK

CHAPTER 33

Going to the movies hadn't been his best idea, Thomas thought as he made himself a cup of tea in the police station kitchen.

Once they'd arrived at the theater, he and Carina couldn't agree on what movie to watch. Thomas wanted to see something uncomplicated, something that didn't engage his brain. Carina, on the other hand, wanted to see a romantic drama with a famous American actress Thomas couldn't stand.

By the time he finally gave up the argument, Carina was in a bad mood and there weren't any good seats left. They had to sit in the back of the theater. Carina didn't warm up until the movie was about half-done. Her hand sought out his, and she began to give him small kisses on the cheek.

Thomas felt silly, like a teenager necking at the movies. He shifted away a few times, and the atmosphere between them chilled again. After the movie, she said she wanted to go home. Thomas understood how he'd messed things up.

Now he walked to Margit's office and sat in her visitor's chair with a heavy sigh. She continued working on her computer for a few minutes before she hit "Save" and looked up.

"You look like something the cat dragged in," she said.

Thomas dismissed her comment with a wave.

"A fight with Carina?" Margit asked. She closed a folder on her desk and set it on the bookshelf.

Thomas looked at her, surprised.

"What does Carina have to do with it?"

Margit looked at him as if he were dim.

"First Carina comes to work looking overcast, and then you come in twenty minutes later looking even worse. Did you see yourself in the mirror this morning?"

Thomas agreed that she had a point. He was tired and worn out, and it showed. But he still didn't want any connection with Carina at work.

"What Carina does on her own time is her business," he said.

"Cut it out, Thomas." Margit sounded impatient. "The whole station knows you two have been dating for a while."

"Is it that obvious?"

"Our job is to investigate and draw conclusions from the evidence. Did you think we'd all gone blind or something?"

"Of course not."

"Persson is probably the only one who's clueless. Without doubt because he doesn't want to know."

Margit gave Thomas a stern look, but then she smiled.

"Isn't she a bit young for you?"

Thomas hung his head. That was the problem in a nutshell.

"I thought I'd feel a little younger when I was with her," he admitted. "Instead, I feel old, worn out."

"Then perhaps it's time you did something about it," Margit said. She sounded like a schoolteacher.

She picked up a piece of paper that had escaped her wastebasket. Then she met his eyes.

"She is very much in love with you. Anyone can see that," she said. "And I don't want her to get hurt."

Thomas agreed. He promised himself he'd deal with Carina as soon as the investigation ended.

"By the way, I talked to Sylvia Juliander again, this time about her husband's drug use," Margit said.

"Did she know about it?"

"Not one bit. She was shocked. Told me there had to be some mistake."

"Another unpleasant surprise for her."

"She's getting a lot of unhappy information about her husband after his death," Margit said. "First, all his mistresses. And now the drugs."

"She must have had some idea . . ."

"Perhaps. But that's not the same thing as *knowing* it for sure. Not to mention reading it in the headlines. I don't envy her one bit."

Thomas got up.

"See you at the meeting in five."

"Carina has located the sender of the e-mail Eva Timell forwarded to us," Persson began.

Thomas could see a hint of fatherly pride in Persson's eyes.

"The message came from an accountant who'd performed some bookkeeping work for one of Juliander's bankruptcies," Carina added.

"Why was his address so strange?" asked Thomas.

Carina gave him a cold look. "The man was in the country without access to his work account, so he used his teenage daughter's Hotmail address."

"Why such a hurry?" asked Kalle. "He seemed desperate."

"He needed payment before the end of the fiscal year," Carina said. "They wanted to finish up by Midsummer, but Juliander had forgotten to pay."

"He had other things on his mind, I guess, like his upcoming race," Margit said.

"Perhaps. The accounting firm's financial department had phoned to tell this guy to contact the client immediately to get payment. So he sent the message."

"And Eva Timell interpreted it all wrong," Margit said.

"A misunderstanding," Carina added.

"How did you figure all this out?"

"I talked to the accountant. And then I called the company's financial department to be sure. That's it."

"That's it for that line of investigation, too," Thomas stated. "Anything else?" Thomas looked at Carina.

She refused to look back. Instead she held up a bundle of paper.

"I've gone through much of his financial information," she said.

"Your conclusions?" asked Persson.

"I know why he stayed married."

"Let's hear it," Margit said.

"The Julianders had no prenuptial agreement."

"Well, well, well," Margit said.

"The houses, the cars, even the boats—everything belonged to both of them."

"So if he wanted a divorce, half of everything would go to her," Margit said. "That would be worth millions."

"Was there a great deal of debt?" asked Thomas.

"The houses carry high mortgages, but he was able to make the payments, interest included," Carina said. "He earned a high salary."

"Any insurance?" asked Margit.

"One life insurance policy. And a great deal of retirement savings. His widow and children will certainly not starve."

"His wife could still have killed him for the money," Kalle said. "She might have tired of all his women and decided to put a stop to the spending."

Carina looked doubtful.

"All the partners in the firm had identical pensions," she continued. "I checked."

"No life insurance policies taken out recently?" asked Margit.

"No, he's had the same one for years—all through the law firm."

"She could have simply asked for a divorce," Margit stated. "She would certainly have been awarded a huge amount of money."

"There's only one thing that looks odd," Carina said.

"What's that?" asked Persson.

"I can't figure out where he got the money for the *Emerald Gin*."

"His boat?" asked Margit.

"It was brand new, right?"

"Yes," Margit said.

"He didn't take out a loan, and it must have cost a great deal. Where did the money come from?"

"He already had a racing sailboat," Thomas said. "He probably sold it."

"For twelve million kronor?" Carina replied.

CHAPTER 34

"Is Margit in?" Thomas called out as soon as he opened the door to the department floor. He wore his leather jacket since the weather had shifted again. Outside, rain fell steadily. According to the weather report, it would clear up by evening.

"Margit!" he yelled. "Come here for a minute!"

Margit stuck her head out of a doorway. Her short hair was more wild than usual.

"What's going on?" she asked. "Why are you yelling?" She yawned as she walked to the coffee machine for another cup of plain black coffee.

"Check this out," Thomas said and ripped open a yellow padded envelope bearing the logo of Swedish state television. He pulled out a DVD and held it up.

"What's that?"

"The video taken by the TV crew the day Juliander was killed. Kalle's been bugging them for days to get it, but every time he called, they said they'd forgotten to mail it. So I picked it up myself. Let's have a look."

They headed for one of the conference rooms equipped with a TV screen and DVD player. Thomas put in the disc and found the remote before he yelled for the others. Kalle was still at lunch, but Erik and Carina came at once.

The screen filled with a panoramic view of the glittering sea. Thomas remembered the feeling of that day. Sunny weather. The water had been packed with boats, and everyone expected a beautiful start to the race. A perfect day for sailing.

The DVD continued with a number of close-ups of the large racing boats. They would all start at the same time: twelve noon.

The TV cameraman zoomed in to focus on the *Emerald Gin* with Oscar Juliander grinning behind the wheel of his elegant Swan. Beside him stood Fredrik Winbergh sizing up the other vessels.

Thomas noted that Winbergh was positioned slightly behind Juliander, just as he'd described during questioning.

"It feels weird looking at a man who's about to die," Carina mumbled.

The helicopter climbed higher to capture a broad view of the starting field. A puff of smoke rose into the air.

"That must be the five-minute warning shot," Thomas said, mostly to himself.

"What was that?" asked Margit.

"That's the five-minute warning shot," Thomas replied. "They fire a warning from the starting vessel at ten minutes and then at five minutes before the race. It's to allow the participants time to position themselves. They also do a countdown on the radio."

They kept watching one boat after another. Thomas glanced at his watch. About five minutes had passed since the warning shot. It was time for the race to begin.

The helicopter flew closer to the starting line, making it easy to identify the participants. They formed a moving line between the two orange flags. Thomas could see the *Emerald Gin* closest to windward.

He watched the exact moment when Oscar Juliander jerked and fell. But was he sure?

"Did you see that?" Erik exclaimed. "Did you see how they caught that? That wasn't on the news!"

"There's something called 'consideration for the family of the deceased,'" Margit said. "I assume you've heard of it?"

Erik looked down.

Thomas stepped closer to the screen to study the events as they unfolded. While the other boats swept forward, the *Emerald Gin* rounded up uncertainly, lost momentum, and finally stopped sailing. The camera swung away to follow the other competitors on their course toward the lighthouse at Almagrundet.

Thomas used the remote to reverse the action. Then he hit "Play."

As the DVD started, they could see all the sailboats at the starting line again.

Thomas concentrated on the screen.

They could see the competing sailboats as well as a good part of the spectator craft. He could clearly spot the Bjärrings' Storebro. About twenty more boats were nearby. To be on the safe side, he watched the scene again.

"We need to print enlargements of these," he said. "Then let's compare them to Fredrik Winbergh's speculation about the direction of the shot. Dr. Sachsen from Forensic Medicine said the bullet entered the chest from the right and slightly forward, which gives another indication of the direction."

A determined look came over his face.

"Now we are going to put the puzzle together," he said. "This is how we'll catch the devil that shot Juliander."

* * *

"Are you asleep?" Nora whispered to Henrik.

It was eleven thirty at night, and they'd just had really good sex, the kind of intense experience made up of both familiarity and desire. For the first time in a long time, Nora had relaxed enough to hold nothing back.

Nora felt a contentment coming over her, and she knew she'd fall asleep any second now. Still, it was pleasant to lie quietly in the darkness and enjoy the moment.

Henrik was already out, and she listened to his light breathing beside her.

Earlier that evening, they'd taken their tiny boat *Snurran* and enjoyed a picnic dinner at Falkenskär, only ten minutes away from Sandhamn. She'd packed a basket with homemade minipizzas for the boys. For herself and Henrik, she'd made tortilla wraps filled with grilled chicken, Västerbotten cheese, and a little sweet chili sauce. She'd included a green salad and a bottle of good rosé. For dessert they'd shared a quart of raspberries and some dark chocolate. It had been a perfect summer dinner.

They'd sat on the warm, smooth rocks as they'd eaten. The silhouette of Sandhamn was barely visible to the north. The water was so still that even the seaweed didn't move, and the only sound came from the small wayward waves gently rolling against the beach.

As twilight fell, they lit some tea lights that burned brightly against the dark-blue sky. The flames made the shale deposits in the hillside glitter like tiny stars coming out from hiding inside the gray rock.

In the darkness, Henrik had wrapped his arm around her shoulders.

Nora simply let go and enjoyed the moment. It had been a long while since she'd felt so content in her husband's presence. She leaned her head against his shoulder, and a warm wave of happiness filled her.

After her conversation with Thomas, she'd made up her mind. She'd rent out the Brand house for two years to someone who could take care of it and perhaps even repair it a bit. She'd buy herself some time to think about what should come next.

If Henrik insisted that they buy a new and bigger house, they could always mortgage Signe's house. As a bank employee, she'd have no trouble getting favorable loan rates.

In the darkness of her bedroom, Nora smiled.

She no longer worried about not caring for Signe's house, and she was no longer upset with her husband.

Even her wretched mother-in-law could not object to this solution.

She snuggled closer to Henrik. Soon she slept like a baby.

"A toast for the newly engaged couple!" his father exclaimed as he poured fat glasses of cognac for the men at the party. Then he took out a Cohiba, his favorite cigar, and waved it around.

Out of the corner of his eye he saw his mother grimace. She wasn't fond of the cigar smoke that would spread throughout the apartment by morning, but she would never dream of mentioning this to her husband.

The bride-to-be chatted with her mother and future mother-in-law in the corner. After all, they discussed one of the season's most important weddings. When his fiancée noticed him looking at her, she gave him a playful smile. Was he imagining things, or did she seem proud to claim him?

His father strolled over.

"Believe me, this is a wonderful match. She's not just a sweet, young girl. She also comes from an excellent family. She will certainly bring wealth and status to your marriage. Her father and I have already discussed it. And, of course, there's more where that came from!" His father laughed, satisfied.

Deep down he already knew he was making a mistake. But there seemed no way out now. It was too late.

He hardly knew how he'd gotten to this point. It had started so inno-cently. He had been part of a large group of friends who went to parties together. He had a certain charm, pleasing to the ladies, and was always a popular dance partner. She was his classmate's little sister, always hang-ing around. Whenever he was at an event, she was there, too. She was not prudish. In fact, she often took the initiative.

One evening, they'd been at her house while her parents were gone and the servants had the night off. She had looked at him with her blue eyes.

"You know, it's time for us to get married," she said. "We can't keep sneaking around. What if someone discovers what we've been up to? My parents would never forgive me."

She took him by complete surprise.

Marriage? He hadn't even thought of it. They were so different. And so young. She was from a wealthy family, true, but not exactly the wife he'd imagined. She was beautiful and spoiled, and now she wanted him.

Just like that.

He didn't know how to get out of the situation. Before he had the chance to realize what was going on, they'd declared their engagement.

Both families were pleased. His father had shaken his hand and con-gratulated him. His mother had shed a tear.

They were a delightful couple.

"A penny for your thoughts?"

His bride-to-be approached him with a charming smile. She was, with-out a doubt, the cutest girl in the room. He smiled back.

"I'm thinking of you, naturally!" he said. "And how lucky I am!"

TUESDAY,
THE SECOND WEEK

Chapter 35

They had waited twenty-four hours for the enlarged photograph from the DVD to arrive. Now it lay on the conference room table. *It was worth it,* Thomas thought.

Thomas had drawn in the longitudes and latitudes and had reproduced Fredrik Winbergh's markings from the sea chart.

Margit leaned over the finished product. It wasn't bad. They could probably identify the boats that had been within range of the shot.

"This looks good," she told Thomas. "Have you taken a course in blueprint drawing?"

Thomas grinned without interrupting his inspection of the photograph.

"If Winbergh is right, there are approximately twenty-eight boats within shooting range. I'm including Bjärring's Storebro, which we already knew about," he said.

"A golden triangle, you think?"

"Look over here," Thomas said. "Even if we enlarge the area, to be on the safe side, we only have seven more boats to check. Thirty-five, that's a reasonable number."

Margit studied the layout more closely. The sea spread from the starting line. The closest island was far away.

"What are the odds the shot came from a cockpit bench?" Margit asked. She reached for the magnifying glass.

"What do you mean?"

Margit pointed to a motorboat with several people sitting in the open stern.

Thomas realized what she was thinking.

"Fairly small, I'd think."

He walked around the table to look at the picture from another angle.

"If you want to shoot somebody without being discovered, you'd certainly pick a boat with a covered cabin," he said.

Margit put down the magnifying glass and pointed to eight of the smaller boats in the picture.

"If my theory is correct, we can eliminate all open motorboats from the investigation."

Thomas saw no objection to her reasoning. He walked around the table and back to Margit.

"That leaves us with twenty-seven boats," he said.

"Twenty-seven. Well, then, how do we identify them?"

"Keep on doing what we're doing. Look for clues."

Thomas brought the magnifying glass as close to one of the boats as he could.

"You can see a logo on the hull of this one. We have to write down every identifiable characteristic and then try and track each boat down."

He took out a marker and wrote a letter by each boat.

"Here they are," he said. "Let's identify them one at a time."

"This will take days, if not weeks."

"Do you have a better idea?"

All the evidence pointed to the shot coming from one of these boats. The report from the technical team showed no trace of a shot being fired on the *Emerald Gin*. Thomas knew they would find the killer on one of the boats in this enlargement.

But which one?

Margit took out her notebook and made a list matching Thomas's alphabetical order.

"By the way, I talked to Winbergh again," Margit said.

"Did he know anything about the sale of Juliander's old boat?"

"He said it would not have sold for more than three to four million, and, in fact, Juliander only owned half the boat. He shared ownership with another guy in the RSYC."

"So he didn't have enough money to buy a new Swan on his own."

"Right."

"So where'd he get the money for it? Did Winbergh have any ideas?"

"No, he didn't."

"We have to look into that."

That morning, Nora received another phone call from Monica Linde.

When Nora found out that Henrik had discussed selling the Brand house with his mother once again, she lost it.

"*Why* are you talking about the Brand house with your mother?" she yelled. "She needs to stay out of it! Do you hear me? It's none of her *business!*"

They were on the second floor, near the bathroom.

Henrik seemed more surprised than anything. "Calm down," he said. "It's not that big of a deal."

"Can't you keep your mother out of our lives? She's driving me crazy!"

"Cut it out, Nora. Don't get so hysterical."

"I'm not hysterical. I'm just sick and tired of Monica always butting in where she has no right!"

Now Henrik got angry.

"As if your parents stay out of our business. They're always dropping by! We only live two hundred yards away from them!"

"There's a difference. They don't interfere the way she does!"

"So there's a good way to interfere and a bad way?"

"That's not what I meant!"

"Yes, you did! My parents do things the wrong way, but yours are perfect. Thanks so much."

His tone was crushing.

Henrik looked at her as if she were seven years old. Suddenly Nora didn't have the energy to argue, even though she knew she was right. Her anger turned into resignation.

Why was Henrik so blind to his mother's shortcomings? Why didn't he ever take Nora's side? Just once?

WEDNESDAY, THE SECOND WEEK

CHAPTER 36

The chair of the RSYC election committee, Anders Bergenkrantz, had just opened the meeting.

Tradition dictated that the previous chairman of the board should lead the process for selecting the new chairman. The meeting at the Saltsjöbaden clubhouse had been hastily called, though this surprised no one.

The meeting would be short. They had only one item on the agenda.

"We must nominate a new candidate as chairman of the board in time for our annual meeting." Bergenkrantz stroked his chin, his face heavy with worry.

The only woman in the room watched him with a trace of sympathy in her eyes. She was intelligent and gifted and aware of the implications of their dilemma. They had little time for the normal nomination process, and the usual candidate, the board's first vice chairman, was no longer available.

With a directness appreciated by the group, she got right to the point.

"Our present chairman is stepping down, and Oscar is dead." She swept the room with her eyes. "We have only one possible candidate, the second vice chairman. We must ask Ingmar if he will take the job."

A few members shifted in their chairs.

Ingmar seemed an unlikely successor to Hans Rosensjöö. He was a decent secretary and had been on the board for many years, but he did not have any leadership skills. Though he was well liked and sociable, with a large network of acquaintances, he lacked vision. And he certainly avoided all conflict. Ingmar had never set his foot down about anything. Certainly not in his marriage.

But right now, they had no other alternative.

They'd discreetly asked around to see if another senior board member might want the job, but everyone had declined just as discreetly. The chairmanship took a great deal of time and effort; the person who took it on would need months to prepare and even more time to spare.

A new candidate from outside the board would go against tradition. Nobody would even consider such a suggestion.

"Personally, I doubt that Ingmar is the right person, but who else do we have?" Anders Bergenkrantz said. "At any rate, Ingmar has been on the board for years. He knows all our traditions. He's one of us."

My predecessor never had to deal with these kinds of issues, Bergenkrantz thought.

The female committee member raised her voice again.

"I do have one suggestion. I propose we ask Hans Rosensjöö to remain on the board in an advisory role for twelve more months in order to assist Ingmar. That will create continuity and alleviate some of our concerns at the same time."

A clever solution, Bergenkrantz thought. *Probably what we need in this bizarre situation.* He'd never heard of it happening in the history of their organization, but right now they didn't have much choice.

The other members nodded in approval. At least nobody objected.

"Well, then," he said. "We have reached a unanimous decision. The nominating committee's recommendation is to choose Ingmar von Hahne as the next chairman of the Royal Swedish Yacht Club."

The discussion was closed.

Chapter 37

Strictly speaking, Martin Nyrén had no good reason to visit the marina in the middle of the week. Perhaps it was his longing for the much anticipated summer vacation that drove him—only one and a half weeks to go.

Or perhaps it was the lovely evening that inspired him to head to Bullandö, where his beloved Omega waited.

His sailboat, which brought him such great joy.

He found a spot in the nearly full parking lot by the dock. Most drivers were already out on the water. Many chose this popular marina due to its proximity to the open water. You could easily set sail, and you didn't have to waste time navigating through the islands of the inner archipelago. Right now, the marina looked abandoned. The wooden piers were mostly empty. A few lone boats bobbed, waiting for their owners.

He intended to go out for only a few hours, hoping to enjoy the pleasant weather and the long summer evening. Many weeks remained before the darker nights of August arrived. He'd packed two beers and a box of sushi bought on the way from his office. It was all part of being out on the water.

He walked along the outer pontoon and saw his Omega tied between two Y-booms with the bow toward the edge of the dock. He'd christened her the *Aurora*, not a very original name, but it fit a sailor who liked to head out in the early morning. The goddess of dawn reminded him of the many peaceful hours when the archipelago had barely awakened and the morning breeze gently caressed the surface of the water.

He'd actually thought about spending the night anchored in a bay and then returning the next day. If he got up early, he could make it back to the office by nine thirty, not too late of an hour during the summer.

He noticed something wrong as he approached. The hull was crooked, and it looked as if the boat were sideways to the dock.

He sped up.

When he got to his boat, he first thought one of the lines had gotten loose. The bow banged against the concrete edge, and a few ugly marks marred the hull's gel coat.

He swore silently. It would cost thousands to repair the outer hull, even if insurance covered part of it. And he was certain he'd tied her up securely when he'd left the boat last Sunday evening.

Then he came to a complete stop, unable to process what he saw. The entire forward end was painted black. It looked like someone had gone crazy with spray paint. On one side he could see the letter *F*, but then the rest of the word was painted over as if someone had emptied the whole can in a fit of rage.

He couldn't hold back tears as he took in the damage.

All that horrible black smeared across the beautiful white hull. There were even black splotches on the wooden deck.

He sank to his knees and touched the dried paint. It reminded him of smeared excrement.

After a few minutes, he made his way to the harbor office. He needed to report what had happened and see if anyone had spotted who was behind this.

This might be some kind of prank, but it was not funny at all.

THURSDAY,
THE SECOND WEEK

CHAPTER 38

She couldn't take her eyes off the computer screen. Though she despised every word in that hurtful message, she couldn't stop reading it.

> Confess your sin, you disgusting whore. The game is up. Don't ever imagine that Oscar loved you. He just played with you, like he played all the others. You were one in a long line. Now you have to do penance for your crime.

The words cut and her entire body shivered. Diana Söder read the message again. Tears began to form, and fear took over.

Who sent this awful message? How had they found her personal e-mail address? And how did the sender know so much about her relationship with Oscar?

She leaned forward and rested her head on the desk. The surface grew wet, but she didn't care. She was alone in the gallery.

She'd had no bad intentions when she'd met Oscar. He reassured her that his marriage was dead. He and Sylvia were just waiting until the children finished their university educations, and then they'd divorce.

He told her this again and again.

She trusted him, believed his reassurances. Why shouldn't she?

She'd never loved anybody the way she loved Oscar. He was the love of her life. And he'd been wonderful with her son. They'd been like a little family, and she'd started to dream of a second child. A child together. She wasn't forty yet. It could still happen. She imagined growing old together. As soon as he got divorced.

If she would just be patient. If she would wait for him.

She could have waited as long as it took. Her time with Oscar had been the happiest in her life.

Suddenly she sat up and pounded the key to delete the horrible e-mail. She deleted it from the trash folder as well. Then she closed her eyes and tried to focus on something positive, something happy.

But she could think only about Oscar. She took a sip of water to calm the sobs rising in her throat. Then she shut off the computer.

Surely this must be somebody's idea of a joke. Someone with a sick sense of humor.

That's what it had to be.

"How long have we been working here?" asked Margit. She rubbed her eyes. It was almost eight at night. They were still in the conference room where they'd taped the enlargement to the table. They'd taken a short break to grab a sandwich wrap, the only food they'd had since lunch.

Margit looked in disgust at the discarded food in the garbage.

"That's one way to diet," she muttered.

Thomas looked up from the magnifying glass.

"Perhaps we should quit," he said. "I'm beginning to get cross-eyed."

He rubbed his neck as he studied the list of the distinctive features on the boats. They'd scrutinized the photograph from every angle, but there were many boats still not identified.

Each time they found something distinctive, they handed it off to Kalle, who compared the details with known boat models and then checked with insurance agencies to find possible owners. A few additional people had come in to help search the Internet and make phone calls.

Thomas considered it a different way of knocking on doors. Knocking via the phone, so to speak. Still, it was slow and detailed work.

Any information we turn up will help, he thought. For a moment he wondered if they were simply chasing a red herring. Either way, what alternative did they have?

The right boat would lead them to the person who'd fired the killing shot.

FRIDAY,
THE SECOND WEEK

CHAPTER 39

It was Friday afternoon, and the homicide unit was about to break for the weekend.

They needed some time to rest and recover. The faces around the table looked tired and irritated, worn down from the tedious work of identifying spectator boats.

Twelve days had passed since Juliander had been killed.

In a well-meaning attempt to provide her colleagues with energy, Carina had bought cinnamon buns to go with their coffee. She looked content in a room overtaken by low morale. She hummed under her breath despite her colleagues' long faces.

Persson took his place at the head of the table, his face blank, lips pressed tightly together. He looked discouraged by the lack of a breakthrough in the case.

"Let's get going," he said. "First, Juliander's finances."

He turned toward his daughter. "Have you found anything to explain how Juliander could have purchased that Swan?"

"Not by making any money on the stock exchange," Carina said. "But I've found something very interesting, well worth exploring."

For effect, she fell silent, still flipping through the papers in front of her.

"Spit it out, Carina," Erik said.

Carina smiled and raised her eyebrows teasingly. She gave herself a few more seconds to enjoy the attention. Then she couldn't hold back any longer.

"I've got Juliander's wallet, and I've gone through it thoroughly. Forensic Medicine sent it over today. And I found a credit card . . ."

"A credit card," Persson said. "Everybody has credit cards."

"Not one like this. This is a personal platinum card from a bank in Liechtenstein. Vaduz Verwaltungsbank."

"Where's Liechtenstein again?" asked Kalle.

"One and a half hours away from Zürich," Margit said. "It's a tax haven. The OECD blacklisted it."

"Why's that?" asked Kalle.

"Money laundering. They work with neither the police nor tax authorities from other countries."

"So how does this credit card fit in?" asked Kalle. "And what's a platinum card?"

Carina smiled at his question and sneaked a glance at Thomas.

"It's a very nice card with no credit limit at all. You can buy whatever you want."

"I'd sure like one of those," Kalle said.

"Me, too."

"Tell us about that card," Thomas said.

Carina held up an enlarged photocopy of a gray credit card.

"You usually get credit cards through your bank. It's either directly tied to your account so that the money is pulled from it immediately, or you pay your bill once a month."

"Yes, we know how credit cards work," Erik said.

"But there's something special about this one," Carina continued. "With a Swedish credit card, the bank has to report the activity to the tax authorities every year. And you have to make sure those figures correspond with your income tax report."

"But you said Juliander's card was not from a Swedish bank," Thomas noted.

"Exactly," Carina said. Hours of surfing the net and putting the pieces together had paid off. She felt like a real investigator.

Thomas had been chilly toward her the past few weeks. It made her feel insecure. But she'd swallowed her anger and decided to show him just how good she was. She would impress him with some serious police work, and he'd look at her the same way he had last summer.

She was so much in love with him it hurt. She longed for him all the time. She'd accepted having to keep quiet about their relationship over the past year. But she was not about to get dumped in secret. She had no intention of letting him go.

"This is how it works," she said. "If someone has a foreign credit card, he or she also ought to have a bank account in a foreign bank. In this case, it must be in a country outside the EU that does not report Swedish citizens' finances to the Swedish government."

"Do you think we're talking about money laundering?" Margit asked. She leaned forward and put her chin in one hand. "Money abroad not reported to the Swedish tax authorities?"

Carina nodded.

"If he were smart, and he most certainly was, he'd only withdraw cash with this card," Carina said. "Then none of his purchases could be traced. We'd never be able to find out what he used the money for."

"So now we know where the rich lawyer kept his money," Thomas said. "Can we assume he bought his fancy boat using this credit card?"

"It's possible," Carina said.

Thomas smiled at her.

"This is extremely interesting," Margit said. "Good work, Carina."

"Yes, well done," Thomas added.

Carina beamed like the sun.

"So where do we go from here?" Persson asked. "Do we know how much money we're talking about here?"

"And where the money came from?" Margit added.

"There's someone I can ask," Thomas said.

CHAPTER 40

Nora stood in front of the ice cream shop in the middle of the Sandhamn boardwalk, waiting to buy ice cream for the boys. Three scoops each. Simon wanted chocolate, strawberry, and vanilla, while Adam asked for blueberry, melon, and chocolate toffee crunch.

The girl behind the counter put bright-red raspberry jelly on top of each cone. They looked so good that Nora bought a small one for herself, a rare indulgence because of her diabetes.

It was already five in the evening, so they'd have a late dinner. Again. As they often did during summers at Sandhamn.

They found a bench where they could see various boats tied close to the dock and tourists strolling up and down admiring them. Henrik immersed himself in the evening paper.

As Simon sat down, the raspberry jelly fell onto the sand. His mouth opened to let out a wail, but Nora stopped it by reassuring him that they could get another one. She walked back to the ice cream shop with the cone, and they fixed it right away.

Simon gave her a big hug.

"You're the best mom in the world!" he said.

He held out his ice cream and offered her a lick, but she declined.

"Thanks, sweetie, but I have one of my own."

Her phone rang.

She fished her phone from the pocket of her red shorts with her free hand. It was Thomas.

"Hi, there!" she said. "How's it going back in the city? How's the investigation?"

"It's going slowly," Thomas said. "Very slowly."

Nora licked the already melting ice cream. Despite her best efforts, a large chocolate drop landed on her shorts. Typical.

"Are you coming out this weekend?" she asked.

"Yes. I need your help with something."

"Sure, what's up?"

"I need information about the rules of bank secrecy. Especially banks in Liechtenstein."

"Liechtenstein?" Nora had to laugh. "What? Are you thinking of hiding some money?"

"No, of course not," Thomas said. His voice remained serious. "But could you look into it for me? I need to know more about that country's banks. Will you have some time to talk on Sunday?"

"Sunday," Nora said. "Just a sec." She turned to Henrik, who was now lost in the sports pages. "What are we doing the day after tomorrow?"

"Nothing in particular," he said.

"Thomas wonders if I can help him with something for an hour or two. Is that all right, or are you planning to go sailing?"

Henrik shook his head and looked up at her, squinting in the bright sunlight.

"Nope."

He disappeared back into the world of sports.

She put the phone back to her ear.

"Sunday's fine."

"OK, we'll meet then. Do you want to go out to Harö, or would you like me to come on over to Sandhamn?"

"Here is easier. Then I won't have to lug my computer on the ferry. What time?"

"Around three?"

"Sure. See you then."

Nora hung up and slid her phone back in her pocket.

Liechtenstein. A place often tied to illegal cash transfers. What did this have to do with the murder of Oscar Juliander?

She frowned at her ice cream, now a sloppy mess between the paper and the cone. She looked down at her shorts and took a moment to appreciate her washing machine—a mother's best friend. She remembered her own mother washing clothes at the end of the dock. Not until the late sixties did they have a Laundromat in the area.

She inspected her shorts again and sighed. She'd have to change when they got home.

SATURDAY,
THE SECOND WEEK

CHAPTER 41

Martin Nyrén realized he'd made a mistake as soon as he arrived at the barbecue. Actually, he knew going there would be a mistake, but he couldn't stay away. It was one of few chances to see Indi during the long month of July. And people might notice if he declined the invitation. They had an easier time meeting in town. They could blame work or a late meeting to allow them to sneak away without raising suspicion. Out here there were no excuses, just the long wait until summer ended.

He regarded the scene before him.

A large party tent stood in front of the house. Through an opening he saw a long table covered with a checkered cloth. Two enormous speakers were set up on each side, probably to supply music for the dance later.

Two large grills occupied one corner of the lawn. Two men in chef's hats and aprons watched over some kind of meat—possibly lamb—rotating on a spit over red coals.

Martin enjoyed grilled lamb, but he found that a meager comfort. His desire to leave kept growing, though he resisted the temptation to sneak away.

The past weeks had been torture. There was still no progress on Oscar's murder, and the vandalism to his Omega weighed on him. In addition, the unpleasant feeling that someone was watching him continued.

People wandered around the lawn laughing and holding glasses in their hands. A cute girl poured drinks for everyone at a temporary bar in the middle of the yard. Martin walked over, and she ladled something from the punch bowl into a glass for him.

"It's sangria," she said. "We're having a Spanish theme tonight. Here you go."

He took a long sip of the pink drink with chopped oranges and ice cubes. Excellent. Not that weak stuff they served on a charter trip to Spain. This was full-bodied and strong. As he took another sip, he understood why the Spanish were so fond of their national drink. He hoped the drink might help him conjure up a spark of party spirit.

Drink in hand, he looked around the party.

To his left was his hosts' summerhouse—a modern white building with a beautiful view. A wide veranda with dining furniture and lawn chairs covered the south wall.

He imagined his hosts lounging on their wooden deck during these lazy summer days, enclosed by a white railing with crossed slats. It reminded him of signal flags used at sea. Rows of tall pines bordered the property on both sides. Toward the road, huge lilac bushes did the same.

A Jet Ski was tied to the dock. Martin Nyrén detested the machines, and, deep down, he missed the days when Jet Skis were not allowed on the water. They were expensive playthings for people with money to burn and served no purpose beyond making noise. He had a fair idea of why it was sitting there. With teenagers in the house, there would be a lot of pressure on the parents to get the latest model.

A small, tarred skiff was docked next to the Jet Ski. The pair looked like a study in opposites. Martin imagined himself rowing the boat out on a peaceful, windless day and then allowing the current to pull him along.

In one corner of the party tent Hans Rosensjöö stood with other board members and their wives. Martin sauntered over to say hello. It would be awkward to leave now. He should stay for dinner at least. He arranged his face into something resembling a smile and approached the group.

Perhaps there might be a chance for a few stolen minutes with Indi that evening, he thought. Something to tide him over, since there would be no moments alone together in the near future.

Perhaps after dessert, when people mingled here and there over after-dinner coffee.

He already felt better.

"Hello!" he exclaimed. "What a nice party! How are things going?"

Friendly smiles returned his greeting.

Then a light scent reached his nostrils, something spicy that disappeared even as he took it in. He tried to remember where he'd smelled it before. Then he did.

In his apartment the evening he'd thought someone was inside.

But even as he tried to capture the scent, it vanished.

Sunday,
The second week

CHAPTER 42

Thomas and Nora went into her kitchen as soon as he arrived. Her home felt unusually peaceful. That morning, Adam had left for Lökholmen for a weeklong sailing camp run by RSYC. He'd return the following Saturday. Henrik had taken Simon to jig for herring.

"I assume you'd like a cup of tea," Nora said. She pulled down two mugs from the shelf without waiting for an answer. "The usual Earl Grey or vanilla flavored?"

She took milk from the refrigerator and opened the cupboard to get the honey.

"Earl Grey is fine," Thomas said. He opened a drawer and took out two spoons. Nora's kitchen felt like home after all their years of friendship.

"Would you like something with it?" Nora asked. She looked at the breadbox. Thomas shook his head.

"I'm fine. I've had several cinnamon buns already." He patted his stomach, and Nora raised her eyebrows. She didn't think Thomas had changed at all since his days as a handball player fifteen years ago.

They sat down at the kitchen table, and Nora served the piping hot tea.

"How are things going for you?" Thomas asked.

Nora had already opened her laptop.

"Look," she said and pointed at the material she'd put together along with her conclusions. "You can read it for yourself."

Thomas leaned forward to see better.

In her write-up, Nora thoroughly explained the concept of bank secrecy and what it meant. Thomas could see that it had been around as long as there had been banks and that it essentially meant that banks were not required to reveal any information about their customers. In many countries, this was set in stone.

But increased financial crimes over the past few years, especially those connected to international terrorism, had put pressure on the tax havens. Both the United States and the European Union wanted these countries to release information to criminal investigators.

"Where did you get all this?"

"Judicial databases. Some of them specialize in international law, especially in these types of cases."

"Amazing."

"I take it that Juliander must have stashed some kind of fortune abroad?" Nora asked.

He nodded. "This is totally confidential. We don't want any of this made public."

"Thanks for trusting me," Nora said. "I do understand. But if you want me to research further about bank secrecy, I should know a little something about why."

She took a sip of tea and looked at him.

Thomas had to agree.

Nora scrolled to another page and continued. "It appears that Liechtenstein is a really secure tax haven. No access is granted to any authority in any other country."

"Which must create some international tensions . . . ?"

"Yes, indeed. The EU has been leaning on Switzerland, who is more than willing to help them in cases concerning drug money and secret bank accounts."

Thomas studied the text on the screen.

"How can we shake loose information on Juliander's accounts?"

"That's pretty hard. Only in cases of terrorism and drugs has anyone broken through the secrecy." She paused and turned to him. "Now you really have to explain what this is all about, or I won't be much help."

Thomas felt uncomfortable about sharing information gathered by his team.

On the other hand, Nora's knowledge could speed up the investigation. Other channels would cost them time. And he had to consider the lack of financial competence in the Nacka Police Department.

"Well?" asked Nora. A wrinkle of irritation appeared on her forehead. "If I don't understand the question, I can't give you a reasonable answer."

She reached for the teapot, half filled her mug, and then held the teapot toward Thomas, who nodded for more.

"You're right," he said. "Let me explain."

He told her about Juliander's foreign credit card.

Nora listened with concentration. When he got to the theory that Juliander had stashed wealth abroad to back up the card, she looked worried.

"You've got a problem, then," she said.

"Explain it to me."

"See for yourself." Nora scrolled down the screen. "You must have a strong suspicion of a crime before the bank officers will even consider working with you."

"But we have it!" Thomas said.

"In their eyes, having a foreign credit card and a secret bank account is not criminal. They don't even think tax evasion is serious. A conviction would be a misdemeanor that carries a punishment of six months in jail, at the most. That's not enough to waive bank secrecy."

"Where does that leave us?"

Nora's words made Thomas feel anxious.

"It will be very, very difficult for you to get information about Juliander's financial situation abroad."

"So what should I do?"

Nora took a sip of tea as she thought.

"Perhaps someone in your Financial Crimes unit has experience dealing with Liechtenstein?"

Thomas grimaced as Nora studied her screen, searching for an answer.

"There's another thing to consider," Nora said. "The amount of time it will take to get information from Liechtenstein."

"How long do you think?"

"Years. It goes like this. First, someone in our justice department contacts his or her equivalent in Liechtenstein to make a formal plea."

"And then?"

"Then the Liechtenstein judicial department contacts the appropriate authorities in their country. After that, you need a decision from their Landgericht, which is the equivalent of our district court, to access the material. Any ruling can be appealed three times."

Thomas whistled.

"Then they need a specific ruling in order to seize the material. Unfortunately, this decision can also be appealed three times."

"That sounds crazy."

Nora smiled at him. "It gets even better. Even if the right to confiscate the material is approved, another separate decision must be made to transfer the material to Swedish authorities."

Thomas groaned. "You don't have to tell me. Appeals can be made three times."

Nora nodded. "Precisely. So the request can be appealed nine times in total before anything can reach Sweden."

"How long do you think that would all take?"

"I'd guess three to four years."

Thomas was starting to lose faith in the judicial process.

"Anything else?" he asked, discouraged.

"Do you really want to know?"

He nodded.

"After all that, the information comes with some strings attached. The material handed over to Sweden cannot be used for tax purposes. It can be used only for your murder investigation. Without a secure promise to follow this rule, you won't receive it at all."

Thomas had difficulty digesting all this information.

Finally he could say only, "I see." He stood up slowly and leaned against the kitchen counter while he tried to think. "So you're saying this is impossible—"

Nora interrupted him.

"What credit card did you say he had?"

"A MasterCard or a Visa . . . why?"

"You can contact their branch here in Sweden. The card might be issued abroad, but the Swedish office may still be able to help you. At least they can help you track the flow of money."

"Of course. Follow the money."

"Something else to consider: Where did the money come from before he put it in the secret bank account?" Nora was thinking out loud.

"Keep going," Thomas said. It was one of the questions he and his team were trying to answer.

"The whole purpose of a foreign credit card is to hold deposited capital as a form of liquid assets, right?"

"I assume so."

"Money from the law firm couldn't have been used. Not in a tax haven. A bankruptcy lawyer must keep his accounts open to the court.

They'd have shut him down in two seconds if his accounts were connected to Liechtenstein."

"And it would be impossible to transfer the money legally." Thomas tried to follow her train of thought.

"No, the authorities would have been alerted. And he would have been forced to pay taxes on it before it left the country."

"Of course, there are people who carry money out of the country in a suitcase."

"Too great a risk. He would have been disbarred if he got caught."

"So the million-dollar question is, where did the money come from to back up that foreign credit card?"

Thomas sat back down and drank the last of the tea. It was cold.

"The card had no limit," he said.

Nora whistled.

"Then it must have been a tremendous amount Juliander kept over there."

On his way back to Harö, Thomas wondered about the mysterious Oscar Juliander. The image of an exceptionally successful business lawyer with a perfect career and a perfect family was now falling apart.

Why would he risk losing all that?

Evading tax by holding secret bank accounts abroad was, after all, a serious crime. If he'd been discovered, his career would have been finished.

Had Juliander become so successful that he felt above the law? Or did he want the Swan so desperately that he was willing to break the law he'd worked his whole life to uphold?

Perhaps Juliander had angered or cheated someone. Someone who then killed him in revenge. In that case, who?

And where did all that money come from?

Monday,
THE THIRD WEEK

CHAPTER 43

"Did you get anything from the credit card company?" Thomas asked Margit as he took a bite of hamburger steak, one of two lunch specials.

They ate at one of the Nacka Strand restaurants, a few minutes' walk from the police station. They'd chosen an outdoor table to get some fresh air and escape the smell of fried food.

"Our dear prosecutor Öhman has arranged it all," Margit said. She looked up from her fried cod. "I spoke with the administrative head of the credit card company before we left. I've sent our questions to him."

"Did he seem willing to cooperate?"

"So-so. Their computer guy was on vacation, and they'd had to call him back in. But I'd guess this probably isn't the first time they've needed to look up data for a criminal investigation."

She took a bite of fish and continued. "The boss warned me that things won't move very quickly. Unfortunately."

"OK," Thomas said. "We can only hope for the best. It'll be interesting to find out what's hiding there."

He took a piece of bread, buttered it, and ate it before he speared the last bite of hamburger steak.

"Would you like some coffee?" He stood up even before Margit answered, knowing she never declined coffee.

He walked through the dim restaurant to where coffee pots sat on warmers. He took two white mugs, filled them with the strong brew, and carried them back to Margit.

"Here you go." He took a sip. The coffee was good.

"The boat identification is moving forward," Margit said.

Kalle and his assistants had succeeded in identifying fifteen of the boats by patiently making one phone call after the other. Then Kalle had the inspiration to ask Axel Bjärring if he recognized any, and he'd given them another three.

After yet another perusal of the picture, Thomas found he recognized one as well. It belonged to a seventy-five-year-old neighbor on Harö who'd known his parents. Now the question remained, did his neighbor know Oscar Juliander?

The owners of the nineteen identified craft would be brought in for questioning.

The wheels of the investigation were moving, however slowly.

Tuesday, the Third Week

CHAPTER 44

Thomas left early that afternoon for Harö. His thoughts had frozen, and he felt like giving up. He abandoned all the printouts and reports on his desk.

He needed to clear his mind.

His breathing relaxed as soon as he got on the ferry. When he made it to his house, he prepared a simple meal, filled a thermos with coffee, packed it all into a watertight cooler, and walked down to the dock. He lifted his kayak from its wooden rack and set it gently into the water.

He stowed the food at the front of the kayak, put on his life vest, and took a deep breath as he sat down.

He lifted the paddle.

At first he thought he'd go past Sandhamn and then, in a wide curve, toward Stora Hästskär, an island a little south of Sandhamn. For years it had been used as a radar installation by the military. All landings on the island had been forbidden, so no one could visit. Though the military had abandoned the station a few years ago, people were in the habit of avoiding the island. It would probably be vacant.

Which is exactly what Thomas wanted. Room to breathe.

With skillful strokes, he paddled toward the southeast. The paddle was over eight feet long, and he made good speed in the calm water. There was hardly any wind. It felt like moving through silk.

He enjoyed the stillness. Finding himself in the middle of the Baltic Sea in such a small vessel humbled him, in a good way. He could see nature close up, almost eye level with the surface. Kayaking offered a completely different view than a regular boat.

As he neared the channel that led to Sandhamn, he looked at the Linde family's dock out of habit. It was just about seven in the evening, and Nora and her family were probably still eating dinner.

He smiled as he thought about Simon; he always enjoyed talking to his godson. Simon reasoned about this and that, revealing the many deep thoughts he carried around in that little head. For the sake of the boys, Thomas hoped that Nora and Henrik would come to an agreement about the Brand house. Bitter arguments like that weren't good for anyone.

Thomas did not know Henrik well enough to understand his reasoning, but the man's ideas were far from his own. Nora's husband measured success through others' eyes. Who you knew and who your friends were mattered most to him. Thomas still found it surprising that Nora had fallen for a man so different from her. An inward sense of right and wrong had always motivated his childhood friend. She would never imagine resting her self-esteem on wealth or social connections.

A gap was obviously opening between Nora and Henrik, exacerbated by the conservative values of Henrik's parents. His upbringing and family traditions were overtaking him, while Nora was becoming more and more unhappy.

But Thomas also knew Nora to be amazingly stubborn. She would fight to save her marriage, even if only for the boys. Nora was one of the most loyal people Thomas knew, and she never made a promise she did not intend to keep. It was obvious that the conflict between Signe's last will and Henrik's demands was torturing her.

In the middle of a paddle stroke, Thomas caught a glimpse of movement from the corner of his eye. He saw a school of fish just below the surface of the water. What a beautiful sight—all the shimmering silver fish swimming to the side of his prow.

When he reached Hästskär, he pulled his kayak into a tiny bay edged by clumps of reeds. He got out his food and ate it quickly. Then he unrolled his towel and stretched out. He closed his eyes and fell instantly asleep, bathed in the evening sun.

An hour later he woke up. His right arm, propped behind his head, had fallen asleep. He massaged it to get the blood moving again. Still sleepy, he reached for his bottle of water and took a few large swallows.

He'd dreamed about the start of the Round Gotland Race.

Thomas drew his hand through his hair and tried to recall the dream. He'd been at sea in a small boat, surrounded by other spectators. Everyone was deeply concentrating on the start, looking at the gray starting vessel towering over the horizon.

In his dream, he stood on the foredeck, legs firmly planted, holding a rifle. The *Emerald Gin* sailed past him. He was about fifty yards from the beautiful Swan. Its hull shone in the sun. With icy calculation, he aimed directly at Oscar Juliander standing behind the steering wheel. He could clearly see Juliander's wide smile and Fredrik Winbergh behind him.

Just as Thomas aimed, a large wave lifted the hull of his boat and it swayed. He lost his balance. He fired the shot but missed the target by several yards.

With one hand on the railing, he watched Juliander disappear against the horizon.

It had been an unpleasant dream with strangely realistic details. He could still feel how the swaying deck threw off his aim.

He realized something else.

The shooter must have been on a large, stable boat.

They'd paid attention to the wrong thing. Because the water was unusually calm and the breeze light on the day of the murder, they'd reasoned that the shot could have come from any boat at all.

He remembered discussing the movements of the waves with Dr. Sachsen at the autopsy, but they hadn't considered that so many boats in a small area could create localized chop even without much wind. It would have affected a smaller boat much more. A smaller craft, in fact, could not have been the platform for a successful shot. There was no guarantee of accuracy.

But on a large yacht with a deep keel, chop wouldn't matter. The killer could have aimed and fired without losing balance.

Thomas felt a wave of excitement.

How many yachts had been in the golden triangle, as Margit called it? Probably not many. Certainly not twenty-seven.

If he were right, they could eliminate many of the boats in the photograph.

As soon as he was back at the station, he'd take another look. Tomorrow morning, he'd take the first ferry from Harö.

WEDNESDAY,
THE THIRD WEEK

CHAPTER 45

The investigators filed into the large conference room at the police station. The room was sparsely furnished: one oblong table and eight chairs, a flip chart on an easel, and, on one of the short walls, a whiteboard.

The only beautiful thing about the room was the view of the water. In the daylight, they could see large ferryboats bringing tourists to the Venice of the North.

The enlargement hung on one wall. Thomas stood next to it, pointing out the vessels carrying spectators.

"There are only three large yachts near the starting line. One of them belongs to Axel Bjärring. He had many RSYC members on board, and we've spoken to all of them. They give each other alibis."

Then he pointed slightly to the right.

"Here are two other yachts in range. One is a Princess 47, and the other is a forty-two-foot Riva Malibu."

He explained his new idea about the shot most likely coming from a larger craft.

"Not bad," Margit agreed.

"We've identified both owners, and Kalle already interviewed them."

"Kalle," Persson said. "Tell us what Holger Alsing had to say."

Kalle said that Alsing, the owner of the Princess, seemed like a happy person. He'd taken his wife and three teenage sons, as well as their Siamese cat, to watch the start of the Round Gotland Race. His children hadn't lasted long. They'd begun to complain of seasickness and boredom.

"You know how teenagers can be," Alsing had said.

Kalle didn't know how teenagers could be, but he'd nodded anyway.

They'd returned to Sandhamn early because of the constant complaining. They'd gone to Värdshuset Restaurant. It was only that evening, while watching the news, that the Alsing family had heard what had happened.

When Kalle had asked if anyone could verify his story, Alsing had grinned and said his wife and sons could. They were all in the same boat, so to speak.

"That's their whole story," Kalle said.

The interview with the people on board the other yacht was similar. Unlike the Alsings, this skipper had been present at the time of the shooting. He realized something had happened on the *Emerald Gin*, but he didn't know what. He thought maybe someone had taken ill.

Kalle finished his report. The room fell silent. The investigators gazed at the enlargement and considered the new information.

Carina spoke up first.

"The hatch. There's a hatch on the foredeck of this boat. Look here." She approached the picture and pointed to the hatch.

Thomas joined her to study the enlargement. It showed the boats all pointing in the direction of Juliander's Swan at the moment of the start. The Princess 47 was the only yacht with a hatch on the foredeck.

Thomas leaned closer. Could someone shoot from the forepeak with the hatch open?

Why not?

If someone kneeled on the bunk, opened the hatch, and aimed carefully? If the vessel didn't careen because it was so large? And if he were protected from anyone seeing what he was doing so that nobody could interrupt?

"Sharp, Carina," he said.

She brightened. It worried him to see how happy his praise made her.

"It just came to me. Just like that."

Persson beamed at his daughter.

"We must talk to Holger Alsing again," Margit said. "Immediately. Where does he work?" She looked at Kalle.

"He's an engineer with his own consulting firm. He often takes clients out on his yacht."

"Any connection to Juliander?"

"He claimed he'd never met him."

"Interesting," Thomas said.

"Very interesting," Kalle agreed.

"Does he have a gun license? For a rifle, like a Marlin?"

"We'll check right away."

Thomas nodded, studying the lineup again.

Had they really found a suspect? And all those other lines of investigation—the many affairs, the Russian mafia, the drugs, the crooked credit card—were they simply red herrings? Events in Juliander's life unrelated to his death?

Could the answer to this riddle be on board the Princess 47, right in front of their eyes?

Alsing's only alibi was his word that he'd spent the day with his wife and sons. Could that be a lie? They'd check with his family. And what might be Alsing's motive?

"We have a bit of a problem," Kalle said.

"What?" Persson furrowed his eyebrows as he drank the last bit of coffee.

Kalle looked unhappy.

"He's not in Sweden."

"He? You mean Alsing?" asked Thomas.

"Why not?" asked Margit.

"He left the country this morning," Kalle said. "He and his family went to Mallorca for a two-week vacation."

Kalle hung his head as if he felt personally responsible.

Thomas and Margit looked at each other.

"Should we try a phone call?" asked Thomas.

"The risk is that we'd warn him unnecessarily," Persson said. "We have no proof, no reason to have him arrested and held while abroad."

Thomas agreed. They needed a great deal more evidence to get someone extradited. He could already hear Öhman, the prosecutor, explaining it to him.

"So when did you say he's supposed to return?" asked Margit.

"Two weeks," said Kalle.

"We'll bring him in for questioning then," Margit said. "Once he's back on Swedish soil."

"Until then, find out everything you can about this guy," Persson said. "More on his job, his financial situation, his gun licenses, and so on."

"Somewhere we'll find a connection to Juliander," Margit said. "We'll be ready when he comes back to Sweden."

The music was deafening. He was drunker than he'd ever been before, but he liked it. He enjoyed the feeling of freedom that alcohol gave him.

Here there is no sorrow, *he thought, as if he were a young man at a college party again.*

They'd gone to Alexandra's, a nightclub catering to the most elegant people in Stockholm. The place everyone who was anyone went, even the king.

His bachelor party had begun with a tour of the Central Baths, where he'd gotten a massage from a scantily clad young woman. Then they continued to the Restaurant Riche, where they enjoyed an expensive dinner and many glasses of schnapps followed by a hearty Burgundy. They finished with cognac and coffee. His closest friend, Ruter, whose real name was Rudolf, delivered a heartfelt speech. Ruter would be his best man on Saturday. He told funny stories until they were all laughing and crying at the same time.

He barely made it from the restaurant to Alexandra's. His good friend the Count held his arm to help steer him. The beautiful owner escorted them to a private corner where glasses and bottles waited.

People danced wildly around them to the blaring sounds of the pop group Sweet. Beautiful women in short dresses and young men with sideburns and velvet jackets surrounded him. Someone put a gin and tonic in his hand, though he hardly needed another drink.

In one week, it would be time. The ceremony would happen at three in the afternoon, at Oscar's Church in the center of Östermalm.

For a long while, he'd ignored the wedding preparations. The unending stream of decisions made him dizzy, from the design of the wedding cake to the seating arrangement at the table of honor. How could it take so much time to plan a celebration that lasted only a few hours?

After the engagement, everything moved forward with surprising speed. His bride's bottomless enthusiasm scared him. It felt like the wedding had become more important than their relationship. She'd spent so much time planning the ceremony the last few months that he'd barely seen her.

He took a long pull from his drink and stumbled over to the Count, who was talking with a pretty brunette on his knee.

"Skål! May the devil take me!" he said. He downed the rest of the drink and ordered another.

Thursday,
the third week

CHAPTER 46

The funeral was set for two in the afternoon, but guests began to gather in front of Uppenbarelse Church in Saltsjöbaden half an hour early.

The beautiful old church, designed by Ferdinand Boberg, sat high up on a hill with a wide view of Ersta Bay. An imposing creation that could hold four hundred people, the church dominated the surroundings with its clock tower and art nouveau architecture. Today Oscar Juliander would be buried here. *They'll need all the space,* Thomas thought. The parking lot had filled up and cars now lined the narrow road to the church.

Thomas and Margit stood apart from the others. He recognized many of the guests, including famous businessmen and lawyers. At the entrance, he saw Ivar Hallén, from the Kalling law firm, standing with a group of men and women dressed in black. Thomas guessed they must be Juliander's colleagues from the firm.

Eva Timell stood with them. She wore dark sunglasses, but Thomas could tell by her flushed face that she'd been crying.

Thomas and Margit waited until everyone went inside. Then, just before the huge wooden doors closed, they entered. Space was scarce because of the crowd, but they managed to find a spot in the last pew before the giant doors opened again for the family.

The minister led the procession with Sylvia Juliander beside him. She wore the darkest black dress imaginable and a hat with a veil. Their three children followed, the daughter slightly ahead of the sons. Sylvia clutched a crumpled linen handkerchief. The sons walked solemnly in black suits with white ties. Each child carried a red rose.

The family sat in the pew closest to the altar. Silence settled over the congregation, then the organist began to play the hymn "Beautiful Savior." It reminded Thomas of the last funeral he'd attended, the one with only a tiny white casket. He and Pernilla had sat in the pew closest to the altar, struggling to understand something beyond comprehension.

Emily no longer existed. Emily was dead.

They'd held the service for only the two of them. They could not handle having anyone else there, not even their parents. They'd barely managed to make it through themselves.

Thomas did his best to set these melancholy thoughts aside, to ignore his sense of failure as he remembered the funeral and separation afterward from the woman he thought he'd be married to for the rest of his life.

If he died tomorrow, there wouldn't be enough mourners to fill a church, he thought in an attack of self-pity. Just one ex-wife and one young girlfriend he was already tired of.

Thomas willed himself to close his eyes and think about the investigation instead.

Until now, they'd only had pieces of a puzzle. Wherever they turned, the media followed. It was hard for the police to work amid all the speculation. There seemed no end to the articles written about this story. The tabloids even turned to pure invention. If Persson hadn't thought to get their media spokesperson involved immediately, they wouldn't have had a moment of peace.

Thomas opened his eyes and looked toward the altar.

The family had chosen a walnut casket. An unbelievable number of flower wreaths and bouquets surrounded it, and an especially beautiful arrangement in white and green tones adorned the top.

The minister delivered a touching eulogy about Juliander's love of life, his ability to find humor in any situation, and how valuable he'd been to so many.

Thomas felt surprisingly moved by the eulogy. His team had developed a picture of an unfaithful liar who manipulated the truth and took his material status for granted. Thomas had come to see Juliander as a deeply egotistical man who put his needs above those around him.

Now, another person came into focus. Oscar Juliander meant a great deal to many. People liked him, the same people who now cried quietly in this church. His widow and children remained in the first pew, inconsolable. And somewhere, far from here, a distraught Diana Söder delivered her own silent farewell. He knew she did not dare attend the service, especially after the newspapers exposed their hidden relationship. A wave of compassion washed over Thomas as he remembered her pale face and tear-filled eyes.

What made the dead attorney so obviously seek all the classic attributes of success? Thomas wondered as the minister prayed for Oscar Juliander's soul to find peace. Was he driven by competition? Was it all about the trophies he'd collected in droves? Did he enjoy being a lawyer with the high salary, the cars, the boats? Or did these things seem hollow once he'd acquired them? Was the house of cards about to fall down?

When the time came for guests to walk past the casket to bid Oscar farewell, Thomas and Margit quietly stepped outside. They'd had no specific reason to attend Juliander's funeral. It simply felt like the right thing to do, especially while investigating the man's death.

* * *

Eventually, the doors opened wide and people exited. They milled about on the gravel pathway below the church, many of them still drying tears.

The family had invited the guests to a reception in the Grünewald mansion not far from the Juliander home. Thomas assumed most would attend. He nodded to people he'd interviewed in Sandhamn and who recognized him.

As he stepped back to let someone hurry past, he bumped into someone. He turned to apologize and found Ingmar von Hahne.

"It's nothing," von Hahne said as he caught his balance.

He shook Thomas's hand and greeted them both. Standing beside him, Isabelle von Hahne did the same.

"How is the investigation going, if I may ask?" Ingmar von Hahne said.

Thomas and Margit glanced at each other; they found it best to give the standard answer in these situations.

"It's moving along," Margit said. "These things take time."

"We all hope you find the bastard!" Ingmar said. "People like that should be locked up for the rest of their lives."

Margit changed the subject.

"I hear that you'll be elected chairman of the RSYC in September," she said. "I read about your nomination in the paper."

Before von Hahne could speak, his wife jumped in.

"Isn't it wonderful? Ingmar has put so much time into the club that he really deserves it." She looked pleased as she continued. "We all know he'll do a fantastic job. It's a big responsibility, and Ingmar is certainly the man for the job!"

She didn't seem to care that she was embarrassing her husband.

"Did you know that Ingmar's father also served on the board? He was first vice chairman in his day. So this is the second generation. Perhaps our son, Marcus, will follow in their footsteps." She sighed briefly. "My father-in-law would be so proud if he could see us today. But unfortunately, he passed away many years ago."

"Now, Isabelle," Ingmar von Hahne said. He looked at Margit and Thomas. "I regard this as a temporary position. Somebody had to take over after Hans, and now that poor Oscar is no longer with us . . ."

He gave a helpless shrug and let his eyes wander along the tops of the trees.

Margit shifted her weight from one foot to the other, unable to think of anything to break the silence.

Ingmar von Hahne glanced at his watch.

"I'm sorry. You'll have to excuse us," he said. "We must go to the reception. We wish you luck with your investigation."

He gave a friendly nod and escorted his wife to their car.

"He seems like a nice guy," Margit said. "In contrast to his wife. Yuck. I wonder what he ever saw in her."

Thomas had not been impressed by either of them.

"They're the worst sort of upper-class people, if you ask me. I've had to deal with a number of their kind in Sandhamn. He's simply the male version of her."

He headed in the same direction as the von Hahne couple.

"Time to get going," he said. "Anything will be better than this."

Chapter 47

Nora's rage grew so intense that it caused her physical pain. She felt her body shaking and her breathing become labored.

How could he?

Exhausted, she collapsed into a corner of Signe's old boathouse, where she'd fled to for some peace. She buried her head in her hands and leaned against the wall. The fishing nets around her smelled of seaweed and salt—comforting and familiar.

She took a deep breath and let it out slowly. Henrik had dashed her hopes of becoming closer to him after the winter.

His words echoed in her head.

She'd be the first to admit that the past year had been incredibly difficult. She'd struggled with dark thoughts. Night after night, those hours in the Grönskär lighthouse returned, and she would wake covered in sweat, smelling smoke. The memory gripped her mind and refused to let go.

Henrik had urged her to see a psychologist. Finally she'd called the therapist one of his colleagues recommended. She had no expectations. Without Henrik's prodding, she wouldn't have gone at all.

The psychologist's office was on Sveavägen in the middle of the city. He was a bald man who wore horn-rimmed glasses, gray pants, and a shirt buttoned to the neck at every session.

She sat in the light-brown armchair across from him. His technique involved bouncing her own comments back to her in the form of questions. He always began by asking how she felt. After she talked about her feelings for a while, he picked her last sentence and reworked it with a question mark. She responded, and he repeated the maneuver. He charged her five hundred kronor an hour for this.

She gave up after five sessions. Therapy was not her thing, she decided, though the dreams became less troublesome after the visits. They weren't as frequent or intense.

But she struggled when she returned to work after sick leave. She remembered immediately why her job made her so unhappy—everything that had driven her to search for a new one remained.

Her anger at Henrik grew. He had insisted she turn down the Malmö job. But at the same time, she desperately wished that their life together would remain the same—that it would return to what it had been in the past.

Last week, when she'd curled up next to him and fallen asleep, happy and in tune with him, she truly believed things might work out. But they quickly reverted to their old pattern: Henrik got his way, his mother got involved, and she shut up and played along.

Now he was allowing the real-estate agent to bring the family living in Switzerland to inspect Signe's house. He'd ignored her suggestion to rent it first. He knew she wasn't ready to sell. She'd tried so hard to explain her reluctance.

Had he listened at all?

Without blinking, he'd told her the family would come by on Saturday at two in the afternoon, after Adam returned from sailing camp.

She'd felt herself turn to stone in her own kitchen, unable to say a word.

"What's wrong, Mama?" Simon had asked. He'd looked worried as she walked away, her face white as chalk.

She couldn't remain in the room with Henrik one minute longer. She didn't remember finding her way to the boathouse. It simply felt like the most natural place to go, somewhere to be alone.

When had money become so important to him? How had it come to this?

CHAPTER 48

Thomas and Margit sat at the conference table with Juliander's financial records in front of them. Most everyone else had left for the day. Thomas planned to stop by Carina's with pizza later that evening.

"This man lived far beyond his means," Margit stated. "There's no way he could have bought that Swan on his own."

"Don't forget all his mistresses," Thomas said. He remembered the ring Diana Söder received for her birthday. That hadn't been cheap. Their interviews with his other mistresses exposed similar extravagances. Oscar Juliander had been a generous man who took his lovers on expensive trips where they stayed in elegant hotels.

"It's odd that no boat payment shows up here. Unless he had a suitcase full of cash, he must have found a different way," Margit said. She shoved the papers aside. "Even if he used the Liechtenstein card, why don't the transactions show up here?"

Thomas took a last sip of tea and thought about the problem. He looked at the statement from the Swedish branch. All the transactions listed had taken place in Sweden.

"He certainly withdrew lots of cash," he said.

They had a list of dates and withdrawals for ten thousand kronor each. The dead man had secretly increased his cash flow, a simple but smart way to use a hidden bank account. Withdrawing money at ATMs kept things discreet. A bank cashier might have become suspicious.

"This guy was one smart lawyer," Margit said. "The credit card isn't even in his name."

She read aloud: "Springfund S. A. It's a name that says nothing. Account in Liechtenstein. Can't see the human being behind it."

"So the withdrawals are impossible to trace directly back to him."

Without the murder investigation, they'd never have been able to get these financial records. Nobody would have connected the card to the owner, Thomas thought.

"But the question remains: How did he pay for his boat?"

"Ah, I got it," Thomas said.

"What?"

"The *shipyard* is *not* in *Sweden*."

"Explain that." Margit looked at him.

"Swan boats are made in Finland. That's why we see no payments here. This list covers only payments and withdrawals in Sweden. The Swedish branch wouldn't include payments made in Finland."

"So now we have a chat with the Finnish branch?"

"Probably. Since the Swedish company only deals with Swedish transactions, I assume that the Finnish company does the same in Finland."

Margit sighed.

"So we contact the Finnish police to help us get the same information from Finland that we got from the Swedish company. We'll need another court order from Prosecutor Öhman."

More wasted time, Thomas thought.

"Well, it's one reasonable explanation for how Juliander bought his Swan. With a foreign credit card that flew under the radar here in Sweden and probably did the same in other countries."

"Elegant reasoning," Margit said. "Even if it's illegal."

"We still don't know where his money came from."

"No, we don't."

"Did he have any dealings with this Alsing guy? Something that wasn't exactly clean?"

"We'll have to figure that one out."

FRIDAY,
THE THIRD WEEK

CHAPTER 49

Martin Nyrén whistled happily to himself as he thought about Indi's latest text message.

```
Coming to town Sunday evening. Longing
for you. -Indi
```

Finally!

Hiding his feelings for Indi at the funeral had tortured him. He'd gotten a seat right behind her, so close he could almost touch his love. He wanted to provide comfort in that heavy place filled with muffled cries.

A couple times, they'd made eye contact, but only for a moment. He kept reminding himself to remain discreet.

As the congregation sang the final hymn, he lost himself in the memory of their last meeting, one of the few times they'd enjoyed an entire night together. Indi's family had been away. They were able to wake up together without making elaborate plans.

He'd hardly wanted to waste time sleeping. He'd dozed lightly and woke often to reach over and reassure himself that he was not alone. The sound of light breathing filled him with joy. What if they could always be like this? He would sacrifice anything to make that dream come true.

It had been a wonderful evening and night—in contrast to yesterday's service at Uppenbarelse Church. What a tragic piece of business.

Martin Nyrén hated funerals. An older person's service, however, seemed natural. Someone who'd lived a long life would eventually die. But sitting in a pew and watching Oscar's children grieve had hurt his heart. The girl's sobs had competed with the organ music, while the sons had acted more reserved. But when it came time for them to approach the casket, they'd broken down and wept.

The only person who did not shed a tear was Sylvia. She'd sat still as stone during the service, but then, she'd received one shock after another the past few weeks. Probably she'd taken a tranquilizer. She handled the reception with grace. She conversed politely with the guests and acted like the perfect hostess.

So typical of Sylvia.

Martin Nyrén shook off the memories of the funeral. He began to page through a cookbook, wondering what he would make on Sunday evening. He wanted something especially fine for his dinner with Indi. Duck breast with orange slices and red wine sauce sounded good. Or perhaps scallops in lobster sauce? He'd find a fine wine at the state liquor store. Or maybe a bottle of champagne. Yes, champagne would be best.

And only the best was good enough for his beloved.

CHAPTER 50

"Will you take the weekend off?" asked Margit. She set her coffee mug on the table. It was nearly four thirty in the afternoon. They spoke in the kitchen of the police station after a long day of follow-up questioning.

"Maybe I'll swing out to Harö. Then tomorrow I can sort through our material in peace and quiet."

"I'll come in then, too."

Margit sounded tired, and Thomas shook his head.

"No need for that. Spend the weekend with your family."

Thomas had a great deal to think about.

Last night, he'd gone to Carina's. They'd enjoyed some pizza and beer. She'd wanted to cuddle, but Thomas hadn't felt like it. The atmosphere became frosty, and Carina went from unhappy to angry. They had a discussion in which she delivered a long monologue critiquing his behavior.

"You will have to make up your mind, Thomas," she said. "You know that I love you. I've been in love with you for over a year, but I have no idea what *you* want."

She was so upset that she got up from the table and stood with her back to the kitchen counter. Her dark hair was held back in a ponytail.

It cut Thomas to the core to see her like this, so young and vulnerable, and to know he was the one who'd hurt her.

"One minute you're kind and sweet," she said. "We have a great time together. Then at work you hardly even look at me. And I don't understand why." She stared at him. "But I won't go on like this. If we're staying together, I'm done sneaking around. I want everything out in the open."

She took a deep breath, crossing her arms tightly across her chest. Her eyes filled with tears as she spoke. "Are you ashamed of me, Thomas? Do you have any idea how hurtful it is that you won't reveal our relationship to everyone?"

She wiped away a few tears.

"I think you should go now," she said. "And think about what you want. But remember, I'm not going to sit here twiddling my thumbs, waiting for you to make up your mind."

Thomas could tell by her trembling lower lip that it took every ounce of her self-control to keep from bursting into tears in front of him.

He picked up his jacket and left without a word.

He felt totally ashamed because everything she said was true. He enjoyed himself with Carina, and nobody had forced him to be with her, but he did want to keep their relationship a secret.

And why? Why did he feel uneasy about publicly acknowledging Carina as his girlfriend? Because she was just a girl? Only twenty-five years old?

Of course not. She was more than a girl. Even thinking that belittled her. What was wrong with him?

He sighed out loud.

"What?" asked Margit.

"I have some things to figure out," he said. He knew he sounded unhappy. The room went silent until Margit spoke again.

"Well, if we've finished here for now, I think I'll head on over to my summerhouse. My sister and her husband are coming over for dinner tomorrow evening, and maybe I'll try to force my daughters to stay home and spend some time with their relatives."

"So they have other things they want to do?" asked Thomas.

"I never see them anymore, especially on the weekends," Margit said. "They're out with friends every evening during summer vacation."

She smiled in resignation.

"I guess that's how teenagers are," Thomas said.

"True, but I get tired of having constant discussions about what they're wearing, where they're going, and when they'll be back."

"Can't you sic Bertil on them?" Thomas said. He half joked.

Margit's husband was a teacher, too friendly to put the fear of God into anyone. Thomas had met him only once but wondered how he controlled his upper-level classroom. That was the age when students tended to be difficult.

Margit's skeptical expression told Thomas what she thought of his suggestion. It also told him that he had no understanding of teenagers.

"Well, it's like this, Thomas," she said in an almost lecturing tone. "There's a special connection between a mother and her daughters, especially when they're teenagers. Believe me, there's no point in getting Bertil involved." She sighed and put down her mug.

"But everything has its time," she said. "On the other side of their eighteenth birthdays they'll become normal people. At least, I hope so."

CHAPTER 51

Eva Timell lay awake in bed. Her eyes were closed, but sleep refused to come.

She missed him so much. And she was so angry.

At the funeral, she and Sylvia had stood only a few yards apart. She'd almost gone over to say, *All day he was mine. And you had no idea where he spent his nights. He was never yours alone. Just so you know.*

But funeral guests surrounded Sylvia, offering their condolences. Eva lost her courage. And what purpose would it serve to create a scandal? It wouldn't bring Oscar back.

So she didn't make a scene. Instead she went to the reception and acted like everyone else. She conversed politely and tried to say as little as possible. As soon as she could, she went straight home. She poured a glass of wine and curled up on the sofa with her cat, Blofeld.

She spent hours reliving memories of Oscar and their time together. Finally she took a long bath and went to bed. Exhausted, she slept for nine hours.

But tonight sleep refused to come. That's how it had been ever since Oscar's death. Almost every evening, it took half a bottle of wine to make her feel sleepy. Then she'd wake up early with the need to cry and a bad headache, unable to go back to sleep, though she knew how tired she'd be the next day.

Now she tried to relax. She tensed her leg and arm muscles for ten seconds, holding her breath. Then she breathed out and let them relax. She did this exercise three times. She inhaled deeply to calm her body and trick it into sleeping.

Sometimes the exercise worked but not now. She found herself full of anger, unhappiness, and disappointment at how her life had turned out. She feared she might never feel sleepy again. She'd sacrificed so much over the years for his sake! All that time she'd waited and hoped! And here she was, with no family of her own and only a white cat for company.

What's left for me? she thought with a bitter taste in her mouth. *Who is going to take care of me now, Oscar? Who will look after me?*

SATURDAY,
THE THIRD WEEK

CHAPTER 52

Why did she agree to this? Would she do anything to keep the family peace?

How else could she explain why she stood here waiting to show the Brand house to Mr. and Mrs. Swiss Cheese? Their real names were Ivar and Ella Borman, but in her imagination she'd already renamed them. She disliked them as much as she disliked that overambitious real-estate agent Severin.

Mrs. Swiss Cheese was now strolling through the ground floor inspecting all the rooms. She'd already seen the kitchen and declared her intentions. "It's pleasingly old-fashioned," she said. "But just think how much more pleasant it would be if that wall were knocked out to allow a view of the Baltic."

Be my guest, Nora thought as she leaned against the dining room wall, arms crossed over her chest. *Go buy yourself a unique old mansion and wrench it into a modern house with an open floor plan. Why keep a classic dining room when you can make it look like a page from a magazine? You can't think for yourself.*

She glared at the woman, who was now evaluating Signe's beautiful antique furniture. A snort came out before she could stop it.

"Excuse me," Ella Borman said. "Did you say something?"

"Sorry," Nora said. "Something must be stuck in my throat."

She pretended to pick up a scrap of paper she found near a windowsill.

"Is the furniture included in the sale?" asked Ella Borman. She pinched the lace curtains, and then she plopped down on one of the dining room chairs and surveyed the table as if she already owned it.

"We hadn't discussed it," Nora said.

"Most of this stuff is trash," the woman said. "But a piece or two can be salvaged. For instance, that cupboard in the corner. It can be made into something fun with a dash of color."

Nora gave a pained smile.

How dare this woman refer to Signe's belongings as garbage. Signe had loved her furniture. Her father and her grandfather had furnished this house, and each piece had stood in its place for as long as Nora could remember.

Now, in the eyes of this woman, it became trash.

Henrik escorted the real-estate agent and the slightly overweight Swiss Swede down the stairs. Severin shone like the sun. He kept pointing out the many advantages of the house. The enormous sums being mentioned were not lost on Nora.

"What day can we take possession?" Severin asked.

"We haven't decided about selling yet," Nora said.

Henrik shot her a look, then smiled at the potential buyers.

"We can certainly talk about it," he said. "We'll come to an agreement that suits everyone."

"Look at this spectacular view!" Severin said. He clearly wanted to change the subject. "You can see all the way to Runmarö in good weather. And the Waxholmsbolaget ferries pass by every day. What a colorful contribution to the scenery! And sometimes the old ship *Norrskär* passes by. It's one of the very last steamships that traverses the archipelago. If you want a really good beef dinner, take a trip on her!"

He patted his stomach to emphasize his words.

"Why don't we look at the dock? Very few properties in Sandhamn can boast such a large anchorage. You can tie up any kind of vessel you please."

"That sounds great," said Ivar Borman. "We have a Fairline at forty feet that we'll need to dock here."

"And think of all the guests we could have!" his wife said. "We have many acquaintances in the archipelago, and there'll be room for them all to come by boat. We're counting on having a lot of visitors!"

She pushed her sunglasses onto the top of her head to hold back her hair.

Nora felt something shrivel inside her. How could Henrik not notice how soulless these people were?

Signe would roll over in her grave if she knew this horrible couple intended to buy her beloved home. But Henrik simply stood back and smiled as if everything were right with the world.

Had she any right to fight him on this? Even her own parents had bowed out of the discussion.

"You will have to make up your own mind, Nora," her mother had told her when she'd tried to talk about her conflicting feelings. "You'll have to decide what's best."

Her father had agreed. Nora would have to decide, but, no matter what, they would support her. They felt they were not in the position to give her advice.

Even Thomas had not taken her side. He'd only reminded her how much it would take to care for the Brand house.

Nora felt deflated as a punctured balloon. Her legs started to tremble. She wanted to get away, go home, pull the covers over her head, and pretend this house viewing had never happened.

"Here are the keys to the boathouse," she said. "You might as well take a look as long as you're here."

CHAPTER 53

"How nice of you to come! Please make yourselves at home!" Isabelle von Hahne said. "Ingmar's preparing the drinks. He'll be right here." She smiled at the Rosensjöös and took their summer jackets. The bouquet Hans Rosensjöö had brought along pleased her.

"What beautiful roses! I love roses! Thank you so much."

She led them to the living room, where bowls of snacks and a tray with eight cocktail glasses waited. Silver toothpicks with three green olives balanced on the edge of each glass. Beside them a large crystal pitcher held ice-cold martinis. Ingmar von Hahne bent over the tray preparing the drinks but smiled at his guests as they entered. He kissed Britta on both cheeks and then shook her husband's hand.

"Arvid and Kristina are on their way," Isabelle said. "And Anders and Ann-Sofie, as well."

She poured them each a drink.

"Ingmar," she said, looking impatiently at her husband. "Could you check outside? It sounds like our other guests have arrived."

It was a command, not a request.

"Yes, dear," her husband said. He disappeared from the room.

There was an awkward silence.

Hans Rosensjöö stared into his glass. He had tried his best to get out of this dinner. It was too soon after Oscar's funeral for a party. How efficient, he thought, with everyone already in the area. A small, elegant dinner to pave the way for Ingmar's election. So typical of Isabelle.

Hans had accepted the idea that Ingmar would be his successor. But he had a hard time dealing with Ingmar's wife. She would surely be an asset to Ingmar in his new role, but he preferred to avoid Isabelle's company. Though many admired her ambition, it made him shy away. Her motives were too obvious for his taste.

Tonight Isabelle's voice and gestures were over the top, not that this was unusual. She enjoyed the social life, and there was no limit to her enthusiasm for organizing charity events.

But that was the problem in a nutshell, Hans Rosensjöö thought. That, that . . . he tried to find the right word . . . that obsession. She measured her life by her social successes in a way he found completely foreign. Foreign to Britta, too, for that matter.

Not for a moment would he have agreed to accept the chairmanship of RSYC for social prestige. It was his duty if asked, and he understood the responsibilities.

He had no doubt that Isabelle would enjoy standing beside her husband as an unofficial representative—something Britta never wanted.

But all of this would not be his concern much longer. Ingmar had chosen Isabelle. Now he'd have to endure her constant social climbing.

Hans looked at his own wife with appreciation. Britta had filled out over the years and was now mostly interested in the grandchildren, but she would never treat him the way Isabelle treated Ingmar. She'd sent him out like a dog to fetch the other guests. What nerve. He would never tolerate such bad manners.

He sipped his martini. It was dry, as he preferred. At least Ingmar mixed a good martini, even if he was not master in his own home.

Ingmar von Hahne escorted the other guests in.

The RSYC committee chair for facilities, Arvid Welin, and his wife, Kristina, walked in. Next came the man in charge of the nomination committee, Anders Bergenkrantz, and his wife, Ann-Sofie.

All the guests had arrived.

Oscar Juliander's ghost hovered over the dinner.

Everyone at the table had attended the funeral, and the ladies commented on the tasteful service, the beautiful flower arrangements, and the moving eulogy.

Then Hans Rosensjöö cut to the chase.

"Has anyone heard about the police investigation? I don't understand why they haven't found the killer yet. It's been weeks. What are they doing!"

He looked around the dining room. The table was set with old family china, silver candleholders, and a flower arrangement. Ingmar sat next to Britta, and Hans had been placed between Isabelle and Kristina. That meant that he would give the thank-you speech at the end of the dinner, which didn't trouble him. He'd done it fairly often in recent years.

Arvid Welin cleared his throat.

He was a well-spoken man with an active intellect. As a young student, he'd written a number of radical articles for his university's student newspaper. Though he'd grown more conservative as the years rolled by, after a few drinks he'd sometimes spout ideas from the wild sixties.

"They don't seem to have much to go on yet," he said. "But what can you expect these days? Budget cuts affect everything. You never see patrol cars around anymore."

"I wonder if they'll ever find out who killed poor Oscar," Kristina Welin said.

"It's a scandal that they haven't gotten anywhere," said Anders Bergenkrantz.

"Don't say that," said Britta. She put her hand on his arm. "Of course they'll catch Oscar's murderer. I'm sure they will. I think it was someone from the underworld. Oscar was a lawyer. So many criminals want revenge."

She shivered.

"Dearest," her husband said. "Oscar was a bankruptcy lawyer, not a defense lawyer. He didn't handle criminals."

"But who else would do such a thing?" his wife said. "Oscar had no other enemies. And think about dear Sylvia. My heart breaks for her. What a tragedy."

"What if it was all a mistake?" Ann-Sofie Bergenkrantz said. Her slight double chin quivered. She smoothed an imaginary wrinkle from her dress. "I read about a man who was shot to death moose hunting," she continued. "Perhaps someone was shooting seabirds and aimed badly?"

"My dear," Isabelle von Hahne said, "you can't be serious. Who would try to pot a seabird in the middle of the Round Gotland Race?"

Isabelle chuckled and refilled everyone's drinks.

Ann-Sofie Bergenkrantz understood that everyone thought her suggestion ridiculous. She looked at her plate. Isabelle was so adamant about everything. No one could change her mind. Ann-Sofie felt even more embarrassed when she felt herself blushing. Then she mustered up some courage. Isabelle would not have the last word this time.

"Maybe he engaged in some shady business. I've always wondered how he maintained that standard of living. Oscar didn't inherit wealth, did he?"

Ann-Sofie looked awkwardly at the others. It was impolite to talk about money. She knew that, but wasn't there something odd about Oscar's finances?

Although Ann-Sofie would never admit that she kept tabs on her friends' financial standings, she did follow the tabloid lists of wealthy Swedes. They never named Oscar, though many of his friends were included. It was unusual that a person with his lifestyle did not have a noticeable fortune. The Swan, for example, must have cost an incredible amount of money.

Isabelle's mouth closed tightly. Isabelle, born wealthy and too well bred to discuss money.

How come Isabelle always feels superior? Ann-Sofie wondered. *Why does she need to cut others down? Everyone acknowledges how elegant and worldly she is. And thin, of course.* Unlike Ann-Sofie, who struggled with her weight.

Ann-Sofie felt suddenly fat and awkward.

Ingmar von Hahne, always more pleasant than his wife, came to her aid.

"Perhaps someone was jealous of Oscar's success," he said. He gave her an encouraging look. "He led a privileged life. Am I right?"

Ann-Sofie smiled in gratitude. She never understood how such a sympathetic person put up with such an exhausting wife. She'd never heard him say an unpleasant word to Isabelle. In fact, he would often soften her interactions with an ironic observation or a witty comment.

Ingmar was a true gentleman. And he was nobility to boot.

"What if someone thought Oscar let his success go to his head?" Ingmar continued. "The Greek gods would often punish someone who had such hubris—a person who believed he could do no wrong. Oscar seemed to have everything. Perhaps someone felt it was too much for one man?"

"How can you even suggest a thing like that?" his wife said. She looked annoyed. "It must have been a criminal, just like Britta said. A killer from the underworld. Probably an immigrant."

She turned to Hans Rosensjöö.

"Would you like more lamb fillet?"

Ingmar von Hahne shrugged and sipped his wine. It glittered deep red in his crystal glass.

Almost like blood. Oscar's blood.

CHAPTER 54

Diana Söder looked around her apartment and shivered. Though nothing appeared out of place, it had felt soiled since the mysterious e-mails had started, as if someone had sneaked into her sanctuary and left muddy footprints all over her fine, bright rug.

The text on the screen flickered. She pulled her robe closer around her body. She was freezing, though the room wasn't cold. She felt unprotected, exposed, even in her own home with the door bolted and chained.

She went into the kitchen for another glass of wine, and her hand shook as she unscrewed the bottle. She spilled a few drops.

She tried her best not to give in to panic, but her eyes began to tear up.

Four e-mail messages in the past few days, all full of hateful words describing how she'd gotten a rifle, gone to sea, and shot Oscar. *You'll regret it if you don't confess.*

What should she do? Go to the police? Show them e-mail messages accusing her of killing Oscar? Maybe they'd take her son away. They couldn't take Fabian! Ever!

She drank half the contents of her glass and went back to her bedroom. She left the computer on. She didn't even want to touch the thing. Cold blue light cast a spooky glow across the room.

Who could be so cruel? So hateful?

What if someone wanted to hurt her or her boy?

She crept under the blanket with her robe still on, cold, her teeth chattering as if she were a little child.

"Oscar," she said. She cried into her pillow. "Oscar, you can't be dead! You can't leave me like this! Come back!"

Sunday,
The Third Week

CHAPTER 55

Thomas woke to an insistent knocking. He'd finally arrived at Harö late Saturday evening after spending all day at the police station reading interrogation reports. It was six in the evening when he'd given up.

Once he arrived, he had two sandwiches and a beer and then fell asleep so quickly it felt like someone had pressed an "Off" button. The glass of whisky on his nightstand sat untouched.

It was almost ten in the morning now, which meant he'd been out for over eleven hours.

The knocking continued, and someone called his name. It was a child's voice. He pulled on some underwear and climbed down from the sleeping loft. When he opened the front door, he found Nora with Simon and Adam. Thomas looked at them in surprise.

"Hi, Thomas!" Simon said. He gave his godfather a big hug. Simon's head barely reached Thomas's waist.

Adam, four years older, considered himself too big to hug anyone. He nodded a greeting.

"What's going on?" Thomas asked. He opened the door to let them in. Nora's face made it clear this was more than a friendly visit.

She gave an unhappy smile as she held out a bag from the Sandhamn bakery. It smelled like freshly baked bread.

"Mom said we should surprise you!" Simon scurried inside, underneath Thomas's outstretched arm. "Do you have any juice? Especially orange juice? I don't like that red stuff we get at day camp."

Simon opened the refrigerator to see what he could find.

Thomas moved aside so Nora and Adam could come in.

"I'm sorry, Simon," he said. "No juice. But how about a glass of milk? If you want to grow big and strong like me, you'll have to drink a lot of milk." He winked at the boys as he flexed his muscles. "Just let me get some clothes on," he said. "You two can find something to drink while your mother and I have coffee." He turned to Nora. "How did you get here from Sandhamn? Did you take the *Snurran*?"

He meant the fifteen-foot-long motorboat the Linde family used to get to beaches for swimming.

She nodded.

"I tied it up next to your Buster. I'll start the coffee while you get dressed. I thought you would already be up. It's not like you to sleep in."

Thomas disappeared into the bathroom to get ready for the day.

He wondered what had happened. Nora's red eyes made it obvious she'd been crying. It probably had something to do with that house. Maybe it would have been better if she'd never inherited it. Too late for that now.

Thomas could imagine how Henrik and his witch of a mother were leaning on Nora. He thought Henrik's father, Harald, was a pretty decent guy. At the wedding so many years ago, they'd shared a bottle of whisky, and the alcohol had loosened him up. By the time dawn had begun to arrive, Harald had revealed a more human side. They'd shared interesting conversation about the Swedish national hockey team's chances of becoming world champions again.

But Henrik's mother was a real devil, and her son seemed blind to her faults.

Nora and Henrik had been married for over thirteen years now, and Thomas suspected Henrik always took his mother's side over Nora's. Henrik grew up an only child, extremely sheltered. He didn't see how overbearing Monica could be, not to mention how she treated her daughter-in-law.

Thomas liked his own mother, but he would have said something if she'd ever treated Pernilla the way Monica treated Nora.

Thomas came out of the bathroom to find Nora had set the rolls on a plate on the table. The boys sat waiting to eat. The moment Thomas nodded, they launched into action.

Nora poured two cups of coffee.

"Boys," Thomas said, "you can take your plates outside and sit in the sunshine if you'd like. Then you don't have to hear our boring talk. OK?"

They ran outside at once. Thomas looked at Nora with compassion. "Now tell me what's going on."

Nora's eyes filled with tears the moment he asked the question. She looked more distraught than she had in a long time.

What's the deal? Thomas thought to himself. *Wherever I go, women start crying.*

He walked around the table and gave her a hug. Once she'd had a good cry, he offered her a paper towel to dry her eyes and blow her nose.

"What happened?" Thomas asked. "It's Henrik, right? Did you have a fight?"

Nora nodded and blew her nose again.

"It was awful, the worst fight we've ever had. Henrik insists we sell Signe's house. He said I was egotistical and thought only about myself." She paused to catch her breath.

"He said my sentimental streak shouldn't keep him and the boys from living in a real house in the city. And then . . . he said . . ." She stopped for a minute and looked like a scolded puppy. "He said my behavior made him ashamed."

"Why?"

"That couple from Switzerland came to look at the house yesterday. They acted like they'd already bought it. They showed no respect at all."

Nora described the walk-through and what had happened afterward: how angry Henrik had looked as he stood in the kitchen and pounded the counter in absolute rage. Hurtful words had flown from his mouth, a stream of viciousness that seemed endless.

"How could he say such things to me? He's never said anything like that before. I can't understand why he demands we sell the house, even after we discussed renting it."

Tears ran down her flushed face again.

"There, there," Thomas said. He patted her shoulder in a vain attempt to comfort her. It didn't seem to help much.

Nora tried to smile but failed. "I'm so sorry I woke you. I really needed someone to talk to. Henrik went into the city on the first morning ferry."

"Do the boys know about it all?"

"No. I told them he got called in to the hospital. I had to tell them something."

Thomas fought an irrational impulse to call Henrik and give him an earful. Nora had suffered so much this past year. He knew they'd had troubles in their relationship, but Thomas thought they'd worked things out after what had happened on Grönskär. Why Henrik pressed her so hard now he didn't understand. But he said nothing. He needed to help Nora calm down. It wouldn't help to get angry, especially not with the boys around.

He handed Nora another paper towel.

"You won't have anything left to clean up messes if I keep going like this."

"It's nothing to worry about. You know, Nora, maybe it's good that Henrik left for the day. When he's had the chance to calm down, he'll see he overreacted."

"Do you think so?"

"He can't force a sale if you refuse. You know that. And he loves you. In the heat of the moment, people sometimes say things they don't mean."

"I hope so." Nora's voice trembled.

She pushed the reddish-blond strands of hair from her face and wiped her eyes again. They were swollen, but she looked more hopeful than when she'd come.

She rolled up the sleeves of her pale-blue sweater and blew her nose one last time.

"We both know how Henrik is," Thomas said. "He can be hot-headed, but he would never want to hurt you."

Thomas wasn't certain those words were true. Henrik had an ego-tistical side Thomas also saw in Monica Linde. But now wasn't the time to add another stone to Nora's burden.

"Take your mind off things, Nora. Get a little perspective. Things will work out. Henrik will come to his senses." Thomas hugged her again.

Nora did her best to pull herself together.

"So I'm not a selfish monster? It's not all my fault? One day the boys might like a house in Sandhamn. I'm thinking of their future, too."

She took another sip of coffee before she continued.

"Just thinking of those pretentious Swiss people makes my blood boil. I can't imagine seeing *them* through my kitchen window every day!"

"Are they really that bad?"

"They are! There's not enough money in the world to make me deal with them!"

Nora was a fighter, no doubt about that. She'd get through this, too, Thomas thought.

"You've been incredibly kind," Nora said. "I woke up so unhappy this morning, but I knew I could talk to you."

She looked down at the kitchen table, noticing she'd been tracing figure eights with her finger. Then she glanced at the clock and stood up.

"I should see what the boys are up to. We've been talking for a while."

Her voice sounded stronger now, shedding the last trace of her melancholy.

"I'll sort this whole thing out. Everything can be handled, right?"

CHAPTER 56

As usual, Henrik found the gate to his childhood home unlocked. He drove up the familiar gravel road. After the first hundred yards, the landscape opened up and the pine forest gave way to a large lawn dotted with apple trees.

His parents' summerhouse sat slightly to one side, near the water. Henrik had spent every summer here since he was small. His paternal grandfather had bought the property in the forties. He'd wanted a summer place to share with children, grandchildren, and guests. In those days, summerhouses on Ingarö were unusual. The spot became popular later on.

The building burned down in the late seventies when some people broke in to spend the night and fell asleep with candles burning. They'd probably been trying to keep warm. Henrik was only a boy then, but he remembered how distressed his grandparents had been. His grandfather mourned the house as if it were a living thing.

They soon built a new house with modern facilities, including an indoor bathroom. They also enlarged the kitchen and added a dishwasher, to his grandmother's delight.

Within a few years, however, his grandparents passed away and left the summerhouse to Henrik's father. When his father was stationed abroad, Monica and Henrik spent their summers on Ingarö. Henrik had made Swedish friends, including Johan Wrede, who still raced in sailing competitions with him.

He'd been given his first boat here. A little daysailer. It was later replaced by a Laser, which was replaced by a larger Flying Dutchman with a dark-blue hull.

Near the end of his teenage years, he took part in a competition with a friend and the friend's father, who sailed a six-meter. The race hooked him, and he convinced his father to buy him a six-meter, too. He and Johan, with other friends crewing, kept sailing. Sixth place in the European Masters was their all-time best.

Sailing remained his favorite occupation. Nothing could top the feeling of the bow striking through water. That was why he kept on sailing, even as an adult with a demanding job and family.

The thought of Nora darkened his mood. He sighed deeply as he parked next to his parents' Audi.

She'd been impossible last night. First, she sulked for hours. Then, once the boys were in bed, she accused him of being money hungry and inconsiderate.

Henrik had tried his best to stay calm. He hated it when Nora got so emotional. It always ended in tears and bitter words between them. But he couldn't keep quiet, and finally he'd let it all out.

Why in the world did she feel any loyalty toward Signe, and why would she put that above her own family's well-being? If they sold the Brand house, the boys could grow up in a proper home. They'd have a leg up in life.

Nora always underestimated the importance of raising children in the right environment. You met people in your childhood who became lifelong friends.

He, for one, knew how important that was. He'd seen his father move in diplomatic circles where success revolved around personal relationships. You have to know the right people, or you get left behind. In this big, bad world, social connections counted.

One of his father's friends, a professor at Danderyd Hospital, had put in a good word for Henrik. Without that help, he would have had to wait much longer for a permanent position. His boys shouldn't miss out on opportunities because they lived in that pathetic little town house.

But when he tried to explain all this to Nora, his words fell on deaf ears.

"How selfish can you be?" he'd yelled at her. "Can't you think about someone besides yourself for once? What kind of a mother are you?"

They'd stood at either end of the kitchen table, like roosters in a cockfight, as vicious words flew through the air.

When she began crying, he didn't care.

"I can't believe how you behaved in front of the real-estate agent! I'm ashamed of you! Standing there sighing and carrying on. You could have at least acted like a reasonable human being!"

He was exhausted by the time they finally went to bed. He fell into an immediate but restless sleep. When he woke six hours later, he decided to leave. He couldn't deal with her outbursts. Perhaps if he left for a few days, she'd come to her senses.

He took the overnight case he'd quickly packed out of the trunk.

His mother appeared before he'd reached the front door.

"Henrik, my dear boy!" She kissed him on both cheeks.

"Hi, Mom."

He stepped inside, carrying his suitcase.

"I have coffee ready. Sit down and I'll bring everything. Have you eaten? Do you want a sandwich?"

Her mouth didn't stop moving, and her hands fluttered in small, well-meaning gestures, fast as a hummingbird as she circled her son.

"How are you, my sweet boy? I'm so glad you came so I can spoil you for a while. I really can't understand Nora. She's so . . . so . . ." She tried to find the word. "She's so irrational. Yes, that's it. And selfish. She only thinks of herself."

Henrik had phoned his mother earlier to tell her he was coming. He'd given her a brief explanation about what had happened between him and Nora. As always, she took his side without reservation. Of course he'd be welcome to spend a few days at Ingarö to rest up.

Henrik walked into the living room and relaxed on the striped sofa. He'd always found this room pleasant. It faced southwest and was often filled with light and sun. In addition to the oversize sofa, the room held two comfortable armchairs with matching footstools.

As his mother puttered around the kitchen, he turned on the TV. His mother carried a tray into the room.

"You don't need that on, Henrik," she said. "Your father leaves the TV on constantly these days. On and on without a break."

"Where is Dad, by the way?" Henrik asked. He kept his eyes on the screen.

"He's at the neighbors'. He'll be back soon. In the meantime, let's have a little chat."

His mother set two cups on the table and handed him a plate with several liver pâté and cheese sandwiches.

"Help yourself," she said. "I'll get the sugar and be right back."

She returned to the kitchen and Henrik took a bite of a sandwich while surfing through channels. When his mother came back, he turned the TV off to please her.

"Now tell me all about it, my son," Monica Linde said. She looked at him tenderly and held out a plate of cookies. "Tell me how things are really going."

"I love you," he whispered in wonder.

Those words came so easily.

He hadn't even believed himself capable of love after all the years and all the lies.

But there the words were, perfectly clear, as if they had lives of their own.

Gratitude washed over him.

This is how it feels to love and be loved. How had he ever forgotten?

He longingly gazed into the face before him. With the back of his hand, he traced the line of his beloved's chin, throat, and chest.

How could skin feel so soft and smell so good?

"Thank God you exist," he whispered. "I love you so much. What would I ever do without you?"

"I love you, too."

The voice sounded gentle as a caress. They kissed and desire filled his body, making him dizzy.

"I will never let you go," he said. "Never, ever."

MONDAY,
THE FOURTH WEEK

CHAPTER 57

"Hello, is this Thomas Andreasson?"

The high-pitched voice on the other end of the line gave Thomas pause before he realized who it was: Diana Söder, Oscar Juliander's lover and Ingmar von Hahne's coworker at Strandvägen Art Gallery.

It was about nine thirty in the morning. Thomas sat at his desk as gray clouds filled the sky outside.

"How can I help you? You sound upset."

"There's something I have to tell you . . . I think . . ."

A pause on the other end of the line.

"What do you want to tell me?" Thomas asked. He took a sip of water and waited patiently for her to answer.

"I've gotten some terrible e-mail messages. Messages with horrible accusations."

Thomas heard her sniffling.

"What do they say?" Thomas asked.

"They say . . ." She paused to gather strength. "They say I killed Oscar."

"Can you explain a little more?" Thomas asked. He kept his voice mild to avoid alarming her.

"They call me a whore!" She began sobbing so hard she could barely speak. "They say I did terrible things to Oscar. I don't know what to do!"

"We'll need to look at those messages," Thomas said. "Could you forward them to me, do you think?"

"I'll send what I have. I deleted the first one immediately, but they kept coming. They're all so vicious!"

He could hear her blowing her nose.

"That's all right. Just send the ones you have as soon as you can, and we'll look at them right away. If any new ones come, send them to us immediately. Will you be all right?"

"Yes," she whispered. "Thank you so much."

Margit read the first message from Diana Söder.

> I know you murdered Oscar. You shot him because he didn't leave his wife. You're a whore, a disgusting whore. You're going to pay for this. Don't imagine you'll get away with it. You'll see what I mean. Go to the police and confess.

Margit opened the next one, which wasn't much different from the first.

> You disgusting harlot, confess your crime to the police. You have to pay for his death. You damned whore, you lying adulteress.

The third held more of the same.

"*Somebody* believes Diana Söder killed him," Margit said once they'd studied every message.

"The question is, who?"

"The wife?"

"Sylvia Juliander?" Thomas thought about it. It seemed a long shot that the grieving widow would send these messages. But who knew what a deceived wife might do after hearing such hurtful news.

"We'll have to question her."

"Do you think there's anything to the accusations?"

"Hard to say," Thomas said. "But if she were guilty, why would she send them to us?"

"Good point. And she does have a watertight alibi. She was with her brother's family that entire day."

Margit stared at the screen.

"*Harlot* is a rather old-fashioned word. And so is *adulteress*. Nobody talks like that anymore. What does that tell us?"

"I have no idea. Do you think this is some kind of biblical retribution?"

"If so, Diana Söder may be in danger," Margit said.

Thomas nodded. "We should warn her. Too bad we don't have enough evidence to warrant police protection—even if we had the resources."

Thomas reread the fourth message open on the computer screen.

"We need to find out who sent these as soon as possible."

"Give them to Carina," Margit said. "She's good with computers."

Thomas agreed. "Should I interview Sylvia Juliander, or would you rather do it?"

"I'll talk to her," Margit said.

CHAPTER 58

Martin Nyrén sailed his Omega 36 to Stora Nassa, a small collection of islands in the outer archipelago northeast of Sandhamn. Before he left, he'd washed away the black graffiti as best he could. The damage to the hull could be repaired when the boat was in dry dock for the winter.

He planned to stay out until the next morning, when he'd have to be back for an urgent meeting with the Facilities Committee. The owner of a large motorboat had had trouble with reverse as he was docking at Lökholmen. He'd seriously damaged the dock. Now the RSYC had to deal with insurance and repairs. The organization was not wealthy. They brought in enough to finance the operations, but not much more. And they couldn't raise the already high membership fee.

What could they do? The dock had to be repaired.

He adjusted the sheet that regulated the main sail so he wouldn't lose speed. It was time to find anchorage for the night. This part of the archipelago could be difficult to navigate. Stora Nassa was full of sunken rocks, and one could easily strike bottom. He checked the echo sounder regularly to be safe.

After a while he found an isolated bay where he could be alone. Once anchored he sat down and opened a beer. He enjoyed the silence, broken only by the distant call of a gull. Before him the gray archipelago skerries spread as far as the eye could see, filed to perfection by water and wind. The sun had become a reddish-orange ball just above the horizon, reflected in the water as a flaming mass. It was unbelievably beautiful and still.

The only thing he missed was Indi.

It had been a wonderful night. Martin remembered yesterday evening as tender and loving. They'd been completely happy.

Afterward he'd tried to persuade Indi to sail with him out to Stora Nassa. He'd stopped just short of begging. He hardly knew why he thought it so important, but he longed for a few more days together. They would wake up on board, eat breakfast together, and take the day as it came.

But all he got were the same old arguments. Someone would see them. It was too risky. Leaving for a few days would be impossible without planning. They had to think about the children.

Finally he could take no more arguing. He said good-bye the way he always did.

He hated secrets and sneaking around. How humiliating. Teenagers did such things, not adults.

Still, he felt hopeful. For the first time they'd discussed a future together, even if their daydream had been careful and oblique.

But it gave him hope.

He'd sneak around for a long time if there were hope that one day they could be together.

He decided to send a message to say good night. With a smile, he picked up his phone.

CHAPTER 59

One should not read another person's text messages. Everyone has a right to privacy. That must be respected, even within a marriage.

Usually the cell phone on the hall table would be left alone. Any incoming text messages would be left unread until the owner returned.

If only there hadn't been that electronic ping. The sound in the silent hallway made the temptation much too great.

One click and the message appeared on the screen.

Blood boiled, rage ensued, but when the wave of anger subsided, the text could not be unread. The truth could not be deleted.

You've been cheated on. Cheated on and humiliated. There's someone more loved than you. You're going to be abandoned. Everyone will laugh at you. Your life will be ruined.

No doubt what the message meant. Just a few words, but enough, enough. It forced a decision.

```
Thanks for a wonderful night. I can't wait
until we can spend every night together.
-Martin.
```

This was unacceptable. It had to be stopped.

TUESDAY,
THE FOURTH WEEK

CHAPTER 60

A drizzling, almost pleasant summer rain fell. July was giving way to August, the evenings already growing shorter. As darkness fell, the temperature dropped.

The building on Birkalidsgatan sat empty and abandoned.

Built in the thirties, its light façade was darkened from pollution and exhaust. Cleaning would have helped, but it was one of the few commercial buildings on the street. There were no apartment owners trying to increase the value of their property through costly renovations.

At this hour, those who hadn't already left for vacation would have stopped working long ago, left the building, and gone home. Not a single window was lit.

Perfect for the purpose.

The key slipped easily into the lock. A quick turn, and the entrance door opened. The spot selected was a half floor up with a window facing the street. It offered a perfect view of Birkalidsgatan 22B. It would not be hard to make the shot from this distance.

The keys to the individual doors worked as easily as the one to the entrance. Even the black iron security gate slid up without a sound. The dark single-room studio had a toilet and a small kitchen area with a round table and four chairs. It was stuffy and smelled vaguely of turpentine. Paintings leaned against the walls.

It was too risky to turn on the ceiling lights, but the streetlights cast enough of a glow. The small flashlight also helped, even aimed at the floor to avoid being seen from the street. A large lamp hung over the entrance to Birkalidsgatan 22B. That would help. The person who would soon punch in the entrance code and unlock the front door would have plenty of light.

Enough to aim well, in other words. Enough to kill.

The parts of the rifle rested in a gray sailor's bag. It weighed next to nothing—a couple pounds. It took only a few minutes to load the ammunition and the rifle parts into the bag, and only a few minutes to reassemble the weapon. At the bottom of the bag was a little box marked *.22 WMR*; the bronze bullets gleamed under the flashlight.

There was something appealing about the bright metal and the oval form so perfect for its purposes. Remarkable that something so small could do so much damage to the human body.

The rifle's magazine held eleven bullets, every bullet slipped smoothly into place.

The only thing left to do was wait.

This time there was no hurry. Before, everything had to be timed to the second. There'd been no leeway, since the risk of discovery had been much, much greater.

Now only patience was needed.

Martin Nyrén would soon come home to his apartment. If not today, then tomorrow.

There was all the time in the world to wait for Martin Nyrén.

CHAPTER 61

The evening meeting of the Facilities Committee was unusually fruit-less, Martin Nyrén thought. He sighed over colleagues who sometimes seemed incapable of making a decision. The discussions moved in cir-cles, resulting in an agreement to meet again in a few weeks for a final decision on repairing the Lökholmen docks.

He'd gotten a ride from Saltsjöbaden to Slussen, where he took the subway to Sankt Eriksplan. No one else got off at that stop. He was alone on the platform at almost eleven at night.

Even though he usually walked up the escalator for the exercise, he stood still this time.

His relationship with Indi nagged at him. While at sea, he'd thought a great deal about their situation. Should he demand more, even make an ultimatum?

His love was so strong that everything seemed perfect when they were together. But he hated the loneliness that overcame him the min-ute they parted.

He wanted to spend every day together. They'd argue sometimes about whose turn it was to do laundry or who should do the grocery shopping. But he'd always find a light on in the apartment when he came home.

Patience, he told himself. *You must have patience.*

When he walked out of the station, he took a deep breath of night air. The city could be stifling during the summer, and he already longed to put out to sea again. He shivered a bit at the thought of the vandalized Omega. It must have been kids. Who else would have done it?

He still needed to report the damage to the police. His insurance company demanded it. But what would he say about the other odd things? That he thought someone had been in his apartment? He had no proof. That he felt followed when he was walking down the street? That he suspected it wasn't a few kids who had damaged his boat?

He could imagine how the police would grin behind his back if he brought up these concerns. And what could *they* do about it? They couldn't watch over him and his boat twenty-four hours a day.

He looked around a little more than usual in the night darkness. He picked up his pace and pulled his trench coat tighter. The temperature must have dropped ten degrees since sunset.

He took his phone from his pocket and fingered its metal case. Should he send a text to Indi? Just to say good night?

The thought was tempting. Why not?

Just that possibility put him in a better mood. Somehow everything would work out for them. He could sense it.

The solitary figure in the light trench coat was visible from far away.

The street was silent and empty with many open parking spaces.

It made everything so much easier.

It wouldn't necessarily stop things if someone were with him. Not even the most observant witness could register the bullet before it was too late. But it was one less thing to worry about.

It was time to focus. Every move must be executed perfectly: flip up the small sight, push the barrel a few centimeters out the window, check the angle. Wait for the right moment.

Through the sight, Martin Nyrén came into focus.

He walked slowly, lost in thought. He didn't even look up.

He held his cell phone in one hand, but he wasn't speaking into it. When he got to the entrance, he stopped a moment to look at his watch. Then he leaned forward to punch in the entrance code.

That small movement was key.

The body was perfectly aligned, as if he had voluntarily placed himself at the center of the sight. Light pressure on the trigger, and the rifle fired. The silencer muffled the report as effectively as it had the first time.

Martin Nyrén was hit in the temple.

A perfect shot, a nice entrance hole. Flying brain matter. And it was over.

Martin Nyrén stood completely still for a few seconds, as if his fingers were able to punch in the code by themselves to escape his attacker. Then his legs crumpled, unable to support his weight, and he fell against the entrance door. He slid down the glass and collapsed on the ground. It looked like a single graceful movement that he'd trained for his entire life.

Someone might even think he was asleep.

How easy it was to kill another human being. So simple.

The first time it had been absolutely necessary. When everything had been weighed, only one solution had remained: Oscar Juliander had to die.

And now Martin, too, had to go. Before things got out of hand.

It seemed much easier to breathe now. A feeling of peace settled in. This was much more satisfying than rifling through his apartment, better than following him through the city, better than trying to deaden the feeling of humiliation by vandalizing his boat.

Balance was restored. Martin Nyrén had only himself to blame. His death was a result of behavior that could not be tolerated.

Not for one more day. Not for one more minute.

CHAPTER 62

The call came in at 11:55 p.m., just five minutes before Tuesday turned into Wednesday.

The woman who called in was hysterical. The operator had trouble understanding and used many soothing words to calm her down. The woman could then describe what she'd seen.

A man lay in front of the entrance with blood coming from his head. She'd found him when she'd returned home from Stockholm Arlanda Airport—she was a flight attendant.

The alarm went through the provincial central communication system, and, as luck would have it, a patrol car was on the other side of Sankt Erik Bridge at Fleminggatan, not far from the scene. It would arrive in just a few minutes.

They sent an ambulance as well. Although the woman said the man was dead, the operator did not want to take any chances by sending only a hearse, the usual for transporting dead bodies.

And, last of all, a team of crime scene investigators was dispatched from the Stockholm police station.

* * *

The policemen saw immediately that the flight attendant was correct.

The man on the stairs in front of Birkalidsgatan 22B was really, truly dead. The cause of death was most likely the hole in his temple. In addition, there was a great deal of blood and brain spatter on the frosted glass door.

Clearly in shock, the flight attendant sat beside the corpse. She had some blood on her uniform.

When an officer in his thirties tried to speak with her, she began to weep. He helped her up and accompanied her to her apartment. He hoped there she might calm down enough that he could question her.

Conny Malmsten, the forensic technician on call that evening, arrived right before the ambulance. The police had already cordoned off the area to minimize access to the crime scene and secure the evidence.

Conny needed little time to figure out the cause of death.

"I'm assuming he was shot right here," one of the uniformed officers commented when Conny arrived.

"That appears to be the case," Conny agreed.

He studied the scene in front of him.

The blood pooled on the ground under the man's chin, and the spatter of other bodily fluids indicated that this was the primary crime scene.

Conny pulled out his digital camera. His photographs would serve as the basis for the investigation, both in reconstructing the chain of events as well as pinning down any material evidence. As he snapped the photos, he constructed a mental picture of what had happened.

There was no powder mark on the skin, as far as he could see. This indicated the shot had come from a distance. This also indicated there was little likelihood of finding any evidence here about the killer.

When he finished, he put his camera back in its heavy black case. He was meticulous about his equipment. Nothing made him more irritated than finding something out of place—it could ruin his whole day.

Conny Malmsten stepped past the corpse and opened the front door. Luckily it swung inward, so he did not have to disturb the body.

He didn't see anything unusual in the stairway, so he stepped back outside and moved around the corpse with care.

There were pieces of a cell phone on the steps outside. The bottom plate hung open, and parts had fallen out. He put the pieces inside an evidence bag. If they could reassemble the phone, they might discover who the deceased had been calling.

He put on plastic gloves and carefully inspected the victim's skull. He could see more closely where the bullet had penetrated. Then he began to swab for biological evidence.

All bodily fluids at the scene would have to be secured.

It was going to be a long night.

Wednesday,
the fourth week

CHAPTER 63

It was seven thirty in the morning, and the atmosphere in the conference room was gloomy.

"So what do we know?" asked Persson. He looked ill as he blew his nose into pieces of toilet paper from a roll on the table.

"So what do we know about all this?" he asked again.

He took a sip of coffee and looked around the room.

Last night's death had taken much of the fight out of the team. They'd now have to double up on their workload with no solutions in sight.

The news outlets were already calling often enough to keep the police spokesperson busy, to say the least. The murder of Martin Nyrén dominated both the TV and radio news broadcasts.

"Another Board Member of the Royal Swedish Yacht Club Murdered!"

Thomas blinked and tried to focus. He'd been up since five that morning, when a shaken Hans Rosensjöö had phoned to inform him that Martin Nyrén had been shot to death in front of his Birkastan apartment building.

The police had contacted Nyrén's brother, who had immediately phoned Rosensjöö. They both connected his death with Juliander's murder.

Thomas had thrown on his clothes and hurried to the station. There he'd spent an hour trying to find out what had happened. He'd talked to the forensic unit for a description of the crime scene. Conny Malmsten, the technician first on the scene, shared his conclusions.

Thomas repeated the facts to his coworkers. "The victim is Martin Nyrén. He was fifty-three and single. Lived in a three-room apartment in the Birkastan District. Worked at the Legal, Financial and Administrative Services Agency as a manager. He finished law school and was head of the RSYC Facilities Committee."

"What's that?" asked Erik.

"It's the committee in charge of the property and grounds. They care for all the RSYC's buildings, docks, and the like."

"So what happened?" asked Margit.

Thomas held up one of Malmsten's photographs. The position of the body was clear. The curved back, the sprawled legs, the head below a blood-flecked glass panel.

"He almost looks like he's asleep," Kalle said.

"He was on the board with Juliander, and he was also a lawyer," Persson said. He blew his nose again. "Any other connections?"

"We don't know," Thomas said. "We need to find out."

"And the murder weapon?"

"He was shot. In the head. The bullet went right through the brain. He died instantly."

"So perhaps another long-range shooting." Persson sighed as he said this.

"Have they started the autopsy yet?" asked Margit.

"They'll do it this morning. Dr. Sachsen has moved him to the top of the list. He said by lunchtime we could stop by for the results."

"Anything else?" asked Persson.

"Conny Malmsten confirmed that Nyrén was shot from a distance," Thomas said. "There were no powder burns, and the entry wound was small."

"So a rifle?" asked Margit.

"Most likely. We'll have to wait for ballistics to know for sure if it was the same one used to kill Juliander."

"Anything else at the crime scene? Another bullet lodged somewhere, perhaps?"

"No, nothing."

Juliander had been shot with a half metal jacket bullet that had remained in the body. A full metal jacket bullet probably would have gone right through Nyrén's head and out the other side. A moment of silence came over the room. The similarities between the two killings were clear.

"What are the chances that two different killers use the same method to gun down two members of the same club?" Margit asked. She propped her chin on her hand.

"Very small, I'd assume," Persson said.

"So what's it all mean?"

"We have a crazy person at large who does not like this yacht club," Thomas said. "Or, at the very least, does not like the members of its board."

"The RSYC is the natural link," Margit said. "We have to begin with them."

"Members of the board must have police protection," Persson stated. He turned to Margit. "You and Thomas see to that."

Margit noticed Persson's runny nose and swollen eyes.

"Shouldn't you be in bed?" she asked.

Persson gave a dismissive wave.

"We'll have to speak with Juliander's widow again," Thomas said. "She might give us some connection between the two. And we need to track Nyrén and see what he's been up to the past few weeks."

"This sheds new light on our theory about Holger Alsing," Margit said. "Is he still on Mallorca? If so, we can eliminate him as a suspect, especially if the same rifle was used."

"So, we find ourselves back to square one," Persson stated. He blew his nose again to clear it before attending a hastily called press conference.

"You should really go home and lie down," said Margit.

CHAPTER 64

Ingmar von Hahne slowly hung up the phone on his nightstand.

His wife returned from the bathroom and gave him a curious look.

"Who called so early in the morning?" she asked.

"Martin Nyrén has been shot," Ingmar von Hahne said. His eyes widened with shock, and his face turned white.

"What did you say?" Isabelle stood still in the doorway.

"Martin Nyrén has been murdered."

"What? He's dead?"

"Yes," Ingmar von Hahne said. "Hans called. Someone shot Martin last night in front of his building. He died immediately, they said. Good God."

He stared at the telephone as if he didn't believe the news it had delivered. He felt like he might faint.

Isabelle stood speechless for once. Silence descended on the room. Ingmar sat upright on the edge of the bed as if paralyzed. He took short, quick breaths.

"We have to call the police," Isabelle said. She pulled the belt of her robe tighter.

"What do you mean?"

"You need police protection," she said. "If there's some kind of crazy person out there shooting the members of the board, you might be next . . ."

Ingmar could not reply.

"Soon you'll be chairman. Have you forgotten?" she said.

He buried his face in his hands. Then he slowly lay back on the bed.

Isabelle left the room to give Ingmar some space.

What good would it do to call the police? What good would anything do?

Chapter 65

Back to square one, Persson had said.

Those words echoed in Thomas's mind as they parked behind the redbrick building that housed the Forensic Medicine department.

Like before, it took a while until Dr. Sachsen appeared behind the ribbed glass door. He looked tired and worn out. He had been awake since the crack of dawn, same as them.

They followed him through the long corridors to the autopsy room. He opened the door and entered first.

A body lay under a sheet on a steel examination table. Dr. Sachsen showed them the body of Martin Nyrén, already sewn up after the autopsy. It was hard to believe that his chest cavity had been pried wide open that same morning.

He looks younger than fifty-three, Thomas thought.

Despite the flecks of gray, Martin Nyrén was not losing any hair, unlike many men his age. His face looked peaceful. He probably hadn't even had a chance to realize his life was ending.

Thomas walked around the table to examine the body more closely.

There were no unusual marks. He'd been in good shape. Perhaps a tad overweight, but nothing serious. He had a faded scar from an appendectomy.

"What can you tell us?" asked Margit.

Dr. Sachsen took his glasses from his breast pocket and skimmed the autopsy report to refresh his memory.

"Let's see what we have here," he said, leafing through his papers. "His death was instantaneous. The bullet entered the left temple and continued through the right half of the brain, destroying enough tissue to quickly end his life."

"Can you tell us anything about the trajectory?" asked Margit. She leaned forward to examine the entry wound. Barely a centimeter long, it was neat and clean, like a surgical incision.

"The angle seems to be slightly from above. The bullet traveled in a downward trajectory, which indicates that the shooter was higher up than the victim."

"How much higher?" asked Thomas.

"Hard to say. Slightly, perhaps."

"And the distance between them? What do you think?"

Thomas remembered that the shot in Juliander's murder had come from somewhere between fifty and one hundred yards away.

"A fair distance. I found no powder residue, so we're talking several dozen yards. I'd say between twenty and eighty. I can't give you a more exact number."

"And the bullet?"

Dr. Sachsen picked up something small from a steel bowl. He held it up so they could get a good look.

"It's very similar to the previous one," Margit said. "Suspiciously so."

"Yes. The same mushroom shape, the same metal."

"When will you send it out for further analysis?"

"This afternoon."

"How long until we hear back?"

"You'll have to ask Linköping. Perhaps you can persuade them to bump you to the top of the list." Dr. Sachsen continued before Margit could open her mouth again. "Because that's what you'll do anyway. Right?"

"Should we drive out to Birkalidsgatan?" Thomas asked when they were back in the car. "I'd like to take a look at the crime scene, even if it's already been cleaned up. It's a damned shame they didn't call us last night."

Margit shrugged.

"The central station had no way to know the connection. They're not mind readers. The operator followed procedure."

Margit's logic didn't soothe Thomas.

"Persson says we have jurisdiction because of the obvious similarities."

Thomas started the car.

"It won't take long to get there if we take the Solna Bridge."

Five minutes later, Thomas parked on a cross street of Rörstrandsgatan, a few hundred yards from where Martin Nyrén had died.

He stepped out of the car and took in the calm atmosphere of the neighborhood. There were few cars on the street and many small shops and cafés on the ground floors of the buildings. It felt like a small town in the midst of a big city.

As they walked up to Birkalidsgatan 22B, they saw traces of blood on the steps. Someone had tried to clean one of the glass panes on the front door, but there were still noticeable smears.

Thomas held up Malmsten's photograph from the crime scene. Despite the darkness of night, it was surprisingly sharp. Nyrén's face was clear. He looked as peaceful as he had in the autopsy room.

"Stand by the door," Thomas said. "Let's try to reconstruct what happened. We know he was on the way home. He stood at the entrance, probably opening the front door. But he couldn't have done much more than that."

Margit took her place in front of the keypad and bent forward.

"Like this? If he was entering his code and was shot in the temple, he was probably standing here, right?"

Thomas watched her and nodded.

"The doctor said he'd been shot from a distance of at least sixty-five feet. And from slightly above."

Thomas crossed the street until he stood at the right distance, about twenty yards away, but he remained at the same height as Margit.

Thomas turned to look at a slightly shabby building behind him.

Margit joined him across the street.

"Are we thinking the same thing?" She looked back at the entrance to the apartment building. "That the killer was here? For instance, aiming from that window?"

She shaded her eyes with her hand and pointed to the first row of windows a half floor up. Then she leaned forward to read the business names embossed on the plate by the entrance.

"No individuals, only businesses. Nothing else."

Thomas read the names over her shoulder. Then his eyes stopped.

"Strandvägen Art Gallery" was listed neatly on one of the metal plates beside the entrance.

Thomas remembered the elegant script on the entrance to Ingmar von Hahne's art gallery. Ingmar von Hahne: RSYC board member and the boss of Oscar Juliander's mistress.

It could not be a coincidence.

Someone must have shot Martin Nyrén from this rented space. Was it Ingmar himself? And, if so, why?

"Come on," he said to Margit. "Let's go look at Nyrén's apartment. Meanwhile, I'll call for a warrant to search this place."

* * *

Thomas opened a solid oak door and stepped over the morning paper lying on the hallway rug. The apartment smelled freshly cleaned. He nodded at one of the technicians securing evidence.

"How's it going?" Thomas asked.

The man glanced up.

"Not bad. But unfortunately this place is clean as clean can be."

"Any fingerprints?"

"Not yet, but I'm still working."

The spacious three-room apartment showed that the owner cared about his home. The interior design was expensive but not ostentatious, and the apartment was well ordered. Everything had a place. Colorful art hung on the walls, and white orchids in matching pots lined the living room window. Everything looked almost obsessively neat.

This is not your average bachelor's apartment, Thomas thought. He pictured his own sparsely furnished two-bedroom place, a space to sleep and not much more.

They took their time wandering around the apartment, trying to build a picture in their minds of its dead owner.

Thomas used the telephone to check Martin's answering service. No messages had been saved.

The bedroom was as orderly as the rest of the apartment, though the colors were more somber. A stack of books sat on the nightstand. Thomas didn't recognize any of the authors.

They noticed unplugged computer cables on the desk. The technicians had already taken Nyrén's computer. With a little luck, they might access its contents.

They walked into the kitchen, the room as tidy as the rest. A large gas stove dominated the space. Margit opened the refrigerator.

"Not a starving bachelor," she said.

Thomas leaned forward to see.

The shelves were filled. He saw various kinds of French cheese, a number of chocolate bars, and a large chunk of Parmesan beside a package of kalamata olives. Two bottles of champagne were chilling in the wine compartment.

"Was he expecting company?" Margit asked. "Or was this standard for him?"

"Yes, I wonder who was supposed to drink all that champagne."

They went into a bathroom with gray mosaics on the walls.

"Thomas, he was single, wasn't he?" Margit asked.

"Yes."

"Then why are there two toothbrushes in the mug?"

CHAPTER 66

"We need to know where you were last Tuesday evening," Thomas said.

Ingmar von Hahne looked terrified. Dark circles hung under his eyes. The confident, well-tanned appearance from last month at Sandhamn was long gone.

"I was home. At home, in my apartment."

"Anyone there who can back up your story?"

"No." His voice was low. "I was home. Alone. At least until midnight when my wife returned, and shortly after that, my daughter, Emma. Marcus, my son, is still out in the country."

"So you knew Martin Nyrén," stated Thomas.

Ingmar von Hahne nodded without speaking. Thomas pointed to the tape recorder and asked him to speak up so his words could be recorded.

"Yes, yes, I did."

"Can you describe how you came to know him?"

A moment of silence.

"We knew each other from the RSYC," Ingmar von Hahne said. "He was the chair of the Facilities Committee. I'm the secretary of the board."

"How did you find out he was dead?"

"Hans Rosensjöö called me this morning. He said Martin had been murdered!" Ingmar gave them a forlorn look. "What kind of crazy killer is on the loose?"

"Martin Nyrén was found outside his front door in the Birkastan District. We believe he was shot from the building across the street," Margit said. Until that moment, she'd let Thomas ask all the questions. "You know the area, don't you?"

Ingmar von Hahne's eyes darted around the room. A vein pulsed in his throat.

"Did you understand my question?" Margit asked.

The tormented man nodded silently, and Thomas reminded him to speak aloud for the recording.

"Yes. Yes, I know exactly where it is. I have storage space there."

"Storage space?"

Thomas waited for an answer.

"When there's not enough room in the gallery, I keep the overflow artwork there."

"It's close to Martin's apartment?"

"It's across the street."

"Actually, we already know that," Thomas said. "We've already been in your storage space. We received a search warrant this afternoon."

Thomas's comment made Ingmar pale.

"Would you like to know what we found there?" asked Thomas.

"Yes." The reply was a whisper.

"We found traces of gunpowder residue on the windowsill, the one that gave a perfect view of the entrance to Martin Nyrén's building. Is this a coincidence? What do you think?"

"I don't think anything," Ingmar von Hahne said. He choked on the words and put his face in his hands.

"So, I'll ask you again. Where were you Tuesday night?"

"I was at home, as I told you!"

Margit broke in. "Any explanation about why we'd find gunpowder marks in your storage space?"

"Somebody must have broken in."

"The outer door was undamaged."

"But what other explanation could there be?"

The man on the other side of the table looked ready to faint. All he wanted was to wake up from this nightmare.

"You can't think I had anything to do with Martin's murder!"

"Who has keys to the room?" asked Margit.

Ingmar von Hahne looked uncertain.

"Well, I do, of course. And Diana, who is employed at the gallery. And we have a student intern, a young woman studying art history. She helps out sometimes. I know her parents."

Thomas peered at Ingmar von Hahne without expression for a few seconds before asking the next question.

"By Diana, you mean Diana Söder?"

"Yes, how did you know?"

Thomas ignored that and went right to his next question.

"How long did you know that Diana Söder had a relationship with Oscar Juliander?"

"I read it in the paper."

"They met at your Christmas party last year," Margit said. "It seems their relationship lasted almost eighteen months. Didn't you know before it came out in the papers?"

Ingmar von Hahne sank into his chair.

"Oscar had a weakness for women. That's not a secret. But it was only recently I knew that Diana was seeing him."

His hand shook as he took a drink of water.

Thomas studied him during the silence.

Ingmar von Hahne did not look well at all. It appeared as if he'd just thrown on whatever clothes were on hand. The dapper gallery owner he'd met earlier had vanished.

"Do you think Diana would be capable of murdering Oscar out of jealousy?"

"Absolutely not." The answer was abrupt and without hesitation. "I can't imagine Diana capable of killing anybody. She's the sweetest person you could ever imagine. Mother to a little boy. I don't believe she even knows how to hold a gun."

"Do you know if she knew Martin Nyrén?"

"I have no idea. She might have met him at one of our gallery parties, like she met Oscar."

Thomas changed direction.

"Do you know of any connection between Juliander and Nyrén?"

"What do you mean by that?"

"Any business together? Often together socially?" Thomas clarified. "Do you know anything at all which could explain why both of them are dead?"

"I can't think of anything they had in common besides the RSYC. It's the only place I know of where their worlds met."

"Do you have anything against Martin Nyrén personally?"

Ingmar von Hahne's face twisted, as if he were close to tears.

"Me?" he said, his voice trembling. "Martin was my friend! I liked Oscar, too, for that matter."

Thomas considered something else. Ingmar von Hahne had been adamant that he'd really not wanted the post of RSYC chairman. Perhaps the truth was just the opposite? Perhaps he presented those feelings as a smoke screen? The lust for honor and power could be a strong motive, especially for those in the upper tier of society, like Ingmar von Hahne.

He might be telling the truth, but what if all this shock was just an act? Thomas knew from experience how easily some people could lie, so he decided to press harder.

"So, how long have you wanted the chairmanship of the RSYC?"

Ingmar von Hahne seemed surprised.

"What are you talking about?"

"Please answer the question. We want to find any possible motives behind the two murders. Lust for power could be one of them." Thomas kept his eyes fastened on him. "Would you kill someone for it?"

Ingmar von Hahne sat straight up, collecting himself as he stared at Thomas in disgust.

"Are you out of your mind?" His indignation was clear. "I have never wanted that position! My nomination should have no bearing on these deaths. It is bizarre to even imagine such a thing. Bizarre!" Ingmar von Hahne's lips pressed together in a thin line, his earlier indecisiveness now completely blown away.

"The chairmanship was the last thing I ever wanted." He sounded sad. "All my life I have tried to live up to others' expectations of me. If you think I would shoot Oscar over that position, you're not right in the head."

He looked around the room as if searching for strength; then he focused on Margit. It was obvious he thought her the more sympathetic of the two.

"Everyone who knows me knows I could not hurt a fly. I need to go home now."

They compared their impressions of all the interviews conducted that day. Somehow it was already six thirty in the evening. Through the window they heard the song of a blackbird perched on a branch outside.

Margit rested in the visitor's chair in Thomas's office, her tired eyes a reflection of his own.

They'd arranged all possible security precautions for each member of the RSYC. They'd given out personal alarms and an emergency number. They'd also told the board members not to go out after dark, to stay away from unknown areas, and to keep an eye on their surroundings.

Persson had fielded calls from upset citizens, all with the same complaint. What were the police doing to protect the public?

Didn't he understand that people feared for their lives?

Finally his summer cold knocked him out. He would have to stay home for a few days to recuperate. It was hard to tell if the virus or the phone calls had brought him down. At any rate, Persson finally realized he was too sick to work.

Thomas knew they didn't have enough officers to guard every RSYC member around the clock. That was impossible. But the public couldn't understand that.

The media was having a field day, and Thomas feared the National Bureau might take over the investigation soon.

Some more prominent RSYC board members got their companies to provide private security. Although Thomas was, in principle, against such action, he also realized it would take some pressure off them. Another murder would be indefensible. The situation was dire enough already.

Diana Söder came to the police station a few hours after Ingmar von Hahne left. It surprised her to be called in again. When Thomas questioned her about the key to the storage area, she hadn't been much help.

Thomas clasped his hands behind his head and stretched.

"We've just seen two people who insist they had nothing to do with these killings. Diana Söder says she's never held a gun in her life, plus she'd never even met Martin Nyrén. And Ingmar von Hahne swears he's innocent."

"She became really upset when you insinuated she might have killed Juliander." Margit furrowed her brow. "Do you think she's putting on a show?"

"Hard to say. I'm sure that she loved Oscar. She also has an unshakable alibi for the day of his death. So does von Hahne for that matter. And Diana Söder came to us voluntarily with those anonymous e-mails."

"A smoke screen?"

"Perhaps, but I don't think so. Could jealousy drive her to hire a hit man? That does happen."

"Yes," Margit said. "But not very often. And the question remains, what did she have to gain?"

"Maybe he wanted to end it. Maybe he wanted to leave her for someone else . . ."

"Perhaps, but is that believable? And why would she kill Nyrén?"

Margit crossed her arms and leaned back.

"The only person who had anything to gain from Juliander's death is von Hahne," Thomas said.

"For the chairmanship? Do you really believe that?"

Thomas shrugged.

"Don't forget. The shot that killed Nyrén came from his storage space."

"Just a coincidence? Was it simply a good spot to make the shot? But why get rid of Nyrén? As long as we're considering von Hahne as the killer."

"I have no idea. Maybe Nyrén found something on him and threatened to reveal it to the authorities."

Margit looked skeptical. "We have guesses and nothing more."

"Yes," Thomas said. "By the way, what did Sylvia Juliander say?"

"She knew nothing about any connection between Nyrén and her husband outside of the RSYC. Nothing at all."

"So we have nothing, too." Thomas tried to stifle a sigh.

When did he lose his children?

When they were born, a feeling he'd never experienced before overcame him. Those tiny, tiny fingers grabbing his. The downy hair barely visible. Eyes peering at him, struggling to focus.

His joy had surprised him. All during his wife's first pregnancy, he'd been distant, as if the whole business didn't concern him. It was one more thing that happened because it was expected, not because he wanted it. He felt as if no one ever asked what he wanted, so he would not participate.

Children were expected, nothing more, nothing less.

But as he stood there in the hospital and looked into the tiny crib where his son lay, he couldn't imagine life without him.

After their births, he'd spent as much time as possible in the nursery. He could play for hours on the floor with building blocks and teddy bears. Tickle tummies until the kids screamed with laughter. Read stories until their eyes shut and the arm hugging the teddy bear fell away.

Things changed so quickly. The children's voices began to echo his wife's thoughts. Their opinions became foreign to him, and their values veered far away from his own.

His daughter no longer sought out his company. She preferred to go shopping with her mother. She stopped chatting with him and became preoccupied with her appearance.

His son, his firstborn, turned snobbish, throwing hackneyed phrases around and surrounding himself with friends he could barely understand.

The siblings formed a united front where he was barely welcome or desired.

As time went by, he felt more and more superfluous in his own home, to the point where he spent more and more evenings working.

Their mother ruled the family, leaving less and less space for him.

When had he lost his children?

THURSDAY,
THE FOURTH WEEK

CHAPTER 67

Nora couldn't take it anymore.

Henrik had phoned Monday morning to let her know he was going to work all week and come out to Sandhamn that Friday evening. They could talk then.

Nora had been on autopilot the past few days. She made food for the boys, took walks on the beach, bought ice cream as soon as Adam and Simon begged for it. She had no strength to argue with them. A proper upbringing would have to wait.

Finally she became too restless to stay on the island. If she did, she would go crazy pretending things were normal.

On Wednesday evening, she called her mother, Susanne, to see if she could take the children for a few days. Nora said she had to go into the city for work. As usual, her mother was happy to help.

Nora's mother looked concerned but did not ask questions. Nora appreciated her discretion. If she'd asked how things were going with Henrik, Nora would have burst into tears.

And what good would that do?

Nora took a morning ferry into Stavsnäs and then the 433 bus to Slussen. Despite the winding road, she fell asleep and did not wake until the final stop. Then she got off and followed the crowd down to the subway.

The shabbiness of Slussen station surprised her. Slussen was one of the first built in Stockholm. The tiled walls were filthy, and Nora wrinkled her nose involuntarily at the scent of urine. She hurried to the platform, relieved when the train arrived.

Someone had left the free newspaper *Metro* on the seat. Out of habit, she picked it up, skimming an article on the Stockholm court system and the long waits for cases to make it to trial. It could take years for an abuse case to reach the court. During that time, the witnesses could forget what they'd seen or the victim could be frightened into silence. It didn't surprise Nora, since the system was chronically understaffed, but it might upset people and undermine their trust in the judicial system.

And for good reason. It was unfair to make people wait so long for justice. Allotting the police more resources wouldn't solve anything if there weren't enough people to process the cases.

Nora remembered all too well her own time as a law clerk in Visby. Even then, there wasn't enough money. The situation today clearly hadn't improved.

Nora sat still with the paper on her lap. Stockholm District Court: the words felt like a sign.

She'd had a vague plan to wander the city, maybe go for a swim at one of the pools. She'd hoped to find peace for a while, to take a break from thinking.

Now another idea came to her.

As the train pulled into Central Station, she grabbed her backpack and got off. She took the escalator to the bottom platform where the blue line ran. She was in luck. The train pulled in as she arrived. She boarded and was at Stockholm City Hall a few minutes later.

She looked up at the stone building that towered above the station. Stockholm City Hall, home to Stockholm District Court.

It was an impressive building where many court cases of all kinds were handled. Here Clark Olofsson was sentenced to prison after the hostage drama at Norrmalm Square. Here one of the most elusive criminals in the history of Swedish crime, Laser Man, received a life sentence. A divided court suffering under intense pressure from the media had condemned Christer Pettersson for the murder of Swedish prime minister Olof Palme.

But other government offices shared the building. For example, the Financial Supervisory Authority, which oversaw cases involving procedures, like the appointment of bankruptcy trustees. The paperwork for each case was sent here, such as the inventory, the management reports, and descriptions of the measures taken on behalf of the bankruptcy estate. They were updated every six months—all here for safekeeping.

That meant most of Juliander's cases should be here. Not exactly inside this beautiful building, but a few hundred yards away, in an archive built in the nineties at the corner of Scheelegatan and Fleminggatan.

Nora still had the list of Juliander's cases from Thomas. On impulse, she'd shoved them into her backpack when she'd left Sandhamn. She felt bad about not looking at them sooner and thought she might go through them on the ferry.

She could spend a few hours here studying Juliander's case reports in the archives. As a bank lawyer, she'd done her share of inventories and reports. She was no stranger to these documents.

And she longed for the chance to take her mind off Henrik and the Brand house. At Sandhamn, those situations consumed her thoughts. They started first thing in the morning and lasted until night.

Burying herself in Juliander's paperwork would be welcome.

And Thomas would certainly appreciate her help. It was the least she could do after crying on his shoulder last Sunday. He was her best friend. For his sake, she could sacrifice an afternoon of work.

She straightened her backpack and headed off toward Fleminggatan.

CHAPTER 68

Nora opened the archive's huge bronze doors and walked into the reception area.

Though the Courthouse Annex took up almost the entire block, only an unassuming awning marked the entrance.

Inside, visitors found an airy hallway dominated by a large spiral staircase.

Nora explained her errand to the young guard sitting behind a glass window. He wore a neatly pressed uniform jacket, though his hair hung halfway to his shoulders. A small peach-fuzz mustache made him look young, hardly capable of defending the government office against a violent intruder.

Through the bulletproof glass, she could see a game of solitaire on his computer screen. A half-eaten salami sandwich and a cup of coffee sat next to his keyboard.

"You need to go to Department Six," the guard said. "One floor up, the fifth floor."

"Where am I now?" asked Nora.

"The ground floor *is* the fourth floor," the guard explained. "This building has underground levels, which makes this the fourth floor. You can use the elevator or take the stairs." He gestured at the spiral staircase. "I'll let them know you're coming," he continued. "Then you won't have to wait so long. The door is kept locked."

He smiled, and his tiny mustache wiggled. He looked ridiculous, but he meant well.

She thanked him and took the stairs. At the top she found a glass door with a sign for Department Six. A woman in her sixties opened the door.

"Hello, I'm Eva-Britt Svensson." She held out her hand. "I'm the court secretary here."

She wore a red pleated skirt and a white blouse. Her gray hair was so short it curled behind her ears, and her large, round glasses made her look like an owl. She definitely looked like a court secretary. Nora could have sworn that there'd been an exact replica at the Visby court.

She introduced herself and explained she wanted a number of files concerning bankruptcy cases. She took the list from her backpack and handed it over.

The woman wrinkled her forehead and then looked sternly at Nora.

"You really need all these? In one day? I hardly believe you can get through them."

Nora nodded and smiled confidently.

"You must know that we can't retrieve all of these at once," Eva-Britt Svensson continued. "Many of these concluded some time ago. I'll have to go get them from the archives. It can take a while." She sighed heavily.

Nora took out her bank ID card.

"I'm afraid we have to look at some of these cases," she said apologetically. "That's why I'm here. I'm sorry to cause extra work for you, but it *is* extremely important."

She did her best to sound authoritative, hoping no one would call the bank to check her story.

By law, every Swedish citizen had the right to access any public document at any government archive, but a good reason didn't hurt. She knew what government employees thought of the general public whenever they tried to exercise their legal rights. Especially when the citizens were journalists who regularly demanded access to infamous cases.

Eva-Britt Svensson glanced at Nora's ID.

"All right," she said. "We'll do our best to help."

Nora gave her a big smile.

"Is there a place where I can sit down to research?" she asked. There was only one table intended for visitors beside the reception desk.

"It's not really allowed, but since there's so much material involved, you can use this room," Eva-Britt Svensson said. She pointed to an empty room close by. "We're getting a new notary in a month, so nobody's using it right now."

Nora set her backpack on the floor there and hung her jacket on the back of the chair.

"This reminds me of my own time as a law clerk in Visby," she said, attempting to get on Eva-Britt's good side.

It worked.

"Then you know the routine. What shall I start with?" Eva-Britt said. Before Nora even had the chance to reply, she'd decided. "I'll get the two most recent case files first. They're up here. It will take more time to get the others. You do remember that you're only allowed two files at a time?"

"Yes. And how long to get copies?" Nora asked, careful not to push the woman's patience.

"It depends on how many pages are in the file," she answered. "We don't have the resources to do it for you. You'll have to use the copier yourself."

She headed off to get the files.

Nora sat down in the empty room and took out a pen and a sheet of paper. The room's one window faced the Klaraberg Viaduct. Its lush greenery framed the water, reminding her of the archipelago.

What did she expect to find here?

This might be nothing more than a waste of time. But she'd give it a try. She'd do her best.

Friday,
THE FOURTH WEEK

CHAPTER 69

Nora took the 433 bus to Stavsnäs. She'd spent all Thursday afternoon and Friday morning at the archive and hadn't left Department Six until she'd looked at every single one of the files on Thomas's list.

Reading them was monotonous, to say the least. Bankruptcy reports and half-yearly reports were formulaic and tedious.

That first day, she'd taken a break and gone to the corner grocery store to buy something to eat. A plastic-wrapped sandwich and a bottle of raspberry mineral water became her Thursday lunch.

The documents' dry descriptions made her eyes water, and she couldn't stop yawning. Still, she kept on. Something, something—she felt on the edge of grasping something important, but she didn't know what. It was like a butterfly dancing out of reach. So she kept on plowing through the files, report after report.

The stack of files she'd read grew as the hours passed. Nothing seemed to deviate. Nothing caught her eye. Yet she was certain there was something. She just hadn't figured it out yet.

She stayed at her parents' empty house that night to avoid Henrik. But before that, she decided to see a movie. She went to a Swedish comedy and ate a big bag of popcorn, but afterward she felt a little queasy. The taste of the greasy popcorn stayed in her mouth for the rest of the evening.

She didn't sleep well. In her dream, Henrik was at the hospital, surrounded by beautiful nurses, while she tried unsuccessfully to get his attention.

When she woke up, she felt teary, heavy, and not rested. It was hard to get out of bed, but she forced herself up and made a cup of tea. She ate a few crackers she found in the pantry. Her parents had emptied the refrigerator when they'd left for Sandhamn, but it didn't matter. She wasn't all that hungry.

Then she made her way back to Department Six. Eva-Britt Svensson helped Nora with all the copying so she could finish up before the weekend. At the end of the day, Nora carried two large bags of copies out of the building.

The bags now sat at her feet on the hot bus. She'd found a double seat all to herself near the back.

The bus turned off the highway, passing the Wermdö Golf & Country Club, and the swaying movements made Nora sleepy. Before she knew it, she'd nodded off again, just as she had before, with her cheek against the window.

CHAPTER 70

Margit brought two cups of coffee and offered one to Thomas. She sat down next to him and drank half of hers right away. Thomas accepted the plastic cup, though he usually avoided coffee from the machine.

It was Friday afternoon. They'd gone over everything from every angle for hours.

They'd interviewed Martin Nyrén's extended family. They'd visited his workplace and talked to his colleagues. It got them nowhere. The evening headlines agreed. A two-page spread detailed the police's lack of success. A number of so-called experts commented on the state of the investigation and offered opinions on the police work.

Margit found a bag of boat-shaped raspberry candy. "Want any?"

Thomas shook his head. He wasn't feeling well.

"I wonder how long it'll take to get the numbers from Nyrén's cell phone," Margit said. "If they're not here by Monday, I'm going to get them myself."

"Kalle said they're delayed because of all the summer vacations."

"It's a damned shame his phone broke. Otherwise, we'd already have what we want."

"The tech guys said they might be able to fix it."

"Yes, but in a week? Or even two?"

"Do we have that much time?"

Thomas gave Margit a worried glance. They needed a break in the case, and soon.

"What about Nyrén's computer? Have they found the password?"

"They said they'd let us know when they do."

"How hard can it be?"

Margit sank deeper into the office chair, bending a pink paper clip back and forth until it broke simply to distract herself.

"Carina hasn't found any connection between Juliander and Nyrén," she continued. "No business together. Nyrén worked at the Legal, Financial and Administrative Services Agency, and that agency is not involved with bankruptcies."

"Well, they were both lawyers. They're almost the same age. Maybe they were in law school together?"

"Kalle checked all that. No connection in the past. Nothing that can help us."

Margit thought a moment. "Do you think Nyrén might have been having an affair with Juliander's wife?" she threw out. "Maybe after all her husband's philandering, she needed some comfort?"

"But then Juliander wouldn't have died first, right?"

"No, perhaps not." Margit sank deeper down. "She might still be the one who sent those messages to Diana Söder. Carina says they came from Internet cafés all over town."

"That doesn't help. The messages were sent from temporary addresses."

"What don't we see?" Margit asked. "What are we missing?"

Her phone beeped, and she looked at the new message.

"Well, they're finished with von Hahne's rifles," she said. "The bullet that killed Juliander didn't come from any of his guns."

"He didn't own a Marlin, so that's no surprise."

Thomas looked out the window. Clouds gathered, kicking off a rainy weekend.

"You don't need a license to get a gun," he said. "What about Laser Man? He went to Liège, bought a rifle on the street, and drove home without it being discovered. Same thing in Baltic countries. What are the chances someone bringing home a rifle on the ferry would be caught? Probably not even half of one percent."

Margit had to agree.

Customs only intercepted a few weapons a year. Their main efforts went into narcotics and alcohol smuggling. Guns weren't a high priority.

"No killer with two functioning brain cells would use a licensed weapon," Thomas continued. "It's too easy to trace. Ingmar von Hahne wouldn't be stupid enough to use his own hunting rifle. And he does know how to shoot."

"You're really focused on him."

"There's something he's not telling us. I'm sure of that."

Thomas couldn't put his finger on it, but he knew Ingmar von Hahne had a secret.

"If not him, then who?"

"I'm sorry, but we don't have enough to bring a case against him."

"I know."

Thomas's shoulders drooped slightly. His head pounded and his body ached.

"You don't look so good," Margit said.

"You're right. I don't feel well."

He shook himself, but that didn't help. He could feel his nose clogging up by the minute.

"I think you've caught Persson's cold," Margit said. "Go home and go to bed. You won't be any use if it gets worse. Go on."

Thomas looked at the clock. It was almost five thirty. He reluctantly agreed with Margit. He felt terrible.

Saturday,
the fourth week

CHAPTER 71

"Hole in one!" Simon yelled. He threw his golf club onto the sand and danced in delight. His eyes shined, and he made the *V* for victory with his small fingers. Nora couldn't help smiling.

"Did you see, Mom? Did you see?" he called out.

Adam, who hadn't got the ball in after six strokes, was not pleased. He adopted a look of superiority and pretended not to care.

Nora and the boys had gone to play minigolf at the harbor between Sailors Restaurant and the swimming pool shaded by hotels. The twelve-hole course was popular with families on the island.

However, it was risky to bring Adam. He hated to lose, and when he did, he'd ruin the game for everyone else. He'd sulk the rest of the day when he got into that mood.

All morning, the boys had begged to go. Adam had assured Nora that he'd behave, and finally Nora had agreed to take them.

She needed something to do, anyway, since Henrik had changed his mind about coming out to the island as he'd promised. He'd left an abrupt message saying he was going sailing with Johan Wrede on the Swedish west coast. They'd have to postpone their talk.

His brusque tone on the recording made it clear he was still angry. Nora tried to call back, but he'd turned off his phone.

She felt torn. On one hand escaping the confrontation relieved her. On the other hand Henrik leaving her and the boys on their own made her angry.

How nice it must be, she thought, her phone in hand, *to assume I'll take care of the children whenever he decides to take off. One telephone call and he's free to go, knowing his wife will take care of everything.*

She'd love to see his reaction if she left a message telling him she'd be gone for the weekend. Especially when they had so much to sort out between them.

Why was she the one who always had to stay pleasant so that Simon and Adam didn't worry? Why did she have to explain their father's absence?

Sometimes Nora wished she could have time away from the family. Snap her fingers and go, as if by magic.

But she was not that kind of person. She knew that. If she let the children see how upset she really was, her sons would pay a higher price than she would. She'd destroy their sense of security, and that would only make things worse. So she swallowed her feelings and pretended things were fine.

Deep down she wished Henrik had to explain his absence to the children instead of simply disappearing.

Adam mouthed the word "damn," interrupting Nora's thoughts. She gave him a stern look to remind him to behave. He'd promised.

Adam pouted, but after a while his lean body relaxed and his brow furrowed as he prepared to putt.

Luckily it took him only two strokes to hole the ball. The crisis was averted for now. Nora could take a breath.

While she waited for the boys to get to the next hole, a difficult one with blocks and a hill, her thoughts circled back to the bankruptcy documents.

Yesterday evening, after the boys' bedtime, she'd sat on the veranda with a cup of tea and the bags of documents. She'd gone through the files once more but still hadn't found anything unusual.

Now it was her turn to play. It was only a minigolf course, but it was still not easy to make the shot. She concentrated, trying to aim the ball as straight as possible toward the small hole.

The ball sailed off the course entirely on her first attempt, which lost her a point. Adam watched with pleasure while Simon tried to encourage her. There was no doubt which of her boys had a fierce competitive streak. She soon used up her strokes before getting the ball in the hole. She recorded her score on the tally card and thought, *You can't be best at everything.*

Adam made the hole with only four strokes. It was just as well. It put him in a good mood.

As she sat down on the bench and waited for her turn, her thoughts returned to the bankruptcy files.

She'd read them in chronological order. Was there any other way to arrange them? Some way to create a different pattern?

This evening with the boys in bed, she'd take one last look. If she didn't find anything, at least she could say she'd done her best for Thomas.

Sunday,

The Fourth Week

CHAPTER 72

Nora surveyed the files covering the living room table. The evening before, she'd stacked them into different piles. She'd even put some on the sofa when she ran out of room on the table. She sorted them again, but no new pattern emerged.

She sighed as she reached for her teacup. There was nothing to discover. She might as well give up.

The weather was drizzly and chilly. Despite Nora encouraging the boys to get some fresh air, they stayed in their room playing computer games.

But that wasn't *her* problem. She took a deep breath and tried to make herself as clear as possible without being downright rude.

The boys pounded down the stairs in search of a snack. They asked for cinnamon buns, and Nora went into the kitchen to get them. They watched to make sure they got the exact same amount as she poured glasses of chocolate milk.

She noticed how much Adam had grown over the summer. He now stood a head taller than Simon and already came up to her chest. Before long, he'd be a teenager with acne and all other things in his head that would push his mother to one side.

As the boys compared glasses, an idea came to Nora. She hadn't sorted the bankruptcy files by size. She'd never considered the amounts of money involved in the cases, not even yesterday evening when she'd tried to see them in a new way.

She ordered the boys to stay at the kitchen table while they ate their snack, then she hurried back to the living room to explore her latest idea.

It took her almost an hour to sort the files from the largest to the smallest amount of money. By then Adam and Simon had eaten their snacks and gone back to their computer games. Their glasses sat on the counter, crumbs everywhere.

Nora didn't have time to care. Instead, she looked at her work with satisfaction. The difference in amounts was striking.

A mixture of IT companies, travel agencies, and other larger companies made up the first group, with losses in the hundreds of millions or more.

The next category held a wide variety of companies with bankruptcies spanning sixty to seventy million kronor. Juliander often acted as the sole attorney for these cases. The businesses ranged from construction to consulting firms. Many were family owned or involved just a few partners who'd started them.

Finally there were those with losses of twenty to thirty million kronor. These businesses also varied. One was a temp service company that hadn't survived the latest downturn. Others were small IT companies.

One last case stood out. A dental practice with a turnover of just four million kronor, it was remarkably smaller than the others Juliander had taken on.

Why get involved in such a small case when he was already well established as a big-time attorney who could pick and choose his work?

Nora sat down to study the file.

The company was Olof Martinsson Dental Practice.

According to the report, Olof Martinsson had been the sole owner. He employed a nurse and a hygienist. Going over the math quickly in her head, Nora thought his income could have easily covered rent, equipment, and three salaries.

Why had the company gone bankrupt? Dentists rarely did. He had a well-established practice, so it seemed unlikely he'd have a sudden downturn in business.

Nora kept reading. Martinsson had taken out large loans against his practice. In the end, he couldn't make the payments, and his assets went into bankruptcy.

Why did he need such large loans? Where had all that money gone?

When Nora went through the list of creditors, she found her own bank had loaned him the largest amount. The loan was high compared to the amount of money the practice brought in. No bank would normally agree to such an off-kilter transaction.

Nora wrinkled her brow.

Something was fishy here. Tomorrow she'd investigate with her bank's credit department and ask a few questions. Perhaps they could explain why they'd agreed to such a large loan.

Monday,
THE FIFTH WEEK

CHAPTER 73

Thomas's sneeze echoed through the hallway of the station. He'd forced himself to stay home that morning, but he didn't have time to be sick. He needed to work. A killer was on the loose.

"What are you doing here?" Margit asked as he came into her office. "You look terrible."

It was hard to tell if she was offering sympathy or simply stating facts.

Thomas looked at her with watery eyes.

"I don't have a fever anymore. Believe me."

"Just stay away. I don't want to get sick."

Thomas sneezed again.

"Where are we?" he asked.

"Do you want anything? A cup of tea?"

Thomas smiled. "Sure, thanks."

Margit brought back two mugs and looked at him with a mixture of compassion and resignation.

"Are you sure you want to be here?"

"Let's drop it. Where are we?"

"Linköping called. They've analyzed the bullet found in Nyrén's head."

Thomas frowned, and she nodded right away to confirm his suspicions.

"It came from the same rifle that killed Juliander. A Marlin. Right rifled. With twenty grooves," she said.

They both knew what this meant, but Thomas said it out loud: "So we have a double murder."

"Looks that way."

Thomas tried to collect his thoughts, but it felt like he had cotton between his ears.

"One link is obvious," Margit said. "Someone out there really dislikes members of the RSYC Board. And if our suspicions are wrong about Ingmar von Hahne, he could be the next victim."

Thomas nodded. The thought that von Hahne could be their prime suspect or the next victim plagued him.

"Anything else from Linköping?"

"Not much. But that Bäcklund woman can really talk your ear off. She kept going on and on."

Thomas remembered Bäcklund vividly.

"By the way, I asked Eva Timell this morning about any possible connection between Juliander and Nyrén," Margit said.

"Anything?"

"No. She didn't recall any. They didn't even have an e-mail exchange beyond general messages from the RSYC."

"What about Nyrén's computer?"

"Nothing yet. The tech guys haven't contacted me."

"Should we lean on them?"

"Sure. I'll call."

Thomas was grateful for his tea, though he still felt chilled and had a terrible headache.

"You should go home," Margit said. "You don't look well at all."

Margit's tone left no room for a refusal.
Thomas surrendered.
"All right."

Chapter 74

"We haven't made a decision yet," Nora said.

It was the fifth time Severin had called since the showing.

"When do you think you will?" he asked. He came off as pushy and worried at the same time. "I don't want to pressure you, but it would be great to move forward, if you get my drift."

Nora got his drift exactly.

He wanted the house sold so he'd get his fat commission and could move on to the next property.

But that wasn't *her* problem. She took a deep breath and tried to make her words as firm as possible.

"I don't know. This house means a great deal to me, and I want it to be in good hands." Nora heard the vagueness in her voice but didn't know what else to say.

"Of course," Severin said. "It's not always easy to decide. You've got to think through the pros and cons. But you must know these buyers are serious about preserving the house as a cultural treasure."

One cliché after another from the agent's mouth. His sticky, sweet words flowed like honey.

I wonder if he knows what he's saying, or is he just young and naïve? she thought. She recalled that horrible woman who'd looked down on Signe's furniture as if it were something the cat dragged in.

She forced herself to be polite.

"I think it would be better in the future if *we* called *you*. We don't want to waste your time, and it might be a while . . ."

She suddenly felt sorry for the young man. This sale would be a career milestone for him if it happened.

"Oh, don't worry about that," Severin said. "I don't mind calling. But I had something else to tell you and your husband."

"I see," Nora said.

"The buyers want me to tell you that they've raised their offer."

"Raised their offer?"

"That's right. They'll add another million kronor, but they want you to decide by Saturday."

Thoughts whirled in Nora's head.

Make up her mind by Saturday? The last day of her summer vacation? She and Henrik hadn't even talked it through yet, and the tension between them continued to grow.

"One million?" Nora repeated.

Severin had said those words as if talking about Monopoly money. One more million to buy Broadway. Do not pass go. It was just a game.

"This is so exciting!" the agent said. "I've never been part of a deal like this. But anything can happen with such a unique piece of property. This must be seen as an offer you can't refuse!"

I can't? Nora thought. *You have no idea what I can refuse! But if I do, will it cost me my marriage? Can you buy happiness with a Chance card?*

"Have you mentioned this to my husband?" she asked.

"No, should I?"

"Oh, no, no, no," Nora said. "We're still discussing it all. I just wondered if you had." She took a deep breath. "I'll call you in a few days."

"Remember, the offer is good only until Saturday, as I said. A bird in the hand . . ."

Severin didn't need to finish his sentence. She knew the cliché.

Nora put down the phone. A second later, she picked it up again. She had planned to call the credit office of her bank.

She tapped in the number, and when the receptionist answered she asked to be transferred to the credit department. If she remembered correctly, they were two floors down from her own office.

A cheerful female voice answered on the third ring.

Nora gave her name and what she needed to know. She added the file number of the dental practice and then waited on the line. A few minutes later, Nora was told that everything had been transferred to the central archives. However, the woman gave her the name of Niklas Larsson, who had overseen their side of the bankruptcy. He would contact Nora. He knew all about it.

Nora left her cell phone number for him and thanked the woman who had helped her.

Then she simply sat with the file on her lap, pondering it all. There was definitely something fishy about this.

Why would Juliander accept such a small-time bankruptcy proceeding?

TUESDAY,
THE FIFTH WEEK

CHAPTER 75

Thomas woke at noon on Tuesday. Almost half a day had passed, but he felt much better. His nose no longer ran, and his head didn't ache. His body started feeling normal again. He'd slept for almost fifteen hours.

Just like Persson, he'd suffered a real summer cold. That much was clear.

For the first time in days, he had an appetite, so he made a huge breakfast: coffee, Swedish soured milk with muesli, and some sandwiches. Then he took a long, hot shower before getting dressed.

It was two in the afternoon by the time he left for work, but he felt good, and he wanted to get back to the investigation. He got his car keys and headed out the door for the drive to the Nacka police station.

Nora didn't hear back from the credit department until Tuesday after lunch. By then she had almost forgotten about it. The weather had improved, so she and the boys had headed out to Fläskberget to swim.

The boys loved to run down the pontoon dock at full speed and leap into the water. They could do it nonstop. Nora had a vague memory of doing the same when she was small, but now she preferred to stay on land. She no longer liked having her head underwater, especially when that water was cold.

At Fläskberget, she met up with some other mothers who lived in the neighborhood. They sat together, keeping an eye on the children while chatting away. Nora felt herself begin to relax in this circle of friends who'd known each other for years. They shared a little harmless gossip. The news of another murder victim from the RSYC Board weighed on everybody's mind. Since nobody knew him well, they felt free to speculate.

Still, thinking about a man's death made them uncomfortable. It felt both surreal and close to home.

Nora's cell phone rang as she and the boys arrived home. She saw it was someone from the bank. Holding the phone in her hand, she went out to the veranda and sat in one of the wicker chairs.

Niklas Larsson politely introduced himself. He'd pulled the file from the central archives to assist her. It sat on the desk in front of him now.

To avoid explaining her interest in the file, she got right to the point.

"I have looked at the loan picture and wonder why the debtor was granted a significantly higher loan than normal." She tried to make the inquiry seem routine.

"That's correct," he said. "It's a sad story. Do you know anything about Olof Martinsson?"

"No," Nora said. "Not much." She pulled a footstool closer and put her feet up.

"He was not just a dentist. He was also an innovative biochemist. Have you heard of the Brånemark Method?"

Nora thought back. Yes, one of the department secretaries had talked about her mother losing teeth, and the name Brånemark had come up.

"I know a little bit, but please tell me more."

"It's a technique for fastening replacement teeth into the jawbone. A Swedish professor had developed it in the sixties, but Martinsson thought he could improve on it. Unfortunately, he didn't succeed. He invested all his money, convinced it would work out. He was fanatical about it."

"Is that why the bank loaned him so much—probably more than they should have?"

"Yes and no. It's true that we granted the loan even though his collateral was doubtful, but the income from his dental practice seemed secure. That definitely reassured the loan committee."

"But it didn't work out?"

"No, he needed to borrow more and more to finish his research. Finally we had to pull the plug. He'd mortgaged his house and everything he owned, but it was not enough."

"What happened after that?"

"If I remember correctly, he couldn't secure any more financing. He was so disappointed and embittered that he let his dental practice fall apart. Finally he couldn't make the payments on the loan any longer. One thing led to another, and his practice went bankrupt."

"What is he doing now?"

"He had a heart attack and died shortly after the bankruptcy concluded. He couldn't handle the disappointment, I guess. Tragic. It's not easy to be an inventor in Sweden."

"And we lost our money, I assume," Nora said.

She leaned back in the wicker chair while waiting for his reply. She could feel a slight headache starting, but she did her best to ignore it. Probably too much sun. She should drink more water.

Niklas Larsson laughed in embarrassment on the other end.

"Yes, well, most of it. There wasn't much value in the practice anymore. We had to write most of it off."

Nora thought about all this information and thanked him for his help.

She decided to devote one more hour to the investigation, and then that would be it. She wasn't getting paid for all this work.

Inside, she turned on her computer and did a search for *Brånemark*.

The technique used small titanium screws to attach the implanted tooth firmly into the jawbone. Once bone absorbed and anchored the screws, the new teeth were firmly attached. This way patients no longer needed dentures. The patented invention was used all over the world.

Then she searched for *Olof Martinsson* and *dentist*. She found an obituary published in a professional dentistry magazine. She clicked on it with rising interest.

Olof Martinsson was described as a highly capable and dedicated lone wolf who had come within a hair's breadth of an important break-through. His research had earned him a patent for a so-called growth factor that was way ahead of the Brånemark method. A protein skin on each titanium screw sped up the healing process and significantly improved the absorption of the screw by the bone. The author wrote that this process could have been utilized in other procedures, like heal-ing blood vessels during surgery, or even bringing the edges of wounds together.

If the method had been developed to its full potential.

Martinsson never had the chance to finish the clinical trials needed for scientific approval, a prerequisite for worldwide use of the patent.

According to the obituary, financial problems broke Martinsson. With no wife or children, he'd put his entire life into his research. When it was taken from him, his body gave up.

It was a sorrowful, bitter obituary. So many years of work with no reward. How sad that he'd been so close when his business, which owned the patent, had gone bankrupt.

So what had happened to that patent?

She reached for the Martinsson file. There was a list of debts and assets. A patent was mentioned that was worth one hundred thousand kronor at the most. This must be the one Martinsson had invested his life in.

In the report made six months after the proceedings, Nora found a small paragraph about the patent. It sold to an American company for one hundred thousand kronor a few months later.

One hundred thousand kronor. Its exact valuation. A small sum for so many years of work and so many millions of Swedish kronor invested. The work of one whole lifetime.

That's still too much money to pay for an allegedly worthless patent, Nora thought. The buyer wasn't noted, but it should be in Juliander's own file.

The court had appointed Juliander at the request of a small creditor, an American company. Nora had a vague sense of recognition when it came to the name: General Mind Inc. Wasn't that a large biomedical company listed on the stock market?

A foreign company requested to have Juliander, an established lawyer who usually handled much larger bankruptcies than this, appointed as the bankruptcy attorney.

Why?

And which American company had bought the patent? Was it also General Mind Inc.?

Lots of interesting questions here. Time to call Thomas and tell him what she'd found out. He could request all documentation on the Martinsson bankruptcy from the Kalling law firm.

That would make for some interesting reading.

CHAPTER 76

Margit didn't argue with Thomas when he showed up at her office this time. Even if he still sneezed now and then, his color had improved and he no longer looked exhausted.

Thomas and Margit settled into one of the conference rooms to be alone.

While Thomas had been home resting, Margit had interviewed many of Nyrén's acquaintances.

Juliander's acquaintances and Nyrén's all gave similar answers. No one knew of any enemies. Nyrén had been a valued colleague and friend. Shock and confusion were common emotions.

"No apparent motive, in other words," Margit said. "No enemies or anything else."

"Any explanation for Nyrén's two toothbrushes?"

Margit shook her head. "No girlfriend. Everyone says he was a bachelor. Perhaps a visitor left the toothbrush."

Thomas shared what Nora had told him while he was on his way to the station. He was just finishing when Carina poked her head through the door.

"Read this," she said. She held out a sheaf of papers.

"What is it?" Margit asked.

"Printouts from the Internet. I've been researching General Mind Inc. as Thomas requested. Look what I've found."

She smiled expectantly.

"Here are their American press releases from last winter. They announce a new, revolutionary way to implant teeth, a method that ensures the screws fasten into the jawbone."

Thomas bent forward to read.

The English text used a great deal of superlatives, possibly to impress the stock market as well as the general public. Thomas was no better or worse at English than anyone else in Sweden, so he was able to get the gist of the text.

The company boasted about their new technique based on an EU patent that promised to outclass all its competitors. No other method could offer such secure implants and swift recoveries.

Thomas thought about the hundreds of thousands, if not millions, of people in the US and Europe who lost teeth and needed implants. They would certainly pay good money for this.

The American company could cash in on a new procedure that worked better than anything else—a method based on a mysterious EU patent—and Sweden was part of the EU.

"How likely would it be that someone else came up with a patent like Martinsson's?"

"That was developed inside of twelve months?" Margit added.

"Not likely," Thomas said.

If this patent was so valuable, how could they have bought it that cheaply from the Martinsson assets? If General Mind was, in fact, the buyer.

"We have to see Eva Timell again," Margit said. "Let's go."

* * *

Norrmalm Square was much busier than the last time Margit and Thomas had been there. Four weeks ago, in high summer, the tempo had been slow. Tourists had strolled along with ice cream, though there were always one or two people with briefcases, their jackets slung over their shoulders and their sleeves rolled up.

Now a few late summer tourists remained, but the pace had picked up. People were coming home from their vacations and getting back to work. The office buildings filled up again.

Thomas took this as a heavy reminder of how long the investigation had been going on. He knew the first seventy-two hours were critical. Thomas wondered what they could still find after four weeks. He was close to believing that they might never catch the killer. But he wasn't ready to give up yet.

They followed a man in a dark business suit into the building and then into the elevator. They waited in reception for Eva Timell.

She looked even more tired and worn out, her sunken cheeks showing how deeply the death of her boss affected her.

She escorted them into a small conference room. Though they'd come unannounced, a tray with coffee and a few snacks waited. Perhaps this was standard procedure in the higher class of law firms, Thomas thought. Margit immediately took a piece of that fine, dark chocolate.

Eva Timell busied herself serving coffee. She seemed reluctant to begin the conversation. The silence was palpable.

Today she wore high-heeled pumps, a black blouse, and a tight black skirt with a narrow belt around the waist. A necklace with a tiny gold heart hung around her neck. It was an almost childlike touch to her otherwise professional look. It hinted at a softness behind her formal demeanor.

"We just have one question," Thomas began.

"Yes?"

Her voice was quiet even as her narrow fingers drummed nervously on her knee.

"It concerns a bankruptcy case from about two years ago," Thomas said. "A dental practice that went under."

Eva Timell looked at him, confused.

"What was the name of the company?" she asked.

"Olof Martinsson Dental Practice AB, owned by a dentist who was also a biochemist."

Juliander's assistant still looked as if the name didn't mean anything to her.

"And?" she asked, raising her cup to her lips.

"It appears that Martinsson had developed a much faster and more secure method for implanting teeth than was previously known."

"I'm sorry. What does this have to do with Oscar?"

"The patent became part of the bankruptcy proceedings. As the attorney in charge, your late employer sold it."

"That's part of his job," Eva Timell said. "They're supposed to get as much money as they can for the creditors. I'm sorry, but I don't understand where this is going."

"Let me be more clear," Thomas said. "We need to know what company bought this patent." He looked directly at her, his eyebrows raised.

Nobody had worked as close to Oscar Juliander as she had. If anyone could answer this question, it would be the elegant woman before him.

"I don't know," she said. "A dental practice? That sounds like a small company. Oscar didn't normally take on such small cases."

"Yes, we know," Thomas said. "That's why we're asking you. We would like to see the paperwork on this bankruptcy. I'm sure you have it here in your offices."

"Yes, probably, but it would take me some time to find it. We archive our documents with a depot in Dalarna. Do you know the date it concluded?"

Thomas thought. Had Nora mentioned the date? Not that he could remember.

"Why do you need that?" he asked.

"If it is concluded, the files are no longer here. If it's still ongoing, there should be documents in the office. I'll look now, if you don't mind waiting for a moment."

The door closed silently behind her as she left the room.

Almost ten minutes later, she returned with three large binders in her arms. She set them down on the polished mahogany in front of Margit and Thomas.

Olof Martinsson AB was printed clearly on each spine.

"There are a few more," she said. "I couldn't bring all of them at once. These are the first three."

Yes, indeed, the spines were numbered *I*, *II*, and *III*.

"There are many financial pages as well, but I believe the accountant has those. We usually don't keep them here."

Margit pulled the first binder close and began to turn the pages.

"Where would you find a contract?" Thomas asked.

Eva Timell took the third binder and opened it to the contents page. Then she went to pocket number four.

"Here are all the contracts related to the bankruptcy," she said. "Are these the ones you're looking for?"

Thomas nodded. He began to go through the contracts. The next-to-last document was a contract in English, just a few pages long and written in tiny print.

Assignment of patent rights. Oscar Juliander had signed the last page.

Bingo.

As far as he could make out, here was the contract in which Martinsson's patent had been sold.

"Look," he said. He turned the contract for Margit to see.

"General Mind Inc. is the buyer," she read.

"So Nora was right."

Thomas sent a silent thought of thanks to his childhood friend.

They now had the American contract to buy the patent right here in front of them, tightly drawn, well formulated, and irrefutable.

He read through the text to the amount of the sale. One hundred thousand Swedish kronor. Neither more nor less. They recorded the amount in numerals as well as words.

One hundred thousand kronor, just like Nora had said. The puzzle pieces fit too tightly to be a mere coincidence.

"Is this the entire amount they paid, or is this just an installment?" Thomas asked.

"I believe it was the entire amount," Eva Timell replied. "That's what it states in this contract."

"So Juliander just gave away Martinsson's life work for next to nothing," Margit concluded.

"Was he aware he was underselling it?" The question hung in the air.

"Do you think it might still be only a partial payment?" Margit asked Thomas.

"With, perhaps, more coming under the table," Thomas suggested.

"This is a lot to look into," Margit said.

Thomas realized Eva Timell was listening to their conversation. They'd have to continue the discussion outside of the law firm.

"I'm afraid I'll have to take these files with me," Thomas said. "I hope this won't cause any difficulties."

"Is it absolutely necessary?"

"It is, unfortunately, but don't worry. They will all be returned."

Eva Timell didn't look reassured, but she didn't protest.

"If you run across anything else concerning General Mind Inc. please let us know," Thomas said. "It's extremely important."

Eva Timell nodded, still looking anxious.

"I've never heard of this company before, but I'll keep my eyes open."

WEDNESDAY,
THE FIFTH WEEK

CHAPTER 77

Everyone gathered for the morning meeting in the large, stuffy conference room. Persson still didn't look all that healthy. His eyes were red and he was breathing with difficulty, but he came anyway.

Erik sneezed loudly. Another one who'd caught the virus.

Margit recapped the information they'd gathered in the past few days. It supported their earlier picture of Martin Nyrén as a lovable, somewhat introverted man whose coworkers and friends liked him. Many colleagues mentioned his personal integrity. He seldom spoke about his private life but put his soul into sailing and the RSYC. He even kept a photo of his Omega 36 on his desk.

"One thing is interesting," Margit said. "A friend mentioned Nyrén's boat had been vandalized recently."

"In what way?" asked Persson.

"Someone sprayed it with graffiti. It really upset him. It could have been kids, but my gut says no."

"Another thing to look into. Did he report it to the police?"

"Yes. Kalle's checking."

"How is the technical investigation going?" Persson continued. "Did we find anything in Nyrén's apartment?"

"Not much," Erik said. "It was very clean. Unusually so. Any fingerprints we found were sent to the crime lab, but nothing matches."

"Nyrén's computer?"

"Still locked. I'm surprised a lower-level manager had such secure firewalls. We also brought in his computer from work but have found only work-related material on it. Nothing personal."

"He worked for a government agency, so it's most likely that his private e-mail is on his home computer," Thomas said. "He didn't want the government to have access."

"A bureaucrat who protected his privacy," Margit said. "What bad luck."

Thomas spoke again to describe their visit to the Kalling law firm and explain their theory about the Martinsson patent.

"We believe," he said, "that Juliander received money under the table to sell that patent cheaply to General Mind Inc. The money came to him through Liechtenstein, most likely."

"So that's the explanation for his credit card and his extra income," Carina said. "A secret bank account for bribe money!"

"But why would such a large company take a risk by bribing someone?" Erik asked. He sneezed again.

Carina shifted away from him.

"It's not unusual," Thomas remarked. "Weapons manufacturers do it all the time, though they often call it a 'commission.'" He used his fingers to draw quote marks in the air.

"Think about what Bofors did in India," Margit said.

"It wouldn't surprise me to find that General Mind had previously tried to buy the patent," Thomas said, remembering Nora's description of the inventor. "The dentist treated his research like a precious child. It's conceivable he would refuse to sell. When the bankruptcy started, they probably saw their chance. They just had to find a lawyer with a good reputation who wanted to play along."

"They probably studied his background carefully," Margit said. "Millions were at stake. Profit is a strong incentive."

"Think about Håkan Lans," Persson said. His comment came out of left field.

"Who's that?" asked Carina.

"The man who invented an early form of the computer mouse. He was a technical genius. He also invented satellite spyware."

"What happened to him?"

"An American IT company cheated him out of his patents. He's been battling in court about it for years, but no decision has been made."

"That's how capitalism gets its way," Margit said.

"This company is untouchable," Thomas said. "The contract is in order. I'm not a lawyer, but it looks airtight."

Persson nodded in agreement.

"Since Juliander is dead, we have no one to prosecute for bribery," Margit said. "We don't even have a witness. Do you think that's why he was killed? They wanted to keep him quiet?"

"Then they'd have done that as soon as they secured the patent," Thomas said. "And what motive did they have? They were probably sure the bribe money would keep Juliander quiet."

"Considering the facts, it seems impossible to prove that General Mind bribed a Swedish lawyer," Persson said. "We have nothing concrete, just speculation."

"It makes me furious," Margit said, "that Juliander got away with it so easily!"

Persson smiled slightly.

"But the guy's dead," he said. "Don't forget that."

Thomas agreed. Bribes or not, Juliander was six feet under.

Margit remained irritated, but there was nothing more to say.

The door opened, and Kalle came in with a bundle of papers in his hands. He looked excited.

"Sorry I'm late," he said. "We've finally gotten the Nyrén telephone lists. The telephone company apologized for being late, but we now know the people he contacted these past few months."

He arranged the printouts on the conference table for everyone to see.

"Here's the list of who Nyrén called and who called him."

They leaned forward to look.

Martin Nyrén had sent a great many text messages from his cell phone.

"Have you attached names to these numbers?" asked Thomas.

Kalle nodded and pointed to another printout.

"Here are the names with the numbers." He smiled in anticipation.

Thomas realized why at once. The top name on the list was familiar to everyone.

Ingmar von Hahne.

"We have to bring him in again," Persson said.

Thomas and Margit were already standing up.

"We're on it."

CHAPTER 78

"Am I under arrest?"

Ingmar von Hahne's question surprised Thomas. Though it was normal under the circumstances, he hadn't expected the man to be so direct.

"No, we just need to ask you some additional questions."

"I want a lawyer anyway."

Margit and Thomas exchanged looks. Waiting for a lawyer would cost them time and also limit what they could ask.

"Do you have anyone specific to call?" Thomas asked.

Ingmar von Hahne looked unsure of himself, as if he'd expected more resistance.

"You mean I can choose?"

"Absolutely." Thomas kept his expression neutral.

Von Hahne punched a number into his phone. A few minutes later, he turned it off.

"Nobody picked up."

"You can decide how we proceed from here," Margit said.

The man seemed indecisive. He looked at his watch.

"Are you in a hurry?" Thomas asked.

"No. Yes. Well, I have a meeting in an hour."

"You decide," Margit said again.

"You might as well ask your questions, then," von Hahne said.

He appeared much more collected than the last time they'd seen him. His hair was neatly combed, and he wore a dark-blue club blazer with the RSYC logo on the right lapel. His signet ring broadcast his nobility to the world.

Von Hahne's elegant appearance irritated Thomas. *You can't touch me* is the message he sent. *People like us always land on our feet, no matter what you try. I'm a better kind of person than you.*

How had aristocratic privilege so quickly replaced the panic they'd seen from von Hahne earlier? A strong urge to crack the art dealer's elegant façade gripped Thomas.

"Why did Martin Nyrén send you regular text messages?"

"We're both members of the RSYC Board. As you know, I'm the secretary there."

"There were a great many . . ."

"We have many things to discuss." The reply was quick.

"Do you text all the members of the board?"

"When it's needed."

"Did you communicate with Oscar Juliander by text message as well?"

"If it was necessary."

"How often?"

"Now and then."

"Would you mind if we looked at those texts?"

Ingmar von Hahne hesitated a moment.

"I'm sorry. I erased them. I don't save those kinds of routine messages."

"Have you ever been to Martin Nyrén's home?"

"Yes."

"When?"

"I once went to give him some paperwork."

"You never had reason to go there again?"

"I must have had a drink or two with him over the years."

"But you have storage space across the street. Didn't you ever meet for lunch or something?" Margit asked.

"It's possible."

Von Hahne hid behind short sentences, Thomas thought. He kept answers brief to avoid long, convoluted sentences that might contradict each other.

He was on guard. That was obvious.

"You must realize you are in a difficult position," Thomas said. "Martin Nyrén's murderer shot him from the window of your rented room. According to our list of telephone calls, the two of you were in constant contact."

"I had nothing to do with Martin's murder."

Ingmar von Hahne sounded bitter. But he remained composed. Thomas held back and let Margit try a new tactic.

"Do you have any theories about why both Martin Nyrén and Oscar Juliander are dead?"

"No."

"But you must have thought about it."

"No."

"Were you enemies?"

"No."

"So you never argued with Martin Nyrén?"

"No."

"Are you positive about that?"

"Yes. I said no."

A muscle twitched in his temple. Von Hahne's calm was starting to break.

"You might be next," Margit said. "Especially if you don't help us."

"I've thought about that."

"Aren't you afraid?"

Ingmar von Hahne looked back at them with a flash of emotion in his eyes that Thomas could not place. Resignation, or perhaps weariness. As if he found their questions tiring rather than threatening and could hardly make himself care anymore.

"Would you give us your fingerprints?" asked Thomas.

"Do I have to?"

"We believe it could be valuable in our investigation."

There was a long moment of silence.

Finally Ingmar von Hahne said, "I would like to speak to my lawyer before I answer any more questions."

CHAPTER 79

Nora grabbed the keys and walked with determination to the Brand house.

When she saw the beautiful roses covering the southern wall, she almost teared up. Signe cared about her roses as if they were animate beings. But no matter how much Nora tried, she did not have Signe's green thumb. If she hadn't called in one of Sandhamn's own rose experts for help, who knew what would have happened to this beautiful climber?

She unlocked the front door and went to the old veranda facing the sea. She sat in one of the tidy wicker armchairs and drew her legs up beneath her. She smiled at the sound of a moped driving by. She could hear the motor through the transom windows.

How would it feel to live here?

Nora closed her eyes and tried to imagine it. Each boy would have his own room upstairs. They would have to make do with the bathroom, even though it needed renovation. The kitchen was old-fashioned but functional. Some color and a new stove would work wonders. Perhaps she'd even be able to afford a dishwasher.

The beautiful furniture in the dining room would stay. So would the wicker furniture on the veranda, and Signe's white lace curtains. The room next to the dining room could become a TV room. And she could probably wallpaper the guest bathroom herself—small flowers in light gold, like a summer meadow.

Not exactly luxurious renovations, but they would do.

She opened her eyes and gazed across the water where gray clouds loomed over the horizon.

From the corner of her eye, she could see a neighbor watering his pots of geraniums.

So many times she'd sat right here chatting with Signe while her loyal Kajsa had slept on the striped rag rug. They'd drunk so many cups of coffee together from Signe's brown Höganäs mugs.

I wonder what Signe was thinking that last evening? Nora wondered. The thought made her sad. *Did she have regrets, or did she feel she was doing the right thing? As if taking her own life could make up for her past actions?*

Nora never imagined she would miss Signe so much. But when she returned to Sandhamn and was standing in front of this silent, empty house, her grief nearly took her breath away.

She'd been close to Signe ever since she was a little girl. She couldn't fathom not seeing her again. Signe, who'd listened and comforted her through all kinds of problems, from a torn Optimist sail to a lost teenage love.

Aunt Signe, who had knitted tiny blue socks for both Adam and Simon. Summer after summer, she'd baked raspberry muffins for the boys.

Nora's eyes filled as she recalled how thoughtful Signe was, even as she contemplated her own death. She suddenly understood how important it was to respect Signe's last wish.

She made her decision.

Why did he never leave her?

He asked himself that question many times. Turned it over and over in his mind. Analyzed the consequences.

The children. It always came back to the children.

In spite of the fact that their mother had driven a wedge between them, he could not leave his children. He would not force them through a divorce with all the gossip, the loose talk, the condemning looks, and the well-intended comments from friends and acquaintances.

He wasn't an ideal husband. Far from it. Over the years, he'd had affairs. But he'd always been discreet about them. Always discreet.

His wife probably did the same.

At least that wouldn't have surprised him. They hadn't been sexual with each other for so long. She'd likely gone elsewhere to fulfill her needs, but she would also be discreet and follow the unspoken rules.

Truth be told, he didn't care one way or another about her affairs.

With his newest love, however, everything had been different. It brought out something in him, something he'd thought long dead. He felt young and alive again, filled with energy and enthusiasm. He began to hope for another kind of life.

Perhaps he could have a second chance. Should he leave her?

THURSDAY,
THE FIFTH WEEK

CHAPTER 80

The run-through had to be short. It was past five, and everyone in the room looked exhausted.

It had been a hectic week with no solution in sight. Two murders and no murderer in custody. The situation was stressful, to say the least.

Persson cleared his throat and silence fell, stifling small talk.

Thomas played with his pen, unable to concentrate. *Martin Nyrén.* He scribbled the name over and over. *Oscar Juliander. General Mind.* He soon filled his entire page.

"So what do we do with von Hahne?" asked Persson.

Margit sighed deeply.

"Not enough to hold him on yet," she said. "And now he's giving us the cold shoulder. He won't volunteer anything."

"Any technical evidence?"

"We confronted him with the phone lists, and he's provided a logical explanation for the calls and messages. The only light at the end of the tunnel now is gaining access to Nyrén's computer. That should happen tomorrow. That could lead to something."

"What about Nyrén's phone? Did it get fixed?"

"No. The fall broke it completely. It's dead."

Thomas drew in a breath. So simple and yet so hard to see. He started writing again.

Persson gave him an irritated look. "Are you too busy to listen to what we're saying?" he said to Thomas. "Or perhaps you have something to share?"

Thomas looked up.

"It's an anagram."

"What?" Persson said.

"What do you have?" Margit asked him abruptly.

"The name of the Swan. It's an anagram. He's rearranged the letters. If you had any doubt he got the money from that American company, put your minds at ease." Thomas started to laugh.

"What's so funny?" Margit sounded impatient.

"*Emerald Gin*, General Mind. The name of Juliander's boat was an anagram! He christened his boat after the company that financed it!"

He now chuckled so hard he could barely speak. "What a jokester! What a sense of humor!"

Little by little, the laughter spread around the room. Even the prosecutor smiled.

The laughter brought relief and lightened everyone's mood.

"So, anything new on a possible connection between Nyrén and Juliander?" Persson asked. He got the discussion back on track.

"Nothing beyond the RSYC," Thomas said. "No illicit income. Nyrén had few possessions. Just the apartment and the boat. He was a government employee and lived on his salary. An inheritance from his parents paid for his boat."

"So now where are we?" Persson interlaced his fingers behind his head and looked at the prosecutor.

Charlotte Öhman's conservative outfit differed from the detectives' more casual clothes. Her gray jacket and white blouse showed she came from the legal side of law enforcement. But she was a good prosecutor, and not at all formal. She allowed the police do their jobs without interference unless she felt it necessary.

"I think we should go over von Hahne's house," Thomas said. "If we toss his place, he might break down a little."

"But what if he doesn't?" asked Charlotte Öhman.

"We have no other suspects," Thomas said. He still believed the aristocrat was hiding something.

"Many things point to him," Erik said. "Nyrén was shot from his storage room. We have the telephone records. He had a motive for killing Juliander."

"Becoming chairman of the RSYC is not much of a motive," Öhman said.

"It's still possible," Thomas insisted.

"But he has a good alibi. Have you forgotten?"

Thomas stood up abruptly. He walked to the enlargement of the race's start still fastened to the wall. How much time had he spent staring at it?

Now he took the magnifying glass as close to the *Emerald Gin* as he could.

Everyone in the room was silent.

"I wonder," he said. "Did we make a mistake when we eliminated all the passengers on Bjärring's boat?"

"They gave each other alibis," Margit said.

"But could the shot have been fired from the Storebro?" Thomas asked. "Could von Hahne have sneaked into the forepeak to shoot with no one else noticing?"

Margit followed his reasoning.

"We've taken for granted that the entire company stayed together the whole time. But did the witnesses convince themselves they'd all seen the same thing? Could it be they didn't notice someone missing for a few seconds?"

"In that case, von Hahne's alibi could be in doubt."

Thomas sat down again and leaned back against his chair, still staring at the enlargement.

"We should bring him in," he said.

"The evidence is still too thin to arrest him," the prosecutor said. "And please remember that I need three days to file a detention order, especially with so little to go on."

Almost against his will, Thomas agreed.

If they arrested von Hahne without permission from the court, they'd look like idiots. In addition, the media would go ballistic because the news concerned the future RSYC chairman.

"Could we do a house search at least?" Thomas asked. "I really think this might break him. And we should also question his entire family."

Charlotte Öhman looked thoughtful for a moment. Then she made up her mind.

"Let's see what we find on the computer first," she said. "I'm sorry, but you don't have enough cause."

The meeting concluded.

"Svante Severin."

The real-estate agent picked up on the first ring, possibly because he recognized her phone number. All the Sandhamn numbers started with the same five numbers.

"Nora Linde here." She didn't waste any time with small talk. She simply wanted to give him her answer.

"Nice to hear from you," Svante Severin said.

"I'm calling to tell you the Brand house is not for sale. We are going to keep it."

"But . . . but . . . ," Severin stammered.

His disappointment was so apparent that Nora could almost feel it.

"Why did you change your mind?" he asked.

Nora pitied him for a minute. Then she decided to end the conversation.

"I'm sorry," she said. "The family couldn't agree. The house is not for sale now, and it will not be for sale in the future."

She quickly said good-bye and ended the call.

So easy. She'd stewed over this call so long, anxious about how to make it.

To her surprise, she felt peaceful despite the fact that Henrik would arrive in the evening and she'd not discussed this decision with him.

It had simply become obvious what she should do. The topic was now closed for discussion.

She was going to keep the Brand house whether Henrik agreed or not. That's what was going to happen.

Chapter 81

Everyone but Thomas had already left the police station. He knew he should go home, too, but he'd lost so much time while out sick. He needed to get caught up, collect his thoughts, and go through the materials in peace and quiet.

Not to mention the mountain of paperwork. He hadn't sorted his mail for an eternity.

With a sigh, he headed toward the mailbox slots near the door.

Some friendly soul had left a box of chocolate by the coffee machine. Probably Carina. She always did things like that.

He felt guilty immediately.

He hadn't seen her since the evening they'd argued—a while ago now. Time had flown, mostly because he was out with his cold. Plus he found it easy to ignore his private problems by concentrating on work.

He knew he had to deal with the issue. She deserved to know how he felt, even if she wasn't going to like it. He didn't think they should see each other anymore. At least, not for a while.

Guilt overwhelmed him. He should have known from the very beginning that they weren't a good fit. He was one year shy of forty. Almost all his friends were married and having children. How he longed to hold a newborn in his arms again. But Carina was focused on a career in law enforcement. She might even go back to school to further that dream. They were in different phases of life.

He'd had trouble resisting Carina's desire at first. The fact that she so clearly wanted him was intoxicating. Right from the start they'd enjoyed good sex. Really good sex. Something he'd been missing since his separation. The sex was so good that he thought it might be enough to make the relationship fulfilling.

But once the novelty wore off, he could see how much they differed. Carina was a sweet, smart girl, but she couldn't share his sorrow over Emily. The only person who could understand that was Pernilla. Sometimes it was difficult not to talk about his daughter with Carina, which created a bigger gulf between them. When she wanted to go out on the town during the weekends, he'd make excuses.

More and more, he escaped to Harö to be in peace. He felt ashamed that he'd used Carina that way. He'd enjoyed what she offered without any consideration for her feelings.

It was simply easier that way. He had longed to be with someone, anyone, but lacked the energy to search for a partner. And then she came along, offering him everything. He couldn't resist.

And now it had to end. He felt guilty, and she was unhappy.

Again, he swore to settle the matter. As soon as they found the person who'd killed Juliander and Nyrén. After that, he would talk to her.

Chapter 82

"Have you lost your mind?" Henrik said. He stared at Nora with dismay and disgust in his eyes. "You really told Severin we aren't going to sell without even talking to me first?"

They sat on the dock with their coffee.

Henrik had come on the six o'clock ferry from Stavsnäs. After a number of days on call, he now had three days off. Nora had dinner ready when he arrived, so they'd eaten right away.

She hadn't put much thought into dinner. She served grilled steak with baked potatoes and carrots. Then she gave the boys ice cream pops while she made coffee for Henrik and herself.

Now Simon was at a friend's house playing a new computer game, while Adam had left to play soccer with some older boys.

It was the perfect time for a married couple who hadn't seen each other for the past two weeks to sit down and talk.

As usual Nora had butterflies in her stomach before they began. She hoped he could understand her decision and why she had come to it.

Did he truly love her enough to listen? It was just a house, after all, a material object, nothing as serious as an illness or a hurt child.

She fumbled her words, trying to explain once again how she felt. How Signe's gift should be preserved for future generations. How the responsibility of Signe's will was both a burden and a blessing.

Finally she told him she'd called Severin and given him her decision. Then she waited for his reaction.

It didn't take long. Henrik turned red with rage.

"How could you? We could have gotten millions for that house! Millions! Don't you get it?" he yelled at her. "We could have gotten out of the town house! Bought a real house! How stupid can you be? Call Severin at once and tell him we've changed our minds. Perhaps he can still persuade those Swiss people to buy, in spite of everything!"

He banged his fist on the table. The coffee cups jumped in their saucers.

Nora looked at him in dismay. Again, he hadn't heard a word she'd said. The father of her children cared only about money and possessions. What had happened to him?

The next thing she felt surprised her: she didn't really care. As this calm detachment came over her, she wondered how to respond. To buy time, she brought the cup to her lips and took a few sips.

"Are you listening to me?" Henrik screamed. He leaned over the table, leaving only a few inches between their faces.

It felt like looking at a stranger, a stranger who moved and spoke like the Henrik she'd fallen in love with. But he'd become someone far from the kind of man she wanted to live with anymore.

"I heard you." She remained calm and looked him in the eye. "I will not change my mind. My decision is final. It was Aunt Signe's wish that I have the house, and I intend to keep it."

"You're a complete idiot!" Henrik said.

"No, I think *you* are!" Now she grew angry, too. "I've had enough!" she yelled. "I am done walking on eggshells trying to keep you happy! And your damned mother, too. I know where you got all this. From Monica! She's the one who wants us to move, isn't she?"

Henrik jumped as if she'd stabbed him with a needle.

"Keep my mother out of this! She has nothing to do with it!"

"She's always got her nose in our business! I am sick to death of her snide comments. Nothing I ever do is good enough for *her*. No matter what, she wants things *her* way! And all these dire warnings about how the boys are raised . . . if I never see her again, it will be too soon!"

Suddenly Nora felt her face growing hot.

"I have no idea what you're going on about. My mother has always supported us. You have to listen to me!"

A laugh escaped Nora. Supported them? Monica Linde?

When it came to his mother, Henrik was so blind she saw no way to reach him. Her mother-in-law was a nightmare, and everyone except her own son knew it.

Nora took a deep breath to regain her composure. Then she looked her husband in the eye and slowly said, "I do not intend to sell Aunt Signe's house. No matter what you say. Are *you* listening to me?"

The blow surprised them both.

Henrik's hand flew up and smacked her left cheek. She remained totally still, her eyes wide open, staring at him. The shock kept her from feeling the pain at first. After a moment, her cheek began to hurt, and she tasted blood in her mouth.

Henrik sat paralyzed before her.

A wave of sorrow came over her. What were they doing? Thank God the boys weren't here.

"I had no idea you were the kind of man who would beat his wife over money," she said.

Her steady voice and her self-control surprised her.

Henrik said nothing at all.

She used a napkin to blot the corner of her mouth. It wasn't much, but the red stood out on the white paper. She folded the napkin so the spots of blood were not visible and put it back down.

Henrik still hadn't said a word.

Nora felt heavy as lead.

"I'm going to pick up the boys and get them ready for bed," she said. It took a great effort to speak.

The petrified statue that had been her husband came to life. He seemed totally confused, as if he had no idea what to do.

"I'm sorry, Nora," he said. "Please forgive me . . . I don't know what came over me." Henrik touched her arm.

Nora remembered how last summer they'd argued about her job offer from Malmö. He'd gotten angry and walked out, leaving her standing there with tears in her eyes, begging him to stay.

Now their roles were reversed, a thought that did not make her feel any better.

With a last glance at the ferry glistening in the sunset, Nora got up.

"You can do whatever you want," she said. "I'll sleep on the guest bed in the boys' room tonight. Go home to your mother if you don't want to stay here."

She hadn't intended to say that last bitter sentence, but it slipped out anyway. Years of resentment paved the way.

"Actually I think it would be better if you left Sandhamn," she added. "I think we need to be apart for now."

She picked up the coffee tray and headed back to the house.

CHAPTER 83

It was almost nine p.m. Thomas yawned, happy to find he'd finished nearly all the forms and the reports hanging over his head. He'd gone through that stack of mail as well. Only one thick envelope remained.

The address was handwritten in neat printing. He turned it over. The return address read *B. Rosensjöö*.

Thomas frowned, checked the envelope again, and then picked up the scissors to cut it open. A pile of photographs spilled out along with a letter from Britta Rosensjöö. She'd found her camera at the harbor office in Sandhamn, at the lost and found. She'd probably set it down somewhere when they came back to port the day Juliander was killed. In all the excitement, she'd forgotten where she'd left it. Some kind person had turned it in to the lost and found, and she'd eventually thought to check there.

She included all her photographs from the start of the Round Gotland Race.

Thomas tried to recall Britta's words in that Sandhamn interview right after the killing. She told him she'd taken photos that day but also that she'd misplaced her camera. They'd agreed she should keep searching and that she'd let him know if she found it. He'd forgotten.

Bad police work on my part, he thought. He should have remembered to follow up. Luckily Britta was not as forgetful.

He rubbed his eyes and shuffled through the photos: thirty-six in all. He recalled that thirty-six used to be standard on an old-fashioned roll of film.

The photos could be divided into two categories: one showing the boats on the starting line from different angles and the other of the people aboard her boat.

A number of pictures captured the von Hahne couple, the Bjärring family, Sylvia Juliander, and, of course, Hans Rosensjöö. In one of the photos, Britta stood beside her husband, but otherwise she was absent from the pictures. Not strange, considering she was the photographer.

Thomas looked for other views of the vessels carrying spectators, but he found nothing special in any of them. The TV coverage had served the same purpose.

Typical vacation pictures. Beautiful scenery and smiling people. They revealed nothing new.

He shoved the photos back into the envelope and set them aside. He was worn out, ready for home and bed.

FRIDAY,
THE FIFTH WEEK

CHAPTER 84

The sun shining through a gap between the window shade and the sill woke Thomas up at six a.m. His two-room Gustavsberg apartment had one obvious advantage—it was light and sunny.

He hadn't gotten to bed until midnight. On the way home he bought a calzone at Gustavsberg Center's pizzeria. At home he drank a cold beer and ate the calzone while watching TV.

An old Clint Eastwood movie on Channel 2 caught his attention. Once it was over, he turned in. But he had trouble falling asleep and then had strange dreams about the investigation—Britta Rosensjöö's photos flickered like flames in his mind.

His guilt about Carina troubled him, too.

Now his eyes blinked open and he realized he would get no more sleep. He might as well get up and go into work.

Thomas was at his desk by seven thirty. His office felt pleasantly cool, and he took his time spreading out the contents of Britta Rosensjöö's envelope.

His subconscious nagged at him. He had missed something.

He focused on the photographs again. Yesterday evening he'd been too tired to note the time stamp on the corners. Now he could see exactly when they were taken. He sorted them by time.

The photographs started at eleven thirty in the morning, about an hour before the race began. The last was at thirteen minutes past twelve, just before Bjärring moved his boat next to Thomas's police boat.

He kept studying them, searching for a clue.

And then he saw it, clear as day.

Now he understood why Britta Rosensjöö's hotel room had been broken into—for the camera.

Britta had taken pictures at regular intervals during the half hour before the start of the race. Everyone on board was photographed. Even Britta was in one photo. But between 11:57 and 12:03, one passenger went missing. One person they could now prove had not been with the others the moment Juliander had been shot.

Six minutes.

Long enough to go to the forepeak, assemble the rifle, open the hatch, and fire off the killing shot. From a perfect position, too, thanks to an experienced skipper who wanted to give his friends the best view of the starting line.

Thomas felt his pulse speed up.

He now had the evidence they needed in his hand.

He picked up his phone to call Margit. He hoped she was already on her way into the station.

CHAPTER 85

"Do you think they'll be up this early in the morning in August?" Margit asked.

Thomas concentrated on navigating the crisscross of one-way streets through Östermalm.

"Whoever designed this street layout was a complete idiot," he muttered as he circled Karlaplan the third time in search of the right street.

"Do you think they're even in town?" Margit asked. "They might be out in the country."

"What?" Thomas ignored a "Do Not Enter" sign and turned down the street where the von Hahne couple lived.

He parked the car, and they walked quickly up the stairs. They rang the bell several times, and a young girl in a light-green robe finally answered. She looked like she'd just gotten out of bed, and stared at Margit and Thomas in confusion as they introduced themselves.

"Mom and Dad aren't home," she said in answer to their question. "They're out of town." She smiled in a friendly way.

This must be Emma, Margit thought. She resembled her father with her blond hair and clean features. Elegant and self-confident. But innocent, at least for now.

"Do you know where they are?" asked Margit.

"They're hunting on the Bjärring estate, not far from Katrineholm."

"Hunting?" Margit asked. "At this time of year? I thought hunting season didn't begin until September."

Emma let out a light laugh.

"They're hunting wild boar. That season is year-round. It's their tradition to hunt during the day and hold a crayfish party at night."

"When did they leave?" Thomas asked.

"Yesterday. They'll be home on Sunday."

"Are there any other RSYC board members there?"

"Sure. They always hang out together."

Thomas frowned, and Margit understood his concern.

A killer with a rifle in the forest. Not good. Who was next on the list?

"Do you have an address or a telephone number for the Bjärring estate?" Margit asked.

Emma shook her head, but then her face lit up.

"Wait. I can check Mama's address book in the study if you want. I've been out there myself lots of times, but I can't remember exactly where it is."

"Please. We'd be grateful."

Emma went back into the apartment while Thomas and Margit waited in the large entryway. It was a typical apartment for the area. High ceilings, beautiful mirrored doors, elegant sconces on the walls along with a number of framed paintings. A reminder this was the home of an art dealer.

To the right, they could see a room with bookshelves covering the walls and oxblood leather armchairs arranged before them. An oriental rug in warm red tones covered the floor.

Margit took it all in: the fireplace nearby, invitations with gold lettering set on a silver plate on the mantle.

A few minutes later, Emma came back with a handwritten note. She held it out to Thomas.

"Here's the address."

"Thanks very much," Thomas said. Without wasting another moment, he turned to go.

"Wait," Emma said. "Sorry for asking, but has something happened?" She watched them nervously. "I mean, there's been so much going on lately . . ."

Margit tried to give a reassuring smile.

"Don't worry," she said, hearing the false notes in her voice. She didn't want to worry the girl. "We've got some more questions for your parents, that's all."

She must have sounded convincing, because the girl smiled politely and explained she just wanted to make sure. As they went down the steps, she said good-bye and closed the door behind them.

Thomas glanced anxiously at his watch. It would take at least an hour and a half to drive to Katrineholm, even longer if they got stuck in rush-hour traffic.

Enough time for another RSYC board member to die.

Enough time to make all their work fruitless.

"Should we call ahead to alert the local police?" asked Margit.

Thomas shook his head, though it went against his instincts.

"We'll put a stop to this ourselves."

Thomas couldn't drive them there quickly enough. He grew more frustrated with every passing minute. He took Essinge highway, past Kungens Kurva, Huddinge, Södertälje, Nyköping—speeding all the way in the left lane.

Margit popped one stick of gum after another, chewing furiously, watching the clock on the instrument panel. They couldn't allow another shooting. They had to get there first this time.

* * *

Finally they turned off the highway and continued until they saw a sign marking a private drive lined by oak trees. The road led up to a manor house.

Bjärringsgård was an old estate from the eighteenth century, with two wings on either side, painted yellow with white trim.

Thomas stopped on a circular driveway in front of the house. They jogged up and pushed the doorbell. The old-fashioned chime rang through the house.

Nothing happened.

Thomas rang the bell again. After a long interval, a gray-haired middle-aged woman wearing a white apron opened the door.

She looked at them quizzically.

"We're from the police. We're looking for the von Hahnes," Thomas said. He held up his ID.

The woman shook her head.

"I'm sorry. I'm the only one in the house right now. They're all in the forest and won't be back until five."

Thomas shifted his weight impatiently.

"We must find them as soon as we can," he explained. "Do you have any idea where they are right now?"

"The hunting party will break for lunch at eleven thirty," she said. "You can go along to the meadow there and wait for them."

She explained how to locate the spot. "It's about fifteen minutes from here by car. Not that far away, but the road is bad."

Then she excused herself, explaining she had to continue preparing the evening dinner.

"There's a lot to do," she said. "It's a dinner for twenty."

It was not difficult to follow her instructions.

They drove back down the driveway and onto the highway.

"Take it easy," Margit said as Thomas took a curve at high speed. "Ending up in a ditch will slow us down."

Thomas let up only a little.

"Don't you think we need backup now?" she added.

Thomas shook his head. "We're almost there."

After four weeks of intense investigation, he didn't want to wait for backup. They were so close. Just a few more minutes.

Thomas turned off the highway onto a forest trail. They bumped along for a few miles until it opened into a parking area. Other cars were there. Thomas parked their Volvo alongside a red BMW, and they got out. In the distance, they heard voices.

"There they are," Margit said. "Let's go."

They followed the sound a few hundred yards until the trees opened up. Simple wooden benches formed a square. Thomas spotted Axel Bjärring talking with a man he didn't know and Ingmar von Hahne emerging from the forest with a rifle over his shoulder. He looked dapper as ever. But his expression was overcast. He seemed weighed down.

From another direction, Isabelle von Hahne also stepped from the forest, about fifty yards away.

Thomas and Margit walked forward. Axel Bjärring looked up and frowned when he recognized the police officers. He excused himself and started in their direction.

Isabelle looked down at first. When she caught sight of them, she startled and then stood stock still, her rifle broken open and loose under her arm.

Thomas walked faster, Margit following two steps back. Now Ingmar von Hahne saw them and, unlike his wife, came to meet them.

Thomas marched steadily toward his goal.

Isabelle von Hahne dropped her rifle, ducked under a branch, and ran back into the forest.

"Don't let her get away!" Thomas yelled. He and Margit broke into a run.

Chapter 86

Isabelle ran as she'd never run before.

Branches with pinecones hit her face. As she forced her way through a wild rose bush, thorns raked her skin. She stumbled over a rock but recovered her balance at the last second.

With a leap, she cleared a narrow tree trunk and ran through a thicket of birch saplings. The heavy hunting jacket was impeding her, and she pulled it off as she ran, letting it fall into some heather.

Sweat streamed down her face and into her eyes. Irritated, she wiped her forehead with the back of her hand.

The only sound she could hear was her own breathing. She worried about all the other noises she was making—the breaking of twigs, the cracking of branches—all revealing her location.

The voices behind her grew fainter. She dared to glance back—she could see nothing through the vegetation.

Adrenaline pumped through her. Her head throbbed, the beats heavy and loud as pistol shots.

Lactic acid was building up in her muscles, but she forced her legs to keep running. They moved with only one goal—to escape her pursuers.

* * *

William Aldecrantz glanced at his watch.

It was time to break for lunch and join the rest of the hunting party. The horn had already sounded, calling them in, but he had hung back. He'd glimpsed a large male boar, slightly out of range, and he wanted to wait a few minutes in case it came back into sight.

He knew he couldn't be too late. Papa wouldn't be happy about that. He'd already been schooled in the importance of following the leader of the hunt. But William desperately wanted to get a boar this time.

He could already picture his return to the elite Lundsbergs boarding school. He'd impress his classmates with a story about taking down a wild boar all by himself.

His own hunting trophy.

When he'd received his first rifle on his eighteenth birthday, he'd thought it the best gift of his life. He'd felt like a man. He couldn't stop admiring his weapon.

It'd be so great to shoot the boar!

William looked nervously at his watch again. He had to give up this good position and get back to the others, or his father would really chew him out. Of that, he was certain.

"Which direction did she go?" Margit yelled.

The trees were close together, and it was hard to force her way through the brush. But Margit caught up to Thomas, who was focused.

"Stand still," he said. "We need to listen."

Margit froze. They heard the wind sighing in the trees.

"Which direction did she go?" Margit said.

"Shhh!" Thomas hissed.

He peered between the trunks, searching for movement. They'd already gone a good distance from the meadow.

One hundred fifty or so yards ahead, something in a thicket caught his eye. It fluttered among the greenery.

"There she is! Follow me!" he called. He and Margit took off again, as fast as they could.

Isabelle was panting; she couldn't catch her breath. She mustn't lose her orientation.

Dear God, *she prayed.* Get me out of this, and I'll never pray for another thing. Please don't let it end like this! Dear God!

Tears of frustration ran down her cheeks. Her jaw and fists tightened. She kept running.

She stumbled over a tree trunk and fell headfirst to the ground. Her nose was scraped and her chin cut open. Woozy, she got back up and leaned against a birch tree.

Blood was flowing from one nostril.

She looked around and tried to collect her thoughts.

There was a highway just beyond the stream ahead. If she could reach that, she could get away. She'd flag down a ride.

She tried to remember exactly where the stream flowed.

She moved several feet forward and then spotted the water through the trees.

Relief came over her. The stream would be her savior. It would wash away her scent so that, even if they sent bloodhounds after her, the water would confuse them. On the other side, she'd be safe.

She continued to make her way through the dense shrubbery solely on strength of will, step by step, her body exhausted.

The instinct for self-preservation was so strong her legs refused to give up.

She was breathing easier. She was almost there.

She saw the sun's reflection dancing on the water, showing her the way. She would make it.

A rustling sound startled William Aldecrantz. In the right square of his scope he saw branches and twigs moving. Something was heading his way, toward the water.

William rejoiced. The wild boar was back. What luck that he hadn't emptied his rifle yet. He was ready. His muscles tensed, and he half shut his eyes against the sun to see more clearly.

He quickly brought up his rifle.

Vegetation obscured his view, but he was sure the boar would rush into his sights any second. His heart was pounding in his chest. His mouth was dry, and he hardly dared to breathe.

As the shadow of the creature moved through the bushes, he took his shot.

Chapter 87

Thomas averted his face as he pushed through branches. He was following a small stream flowing through the forest. Though it was the middle of the day, it was surprisingly dark under the trees. The sunshine barely cut through the thick, looming treetops.

Margit was right at his heels. He could hear her labored breathing.

"Stop, Thomas! Stop!" she yelled. "Look there by the oaks!"

He jerked his head up.

Fifty yards in front of them was a large gray-black boar. The coarse bristles made it look like a creature from the Ice Age. They could tell it was a sow by the udders.

She looked angry.

"Hell," Thomas said. He halted and remained absolutely still.

An angry wild boar was dangerous. A sow separated from her piglets, even worse. Why had she shown up here, when they were in such a rush?

"Do you know anything about wild boars?" Margit whispered. She remained perfectly still, a few feet behind him. "They're pretty aggressive, aren't they? Don't they attack people?"

"Just don't move," he replied. "Maybe she'll go away."

Hope was all he could do. What did he know about wild boars? Could they kill a grown person? What would make them attack?

Margit and Thomas stood without speaking, like two Greek statues.

In the distance, they heard birds singing.

Sweat beaded on Thomas's brow. They didn't have time for this. Every missed second meant Isabelle got farther away.

The sow looked like she might weigh over two hundred pounds. Thomas was not sure his service revolver could even take her down if she attacked, but he released the safety just in case. It felt ridiculously small in his hand.

The sow stared at them with tiny, deep-set eyes, and her short, bristly ears stuck straight up.

A few minutes went by. Margit and Thomas waited. Then they heard something stir behind the trees.

Three small piglets trotted out from underneath a bush. The sow made a deep, guttural sound and led them away.

Thomas exhaled deeply. He wiped his face with the sleeve of his jacket. Margit let out a low whistle and leaned on a tree for support.

"Yowsa," she said. "That was scary."

"Can you hear any sign of Isabelle?" Thomas asked. He listened carefully to the forest.

Suddenly they heard a shot go off.

It was close by. Their choice was simple.

"That way!" Thomas yelled as they crashed on in the direction of the discharge.

CHAPTER 88

The shot had come from nowhere and must have hit her, although, strangely, it didn't hurt. Her left hip felt numb, as if a fist had struck her with violent power. But it didn't hurt.

She'd fallen to the ground and couldn't get back up. She lay on pine needles hidden beneath thick branches.

She gingerly touched the numb area. Her fingers came away wet, and there was warm liquid on her hand.

She was injured.

Bitter tears filled her eyes. If only she hadn't run. They couldn't have proven a thing. She'd carefully eliminated all the evidence. Everything damaging was gone.

But the moment she'd seen that policeman, Andreasson, she'd lost control. In a wild panic, she'd run.

Idiotic. So damned unnecessary. How could she be so stupid?

She shifted slightly to make herself more comfortable. They wouldn't get her. Nobody would. She'd find her way to her sister in Switzerland. She'd be safe there. Her father's money was in a trust in that Alpine country. It would be enough to build a new life.

She smiled slightly at the memory of her father, her strong, clever father. He'd understood years ago that the family fortune had to be moved away from the Swedish tax authorities. Daddy had taken care of his girl—he always had.

First, though, she'd just rest here in the forest. She'd gather her strength. Then she'd go on. She rested her cheek against the moss and pine needles and closed her eyes.

It had been so easy, so surprisingly easy, to shoot that pompous Oscar. And so absolutely necessary.

She'd felt enormous satisfaction when she'd accomplished that. He'd rejected her, too, many years ago, but she'd gotten her revenge. Too many unjust actions.

She'd chosen a moment when he'd feel invincible to give him exactly what he deserved.

A wave of nausea ran through her body. She tried to shift positions again. She didn't feel her blood seeping out as quickly anymore. That was good. She'd lie there a moment longer, then she'd get up and leave this god-forsaken country forever.

She regretted that her plans had gone haywire when she'd been so close. She'd longed to be the wife of the RSYC chairman. She would have met the king and queen and would have sat next to the king when the royals attended the club's parties. She could imagine her photo on the society pages in the newspapers.

She was more than ready to assume that role.

Actually it was she who should have been made chairperson. Neither Oscar nor Ingmar could match her energy or creativity. She was a good leader and an outstanding organizer.

But it wasn't allowed, of course. A woman running such a traditional club? That would never do. The idea would have shaken the entire RSYC Board to the core. They reminded her of her own father in that way. He'd spent a fortune on her private school in Switzerland, where she'd learned home economics, but he could not have imagined she might want a career of her own. Her duty was to get married and have children.

And then Ingmar had come along. Fine, proper, weak Ingmar with all his aristocratic connections.

She'd tried to set an easy path for him using those social connections. She'd encouraged him to put his time and energy into the RSYC. She'd brought him to the threshold of the chairmanship. She'd supported him, attended dinner parties and events, and made sure he met the right people. And she'd eliminated Oscar.

Oscar's death was so very advantageous.

But what kind of thanks had she gotten? Ingmar had cheated on her. Not with just anyone either. A dumb blonde she could have handled. She would even have respected him for finding the balls to have an affair. She'd certainly had her share of men over the years—her husband hadn't satisfied her needs in ages.

But this. This would have brought them down, destroyed their entire social position and everything she'd fought for. She would never have been able to show her face again.

And now it was all over.

A tear of anger and frustration trickled down her cheek. It had been so close—everything she'd dreamed of for years.

She heard voices.

Using all her strength, Isabelle got to her feet, her body struggling to obey her. One hand covered her wound, and the other clung to a branch. She wanted to get out of there. But there was no point anymore. She didn't have the strength. Struggling for breath, she sank back to the forest floor.

The voices were close now. She didn't care. Calm spread over her. She felt no pain, but she was dizzy and weak. Light flickered in her eyes, and her body felt as if it were falling as her head rested peacefully on the moss. Was she going to die here next to this pine tree? The idea didn't scare her. She was content, in spite of everything. She'd been in charge the whole time. Oscar had had his triumph stolen. Martin had gotten what he'd deserved.

Isabelle smiled as she slipped into unconsciousness. The last thing she heard was a man's voice.

"Here she is! I found her!"

SUNDAY,
THE FIFTH WEEK

CHAPTER 89

Nora was curled up in a wicker chair on the veranda, playing Monopoly with her sons. Bit by bit, Adam bought all the expensive properties. She and Simon were definitely losing.

When the game ended, she gave the boys money to go buy ice cream. They thanked her, clutched their twenty-krona notes, and pedaled off on their bikes.

Yesterday evening Henrik had left a message on her phone.

"We can't go on like this," he said. "Call me. We have to talk. Please."

He sounded unhappy, like he wanted to reconcile. He sounded on the verge of tears.

He was right: she *should* call back. For the sake of the children if nothing else.

She dialed his number.

The call went through.

"Henrik Linde."

"It's me."

"Wait a minute. I'm in the middle of rounds. Let me walk away . . ."

He must really want to talk to her—he never took any of her calls in the middle of rounds.

"Nora." He paused. "I am so very sorry. I still don't know what came over me. I regret it so much."

"I see."

What was she supposed to say?

That she had never, in her wildest dreams, imagined he'd hit her? That his actions had destroyed a part of their marriage forever?

That the pain on her cheek was nothing compared to the pain in her heart?

That she was ready to leave him?

"Can you forgive me? We have to work this out. Think about the boys. I miss all of you so much."

She thought of their sons, their tanned faces and expectant smiles. Their questions about when their father was coming back.

"I'll never do it again, Nora, I swear. I'll do what you want, exactly what you want. But think about the boys. Our boys. The three of you mean everything to me. You have to understand."

Tears burned in her eyes. Adam and Simon. They loved their father so much.

They hadn't seen him in days.

"Nora," he said.

He sounded younger on the phone, more like the man she'd met an eternity ago when they were students and crazy, breathlessly in love with each other.

"I was so angry and confused. It's like someone else took over. I'm not really like that. You know me."

She touched her cheek lightly. It was no longer tender, but a bruise of many colors had bloomed.

She told her parents she'd walked into a doorway. Such a lame excuse.

A husband should never hit his wife, she thought. *A woman must leave after the first blow. You don't remain in a marriage where the husband resorts to violence.*

"Darling, we have to put this behind us and go forward. I love you. You know I do." He sounded like he might cry. "Can you forgive me? Please?"

Chapter 90

Thomas nodded at the uniformed officer stationed on a bench beside the hospital room. He and Margit stepped inside.

It was a standard room, the only splash of color coming from the orange government-issue blanket folded across the foot of the bed.

Margit and Thomas regarded the woman lying there. Her head was turned away, and she had an IV in her left arm. She looked exhausted, but her firm expression did not soften.

Isabelle von Hahne had expected they would come. She knew Ingmar would not.

"Do you understand why we're here?" Thomas asked. "We want to talk to you about the murders of Oscar Juliander and Martin Nyrén."

She nodded.

"Can you tell us what happened?"

She nodded again but said nothing.

Thomas pulled a chair from the wall and sat down. Margit did the same.

He got straight to the point.

"You were the one who shot Oscar Juliander and Martin Nyrén, weren't you?"

"Yes, I did." Isabelle's voice was quiet.

"Why?"

She remembered the night she'd met Oscar at the Midsummer's Eve party. She'd gone outside for some fresh air and stumbled upon him in a dark corner near the boathouse.

"I saw him doing cocaine! At a party . . ."

Before she could say a word, he'd attacked her, lightning fast, as she stared at the small mound of white powder.

"He threatened me," Isabelle said softly.

"With what?"

"If I didn't keep his drug use secret, he'd reveal something about my husband."

"What did he threaten to expose?" asked Margit.

Isabelle clenched her jaw. She had difficulty even saying the words.

"Ingmar had a relationship with Martin Nyrén."

Margit and Thomas exchanged looks.

Isabelle shuddered. She'd almost vomited when Oscar had told her. Of course, she'd suspected for some time that Ingmar was seeing someone. But never that the affair was with a man! Never would she have suspected that Martin Nyrén, that dumpy middle-aged member of the RSYC Board, was his lover.

The knowledge disgusted her. Thinking about them naked together made her want to throw up.

After a pause, Margit said, "Please continue."

"I begged Oscar not to do it." She was silent for a moment. "Revealing their affair would have destroyed my life. I would have become a laughingstock. Everybody would snicker behind my back."

She spit out the words.

"Martin and Ingmar! How disgusting. Unnatural."

Ingmar had betrayed her in the worst possible way. In addition, he had been so indiscreet that Oscar had known about it.

A double betrayal.

"And what did Oscar say?"

"He promised to keep quiet. And I promised to do the same."

"Did you trust him?" asked Margit.

Isabelle said nothing for a moment.

She'd humbled herself. Begged Oscar not to tell the truth to anyone. He'd promised, but she knew what Oscar's promises were worth, especially around women. She knew Oscar might say something in the heat of passion and then go on his way when desire lured him in a different direction.

It had been only a matter of time until Oscar, knowingly or not, would spill the secret.

"No," she said at last.

"What did you do then?"

"I tried to find a way out."

She didn't sleep for nights in a row. She worried herself crazy over what to do, debating various solutions, but she kept coming back to the same answer. Oscar had to die.

"So you decided to kill him?" asked Thomas.

"Yes."

There was nothing else to do. It took her only four more days to figure out how. She headed out that Wednesday.

"How did you get the rifle?"

"I went to Riga. It's easy to get weapons there."

"How did you know to do that?" asked Margit.

"I hunt a great deal, you see. I'm a good shot. Much better than my husband. When we have dinner after a hunt, people often talk about ways to get guns cheaply."

She shrugged a shoulder, and the IV tugged at her arm.

"So, how did you get the rifle into Sweden?" Thomas asked.

"I just brought it with me in my car. Nobody checks a well-dressed Swedish woman coming back into her country on the ferry."

"Where is it now?"

"I buried it in the forest next to our summer place."

She reached for a glass of water on the bedside table, but the movement seemed to hurt. Thomas pushed the glass closer to her. She took it, drank, and put it back down.

"How did you plan out Juliander's death?" asked Margit.

"I pretended I had to go to the bathroom just before the start. There is only one, by the forepeak."

"And you fired from there?" Thomas asked.

"I put the rifle together, opened the hatch, and then all I had to do was push the barrel out and shoot."

The Swan was only sixty yards away. Oscar had stood behind the steering wheel, as confident as ever. She was in the perfect position. Axel was a master at maneuvering his Storebro close to the starting line to give his guests the best view.

"It wasn't a difficult shot. I've hunted for years."

"And then what did you do?"

"I took apart the rifle and put everything back in my bag. I returned to the flybridge a few minutes later."

"Weren't you worried that someone would notice?"

Isabelle shook her head.

"Everyone was so focused on the start. And afterward, they were so shocked. In addition"—she smiled slightly—"they were sure I was with them the whole time. I also commented afterward about how I'd been there. Have you ever watched *CSI*? People remember what you tell them."

"You planned it so well," Margit remarked.

"I'm good at planning."

"But why did you pick the start of the Round Gotland Race? Didn't that make things more difficult for you?"

"In his moment of triumph, you mean?"

"Some might see it like that," Margit agreed.

"Because I wanted to. He deserved to die at the moment when he could almost touch his heart's desire." She smiled.

"You were the person who broke into Britta's room to steal her camera, right?" Thomas asked.

Isabelle nodded. "Yes, but I didn't find it."

"She'd misplaced it, set it down somewhere, and found it later at the harbor office lost and found."

"So I heard."

"Why did you kill Martin Nyrén?"

"You don't understand?"

After discovering those disgusting texts to Ingmar, she knew Martin's death was necessary. She could tolerate no more. She wasn't safe as long as Martin lived. If Ingmar was careless, his affair might still be exposed. And if Ingmar ever decided to leave her for Martin . . . she couldn't risk it. All would be lost.

A primitive hate carried her through, though he'd never injured her the way she would injure him. She took his life.

"He didn't deserve to live," she said.

"You mean, you couldn't risk his relationship with your husband coming out," Margit said. "He was a threat to you."

Isabelle didn't bother to answer.

"How did you do it this time?" asked Thomas.

She took a few more sips of water.

"I made copies of Ingmar's keys to the storage room. He never noticed. I did the same with keys to Martin's apartment."

She realized then why Ingmar had chosen the location for his storage area in Birkastan. She'd always thought it too far from the gallery on Strandvägen.

He wanted to be near Birkastan to meet Martin. A pathetic excuse for a pathetic lover.

"And so you shot him, too."

"Yes."

"Didn't you ever think that using Ingmar's rented space would turn our attentions to him?"

Isabelle's heart pounded.

"It's what he deserved! And I thought you would never figure it out. You had no evidence. Ingmar would wonder for the rest of his life how it had happened!"

She sank back onto her pillow, drained of energy. "It felt like a certain kind of justice to shoot my husband's lover from his own property, without him ever knowing how it all happened."

He sat on a bench in the cemetery. Some finches twittered in the background, but he didn't hear them.

He stared at the fresh grave, which did not yet have a marker. Half-wilted flowers lay on top.

He stared at the grave, but his eyes did not see it. Instead he imagined Martin's face. His dear, familiar face. Ingmar knew each wrinkle, each laugh line.

He understood that Martin was not beneath that mound. It was just his earthly remains, his flesh without his spirit. It wasn't Martin, the man he'd loved so much.

Why had he wasted so much time?

First they'd loved each other from afar. Then they'd consummated their love in secret. What joy he'd felt then. He'd considered revealing their relationship and leaving Isabelle but worried about the reactions of the rest of the world. They'd condemn him if the truth came out. He hid behind his consideration for Isabelle and the children. He brought them up whenever Martin pushed for a decision.

Was this his punishment for not standing up for their relationship? He was too cowardly to step out into the open.

Now who would call him by his old nickname? Who would say it with love? The name from the days when he'd play cowboys and Indians as a boy. He'd loved being an Indian and wearing feathers in his hair. His friends had called him the Indian, Indi for short.

Now "Indi" was gone, leaving only Ingmar behind. Cowardly, unhappy Ingmar, who'd lost the only person he ever truly loved.

What would he do now?

He touched the wedding band on his finger, a ring representing thirty years of unhappy marriage. He still wore it, though his wife had killed his beloved. How traditional.

He pulled off the ring and threw it into the bushes.

"You are the love of my life," he whispered. He lowered his eyes to the mound of earth at his feet. "I will always love you, Martin. Always."

CHAPTER 91

Eva Timell fastened her seat belt and smiled at the cute flight attendant who offered her a drink from a tray.

She took a glass of champagne and slowly sipped it. The fresh, dry drink tasted harsh on her tongue, just as it should.

Who was the one who said champagne should be cold, dry, and free? Was it Churchill or was it de Gaulle? Either way, they were wise words.

She lifted her glass in a silent toast to her cat, Blofeld, who sat in his carrier beside her. She was thankful for the latest EU regulations permitting vaccinated pets to travel between EU countries. She couldn't leave him behind in Sweden or quarantine him for six months.

The flight attendant asked if she wanted a refill. Eva shook her head, content for the moment.

Business class. She loved business class. It was extravagant, of course, but in Liechtenstein she had millions of reasons to indulge herself a little.

The banker she'd talked to had helped her book a meeting to transfer the account. Everyone *made* time to accommodate Frau Timell!

He even reminded her to bring the ten-digit code needed to access the account.

Aber natürlich, mein Herr. She'd remembered to bring it.

Oscar had been a wonderful bankruptcy attorney, but, in the long run, it had become impossible to hide anything from her. She had organized his life for decades and knew him better than his own mother.

Over the summer, she'd gone through all his cases to carefully archive his documents and files. The last thing she did was clean up his desk. It was as large and extravagant as Oscar. She'd carefully emptied all the drawers, finding a secret compartment so common in old desks. Oscar had shown it to her when he'd first brought it home from the auction house.

It stuck a bit, so she had to spring the hidden lever with a bread knife. Inside she found an envelope with foreign bank account papers. The bank's name was inscribed on the outside of the envelope.

The Internet revealed it was one of the largest banks in Liechtenstein, the same bank where the American company had sent payment for Olof Martinsson's patent. She appreciated the police officers who'd informed her of its existence.

Oscar, Oscar, she thought. *You gave in to temptation in the end. Even after all these years.*

Not surprising that you'd been nervous lately. Did you regret the decision? Did you fear you'd be discovered? Did you use cocaine to calm your nerves?

When she found the envelope, she knew what to do. And what she didn't know, the kindly bank officer did.

Now ten million American dollars, minus the cost of one sixty-one-foot Swan boat, sat in the Liechtenstein account. The price of a patent, worthless on paper, paid for mostly under the table.

It was a great deal of money, but the company stood to gain much more. If the patent had gone to auction, they'd have paid through the nose.

And the only person who knew about it was now dead.

Eva took another sip of champagne and looked out the window as the last drops rolled across her tongue. In a few minutes, the plane would take off, and she would forever leave this country behind.

She didn't regret sending those anonymous messages to Diana Söder. She thought Diana had killed Oscar. A woman feeling scorned when she got tired of her married lover's endless excuses and delays—who else could it have been?

She never suspected that crazy von Hahne woman. Though the trial wouldn't take place until Isabelle was released from the hospital, everyone knew she'd go to jail for a long time.

Eva didn't feel bad for either of them. She'd hated Diana Söder from the start because, for the first time in many years, it had appeared Oscar might be in love.

The impatient bookkeeper's message had given her the idea to use the daughter's Hotmail address. The happiness she felt every time she wrote another message helped ease the pain in her heart. She felt better when she hit "Send." Leaking the news to the papers was icing on the cake.

The flight attendant offered her more champagne. Eva smiled and held up her glass. The liquid sparkled in the sunshine.

She now had over eight million American dollars.

That would be more than enough for a spacious apartment in southern France, one with an enormous balcony. The rest of the money would go into secure investments that would take care of her for the rest of her life.

Once things died down a little, she would sell her Stockholm apartment. After she'd completed her six-month sick leave.

It hadn't been hard to get the doctor to sign off on that. He'd been sympathetic and understanding, offering to lengthen her sick leave if she needed it. Nobody questioned her grief.

The money from the sale would go into the investment pot, too. Perhaps she'd eventually open a small business on the Riviera. She was a smart businesswoman with many options.

But right now, she planned on enjoying life. Indulging herself. Perhaps taking a lover. A passionate Frenchman who knew how to treat a woman right.

Thank you, Oscar, she thought. She lifted her glass and toasted silently again. *I knew you wouldn't forget me in the end. I didn't doubt you for a minute.*

Acknowledgments

This entire story is fiction with no resemblance to any person living or dead.

As I came up with the plot, I was thinking about how ambition and the love of power could develop in a close circle of people. The RSYC, with its connections to Sandhamn, became a natural launching point. I have been active in that club for many years and have witnessed the great amount of work it puts in to support the sport of sailing. I also would like to mention that its annual meeting is in February and not September, and also many vessels, not just Swans, are capable of racing in and winning the Round Gotland Race.

During my work, a number of people have generously assisted me with their expertise and knowledge.

I would like to thank Jan Fellenius, an attorney from the Fylgia law firm, who explained to me what a bankruptcy lawyer does. Criminal Inspector Sonny Björk described forensic technology and ballistics. Dentist Hans-Olof Örnefeldt explained the Brånemark method. I have also received the assistance of radiologist Katarina Bodén and visited

Marie Frykberg at the bankruptcy unit with the help of acting senior judge Cecilia Klerbro.

A warm round of thanks goes out to family, friends, and colleagues who took time to read the manuscript and give clever suggestions: Lisbeth Bergstedt, Tord Bergstedt, Anette Brifalk, Helen Duphorn, Carin Hildebrand, Gunilla Pettersson, and Göran Sällqvist.

I stand in deep gratitude to my efficient publisher, Karin Linge Nordh, and my unbelievable editor, Mathilda Lund, as well as everyone else at Forum who put so much energy into my books.

As always, my daughter, Camilla, is my biggest fan, and she's been the first to read and give her opinion on my work. My wonderful husband, Lennart, also supported me all the way. He answered many questions about hunting and ammunition and also took over running the household efficiently as I disappeared mentally and physically during the final stages of this book. My wonderful sons, Alexander and Leo, have always given me encouragement through their hugs.

Sandhamn, November 2008

Viveca Sten

ABOUT THE AUTHOR

Photo © 2010 Anna-Lena Ahlström

Swedish writer Viveca Sten has sold almost three million copies of her enormously popular Sandhamn Murders series. In 2014, her seventh novel, the hugely successful *I maktens skugga* (*In the Shadow of Power*), was published in Sweden and cemented her place as one of the country's most popular authors. Her Sandhamn Murders novels continue to top the bestseller charts and have been made into a successful Swedish-language TV miniseries, which has been broadcast around the world to thirty million viewers. Sten lives in Stockholm with her husband and three children, but she prefers to spend her time visiting Sandhamn to write and vacation with her family.